DEFAMED

Michael Llewellyn

For Judy Leger

DEFAMED

Scaramouche Publishing

"He was born with a gift of laughter and a sense that the world was mad."

FOREWORD

*"When traveling in Virginia, you must be prepared to hear
the name of Randolph frequently mentioned."*
–The Marquis de Chastellux, 1782

Virginia in the late eighteenth century demanded
manners and social dictates almost impossible to comprehend
today. Honor was everything, an essential commodity as
much about survival as pride. Duels were fought over it; lives
and entire families were destroyed without it. If a
gentleman's good name was sullied, whether genuinely or
merely perceived as such, he found himself relegated to the
outer fringes of society, deemed unworthy of holding public
office, unable to secure a loan or line of credit, and without
social peers to provide crucial business connections. Ladies
fared even worse. The slightest social peccadilloes made
public could forever savage a genteel reputation, the worst
offense, of course, being loss of virtue. If a woman bore a
child out of wedlock, gentlemen shunned her as damaged
goods, and she was doomed to life as a family ward. What
befell those poor souls without kin was unimaginable.

No family better exemplifies these dictates than the
Randolphs who, for over a century, enjoyed rarefied wealth,
power and privilege, and lived like princelings in a class-
conscious replication of England in the New World. Farmers
doffed their hats when Randolph gentlemen appeared on their
thoroughbred steeds, and Randolph ladies were paid equal
obeisance with curtsies and nods. Their elitist world was the
legacy of William Randolph who arrived in Virginia in 1669
at age nineteen. William was hardy and industrious, a breed
that not merely survives but thrives, and he soon became one
of the colony's largest tobacco planters. He was one of the
founders of the College of William & Mary, and, as Speaker

of the House of Burgesses, the first of numerous Randolph politicians. William and his wife, Mary Isham, have been called the "Adam and Eve of Virginia," with such illustrious descendants as Thomas Jefferson, John Marshall, Robert E. Lee, and John Randolph of Roanoke. Native American blood was introduced to the line when Richard Randolph married Jane Bolling, a direct descendant of Pocahontas.

The Randolphs lived and spent extravagantly, not solely for love of luxury but because not doing so risked social censure. This cavalier overextension proved cataclysmic when the Revolutionary War collapsed the tobacco market and left Virginia's planters heavily indebted to British merchants. More catastrophe ensued when demands for equality thundered throughout the newly independent nation, and class hierarchy was upended. Common citizens serving with distinction in the war were given county-level judicial appointments and other prestigious positions previously open only to high-born gentlemen. Under assault socially as well as economically, the Randolphs were helpless as their glittering province of privilege faded and collapsed.

It was into this fragile, troubled society that Ann Cary (Nancy) Randolph was born in 1774. She would pay an unimaginable price for bearing that prestigious surname. What once provided entrée to the finest parlors in Richmond and Williamsburg would become a curse.

Part 1

"I am an aristocrat. I love justice and hate equality."

-John Randolph of Roanoke

1

A bulwark of thunderheads massed alongside Virginia's Blue Ridge Mountains and rumbled like angry beasts as they marched toward the sea. Nancy Randolph ignored them, aware only of the empty grave at her feet and the harsh scrape of rope as the coffin was lowered into the ground. A discreet rustling followed as straw was scattered atop the casket in a futile attempt to muffle the sound of shoveled dirt. Straw, Nancy realized, would forever remind her of death. She lingered alongside her mother's grave while the others dispersed, waiting until the last mourner was gone. Only then did she whisper a final farewell to her namesake, Anne Carey Randolph, and seek solitude in the garden.

The spring of 1789 had come early to Tuckahoe plantation, transforming the grounds with clouds of flowering dogwoods. Caught by a breeze, the white blossoms lifted and fell as though beckoning Nancy to the boxwood maze that had enchanted her as a child. As she continued to the heart of the maze, each twist and turn spawned memories of playing hide-and-seek with nine brothers and sisters. She sat on a marble bench and sighed with the relief that comes after standing for a long time.

"Oh, Mama."

A sharp pain in her chest fluttered and faded as Nancy struggled to reconcile her mother's death five days ago. Much loved and admired, Anne Randolph was the glue that held Tuckahoe together, and her sudden, inexplicable passing left everyone on the plantation bewildered and adrift. None more than Nancy. She had been her mother's favorite and, to help stem another wave of grief, she relived their last moments together.

Finished with her tutors, Nancy went upstairs to the bedroom she shared with her sister Judith. At the top step, she heard raised voices in their mother's room. Before she could investigate, Judith burst into the hall, face taut with anger.

"Judith!" Nancy cried. "What's wrong?"

"Get out of my way!" Judith ran into their room and slammed the door. Nancy started to follow but was stopped by another voice.

"Nancy?" Her mother Anne stood in the doorway to her bedroom. "Come here, darling. I need to talk to you."

Nancy hurried over, always eager for time alone with her mother. With nine siblings, such moments were rare, and she cherished any chance to trade confidences and share secrets.

"What is it, Mama?"

"Close the door please." Anne sat on a divan by the window, arranged her long skirts and patted the seat beside her. Nancy nestled close, welcoming her mother's familiar scent of lemon verbena.

"What's the matter with Judith?" she asked.

"That's what I want to talk to you about." Anne kissed her daughter's cheek and brushed a wayward strand of hair into place. "She's angry with me because I won't agree to the wedding."

"Oh." Nancy was disappointed. These days, all anyone at Tuckahoe talked about was her Judith's engagement to their cousin, Richard Randolph, and she was sick of hearing about it.

"I like Richard well enough, and it will probably be a good match, but I want her to wait a year, until she's eighteen."

"Weren't you sixteen when you married Papa?"

"Yes, I was. Not much older than you are now, and that's precisely why I want Judith to wait. Heaven knows I wish I had." She gave Nancy a wistful look. "My mother prepared me as best she could, but she was ill-prepared

11

herself. I know Judith believes herself in love, but girls her age are prone to infatuation and liable to be sour when the delirium of love is over and reason sets in. I know what I'm talking about Nancy because I made those mistakes."

"I'm not sure I understand."

"I was little more than a child when I married your father, and I had two babies my first two years of marriage. I dearly love all you children, and my lost babies, too, of course, but—" Anne looked outside at the clipped hedgerow and the family cemetery beyond where three infant sons were buried.

"But what?"

"You must never tell anyone what I'm going to say." Anne glanced at the closed door before making her confession. "Given the choice, I would've much preferred spending those two years in other ways. I assure you that balls and garden parties are much more fun than morning sickness."

Nancy was uncomfortable with such a serious confidence. "Why are you telling me this, Mama?"

"Because I want you to promise something I couldn't request without explaining why." She took Nancy's hands. "Your other sisters waited to get married. Molly was eighteen, and Elizabeth, bless her heart, was twenty. Since I've failed with Judith, I want you to promise you won't marry until you're eighteen."

Ever the obedient child, Nancy agreed. "Alright."

She squeezed Nancy's hands. "Let me hear the words."

"I promise I won't marry until I'm eighteen."

"Thank you, my angel." She smiled and folded Nancy into her arms. "I will rest much easier now."

The intimate moment ended with a knock at the door and a servant delivering afternoon tea. Nancy kissed her mother and went to her own room where she endured Judith's tearful rants. Neither imagined they had seen their mother for the last time.

Nancy conjured those precious, final moments in the midst of the garden maze, closing her eyes to lose herself. She was jarred from her reverie by loud footsteps on the gravel path. Her eyes flew open, and she called out in alarm as her three-year-old sister, Virginia, stumbled toward her.

"Be careful or you'll fall," Nancy cried.

"No, I won't!"

Stubborn as a mule, Nancy thought when Virginia clambered into her lap and hugged her tight. The child had always been affectionate, but Nancy was caught off-guard by her enthusiasm. "Do you want to strangle me?" she laughed. Virginia eased her grip but remained at Nancy's breast. "Now tell me what you're doing out here by yourself."

"She's not by herself."

Judith appeared, breathless from chasing her high-spirited charge. Only two years Nancy's senior, she seemed much older. Both were comely brunettes with oval faces and dark eyes, but Nancy was softer and prettier. There were other differences. As children, Judith was more adult than playmate, much too aloof to share girlish secrets, and her superior attitude often clashed with Nancy's natural ebullience. These disparate personalities were even evident in their appearances. While Judith swathed herself in black mourning crepe and wore a taut chignon, Nancy wore a daytime dress of pearl-gray silk with her long hair becomingly framing her face.

Judith frowned. "I thought I'd find you here."

"I needed a few moments alone."

"A few moments are understandable, but vanishing for an entire hour when the house is filled with guests? Shame on you."

"Please don't scold me, Judith. I simply lost track of time."

"That's no excuse."

"Alright." Nancy tried to get up, but Virginia still commandeered her lap. "Hop down, darling. We need to go inside."

"No, no!" Virginia hugged her tight again. "Want to stay here."

"We can't always have what we want," Judith declared sternly. "Now come along." Virginia pouted but obeyed, and as they wound their way free of the maze, Judith turned back to Nancy. "The Randolphs of Matoax have arrived."

"Good. Theo always makes me laugh."

"This is hardly a day for merriment, sister."

Nancy ignored the rebuke. "I always thought it remarkable that three brothers could be so different. Theo is fun-loving and cavalier with a steak of wildness, and John is as mercurial as he is intelligent."

"And not a little prickly."

"True enough. And how would you describe your beloved Richard?" Nancy ventured.

Judith's voice softened when she spoke of her fiancé. "Dashing and charming and spoiled like all firstborn Randolph sons." She glanced at the gray skies before adding, "And with a roguish past."

Nancy was shocked by the frank admission. "But how would you know?"

"Because I move in adult circles, dear."

Vexed by the insult, Nancy volleyed back. "Then pray enlighten this ignorant fool."

Judith ignored the sarcasm. "I'll say only that marriage to Richard will be a challenge. Heaven knows love directs us down unexpected paths, and we must follow God's will."

"You could do worse, Judith. The man is handsome enough."

"I suppose." Judith squinted when a blinding shard of sunlight broke through the clouds before being swallowed again. "Theo asked for you straight away."

14

"Did he?"

"Stop pretending surprise, girl. You know very well he's not merely being polite, and I do wish you'd start taking him seriously. For that matter, John might be interested too, if you showed a whit of encouragement."

Nancy's cheeks colored whenever her sister attempted to play Cupid. After becoming engaged to Richard, Judith had been less than subtle in directing his brothers' attentions to Nancy.

"I enjoy talking with Theo and John, but I'm not interested in serious suitors."

"Nonsense. You're almost sixteen, Nancy. When I was your age—"

"I don't care what you did at my age." Nancy retorted. "I'm not ready for marriage, and neither are you. Mother said so herself. She also said that girls our age are prone to infatuation and liable to—"

"'Liable to be sour when the delirium of love is over and reason sets in.' Judith finished. "Heaven knows she said it so often I'm surprised she didn't stitch the words onto a sampler and make me wear it around my neck."

Despite the sorrowful day, Judith's bitter quip struck Nancy as funny, and a much-needed release triggered laughter. Judith was appalled, but when little Virginia developed an uncontrollable case of the giggles, she laughed too. The jollity ended when their father abruptly materialized around the next twist of the hedge. Colonel Thomas Mann Randolph, Sr. was a sturdy, commanding figure as befit the master of an eighteen-thousand-acre tobacco plantation, and he wore an authoritarian air which few challenged. His children were all too familiar with his stern demeanor, and, knowing he had heard the laughter, Judith hastened to apologize.

"Forgive us, Papa. We didn't mean to be disrespectful."

"No, Papa," Nancy said.

"So," he said, "not one but three of my daughters are making merry outside when the house is overflowing with mourners come to see their dear mother."

"I'm sorry," Judith said again. "I came looking for Nancy and the baby ran out here too." Virginia stumbled toward his towering bulk and raised her arms, begging to be picked up.

"Papa! Papa!" she wailed.

Randolph acknowledged neither Judith's explanation nor the noisy mite grabbing at his legs. He looked at the threatening heavens and grunted his order. "All three of you. Get in the house at once!"

2

Nancy hurried upstairs to freshen up before returning to the great hall where she was swallowed by mourners. She moved through them like a wraith, barely hearing tendered words of comfort or feeling the embrace of aunts and cousins, friends and neighbors. She remained numb until a warm breath caressed her neck, accompanied by the smell of bourbon and tobacco smoke.

"I was exactly your age when my mother died."

Nancy turned to see a young man with curly brown hair, ruddy cheeks and a toothy Randolph smile. He was smartly dressed in a pecan-colored jacket and two waistcoats, gold beneath white, and breeches buckled below the knee. A few older people disapproved of his insouciance, but Nancy welcomed it along with his warm embrace.

"Theo! How good to see you!"

"You as well, although I regret the circumstances and apologize for missing the service. We left Matoax two days ago and spent the night in Richmond. Richard had business there, so we took the occasion to have an adventure. I fear it took longer than expected."

"No matter. You're here now." Nancy scanned the crowd for his brothers and saw Richard talking with Judith. "Where's John?"

"He was here a minute ago, but you know he loves to disappear. We were so shocked to hear about your poor mother. Had she been ill?"

"Not at all. I consider myself fortunate because we had some time alone the afternoon before she died." She glanced past Theo when she heard raised voices and spotted her brother, Tom Junior, in a far corner. He was in an animated conversation with a cousin whose name Nancy never could remember. Tom's temper was infamous and she prayed he would control it on this of all days. She grimaced.

17

Theo noted her expression and gestured at the crush of hushed voices and long faces. "Something tells me this is the last place you want to be just now."

"I'm ashamed to agree, but I have no choice. I already embarrassed myself by lingering outside after Mama's funeral."

"Then a little added embarrassment can't matter much, can it?" When she saw Theo's mischievous smile, Nancy recalled that streak of wildness she mentioned earlier. "It would be ever so simple to slip out that side door and—"

"No, Theo. I don't dare."

"Then join me on the settee in that alcove. You'll be visible to everyone, but we can at least pretend to be alone."

"Alright." Nancy was always at ease around Theo, a sensation she welcomed when they sat facing each other. As they began talking, everyone else receded as if buoyed away by a wave, conversations melting into a dull hum. "Tell me about school. Do you still like Columbia?"

Theo shrugged. "I like that it's in New York, but I can't bring myself to be serious about my studies. Any day I expect to be told that my presence there is no longer required."

Nancy was surprised. "But why?"

"Would you prefer flippancy or the truth?"

"The truth, if you please."

"I hate studying things to which I am utterly indifferent."

"What would you rather be doing? Managing Matoax?"

"I'm hardly cut out for the life of a planter." The smell of whiskey intensified when Theo leaned closer. "Playing in New York is far more to my liking. It's most fascinating and claims endless diversions."

Nancy's mood lightened as she succumbed to his high spirits. "No doubt you intend to experience all of them."

"I'd hoped so, but, alas, my beloved stepfather does not share my priorities, and because Mr. Tucker has been unfailingly generous, I suffer terrible guilt when we discuss them."

Theo was only a year old when his father John died, and seven when his mother Frances married an ambitious young lawyer named St. George Tucker from Bermuda. Frances' choice raised eyebrows because she had three young sons to support, and the penniless Tucker was not part of the Virginia gentry. To the naysayers' surprise, he not only served with honor in the war with Great Britain, but afterwards built a thriving law practice. In addition to being a good provider, he was a devoted husband and stepfather, and easily scored the love and respect of the three adopted Randolph boys.

"Does John share your feelings about college?"

"John? Heavens, no! I think he sleeps with his nose stuck in a book, which explains his high marks in everything. I've tried my best to broaden his horizons."

"By enlisting him in your escapades?"

"Precisely, although I admit he's not always a willing participant." Theo turned impish. "He was less than pleased when I surprised him at Princeton with some of my Columbia cronies. We tossed his books out the window and demanded he go carousing with us. Oh, he knew it was all in good fun. Then again, he told me if I didn't retrieve his books that he'd tell our stepfather about my misbehavior. I certainly couldn't let that happen. Which reminds me, I must ask you to keep my antics quiet, too."

"I will promise on one condition."

"What is that?"

"I'd like us to correspond."

Theo's eyes shone. "Truly?"

"Truly. Now that I know you're leading such a colorful life, I'm perishing to know more about it."

"I'm honored, but don't forget your father disapproves of me."

To Nancy's dismay, Colonel Randolph considered Theo a spoiled profligate and an embarrassment to the

Randolph name, and didn't hesitate to say so. She leaned close to whisper. "The very reason for keeping our secret."

"Why, Nancy Randolph!" Theo laughed and squeezed her hands. "I never knew you had so much spirit."

"I'm not sure I knew myself!" Nancy laughed too, pleased with their playful conspiracy. "Oh, dear!"

"What is it?"

"I got a disapproving look from Judith. She must've heard me laugh."

Theo frowned. "Judith is always so serious. Critical, too. I wonder if my brother knows what he's doing by marrying her."

"I should hope so. They've known each other since childhood."

"Just like us," Theo reminded her. "And when your sister marries my brother, you and I will be in-laws. Won't that be wonderful?"

Before Nancy could answer, they were joined by a lanky youth over six feet tall. Beneath a shock of black hair was an arresting face that bordered on beautiful. Nancy envied large liquid eyes with lashes longer than her own, but was always uneased by the impetuous soul behind them.

"Hello, John."

"Cousin dear." John gestured grandly. "I'm sorry for the sad occasion drawing us together, but what, pray tell, could be more fascinating than a room full of Randolphs?"

"This is neither the time nor place for sarcasm," Theo chided. "Where are your manners, little brother?"

John sniffed. "Manners merely hide how much we think of ourselves and how little we think of others." Nancy surprised him by nodding agreement. "Your lack of pretense is refreshing, my dear. Tell me. Do you ever stop enchanting people?"

Nancy basked in John's flattery, but Theo was less than charmed. He stood. "I could use a whiskey."

"So could I. Bourbon if you please." With Theo gone, John quickly took his place on the settee. "I'm terribly sorry to hear about your mother, Nancy. I know what that's like."

"So Theo was saying."

"Losing Father was bad enough, but Mother and I had a very special friendship. She spoiled me terribly, perhaps because I was the youngest. Then again, I was a most remarkable child. She taught me how to read as soon as I could talk, and I devoured books like gingerbread. By the time I was eight, I'd finished Don Quixote and Robinson Crusoe, and when I was eleven, I read Plutarch's Lives and Pope's Homer. Voltaire too. Mother loved having me read to her in bed."

"Remarkable indeed." Nancy wondered how much was true and how much reflected John's celebrated conceit. "What did you read to her?"

"Her favorite was Smollett's Expedition of Humphrey Clinker. It made us both laugh out loud. Are you familiar with Smollett's works?"

"My tastes in reading are not so lofty."

"But you do like to read," he insisted, as though something important hinged on her response.

"Mostly sentimental novels. Judith prefers devotional works."

"Female stuff," John said with unconcealed disdain.

Nancy resented his mockery. "You shouldn't criticize something of which you are ignorant."

To her surprise, John was pleased with the admonishment. "How astute that you seized upon that! Is it possible I'm not the only one with the makings of a lawyer?"

Nancy ignored the gibe. "Is law to be your chosen profession?"

"I don't yet know but I intend to explore the possibility. In fact, this summer I'm going to Philadelphia to study with our cousin Edmund. Last year President Washington appointed him America's first Attorney General. Did you know that?"

"Papa may have mentioned it."

"He was Governor of Virginia before that, and before that he was Washington's aid-de-camp during the war and one of Virginia's delegates to the Continental Congress. Beverly Randolph is the current Governor, of course, and you surely know Peyton Randolph was a speaker at the House of Burgesses and the first President of the Continental Congress. Cousin Thomas, who grew up here at Tuckahoe, wrote the Declaration of Independence. Then there was—"

Nancy paid little attention to John's prideful family discourse. She didn't hope for a change of subject because he rarely shifted focus from himself. Nor was it unusual that it took John a while to notice he was losing his audience.

"Forgive me, cousin. Am I boring you?"

"With respect, John. I have no head for politics and scant idea what all those important titles mean."

"Would you like me to explain?" John pursued, undaunted as ever.

Theo handed his brother a glass of whiskey and rejoined the conversation. "No, she would not."

"Why do you say that? You don't even know what we were discussing."

"What *you* were discussing, you mean. Everyone knows about your one-sided conversations and endless prattle, John." Theo took a generous swallow of bourbon. "You could bore the wheels off a wagon."

John's temper, inherited from his indulgent mother, flared. "You're one to talk with your wretched school marks and fondness for debauchery. It's only a matter of time until you're booted out of Columbia."

"Keep your voice down," Theo hissed. "I already said this is no place for you to misbehave."

As the exchange escalated, voices rising, people turned toward the alcove. Lest her behavior be criticized again, Nancy reprimanded both young men, gathered her skirts and hurried up the staircase. Judith, monitoring the interchange, was close behind her.

"What on earth happened?"

"You were right to call John prickly," Nancy replied, grabbing the newel post as she caught her breath. "Theo made a little gest, and John exploded." She jumped at a thunderclap so close it jolted the house. "It was as sudden as that thunder." Both leaned over the banister when Colonel Randolph's voice boomed below, demanding peace between the quarreling brothers. Threatened with the expulsion, John and Theo apologized and fell silent.

"Thank goodness for Papa," Nancy said. "Such discord is not how I want to remember this day."

"Nor I. Shame on those boys. I'm sure Richard will have something to say to them. He can be as firm as Papa when it comes to bad behavior." Judith noticed Nancy tugging on her finger. "What're you doing with grandmother's ring?"

"Come along and I'll show you." Judith followed her sister to a window at the end of the hall, and watched, bewildered, when Nancy scraped the diamond across a pane of glass. Satisfied with the resulting scratch, she etched the day's date and her name and passed the ring to Judith. "Your turn." For once, Judith obeyed Nancy and etched her name alongside her sister's. "This is a much better way to memorialize Mama than a tombstone, don't you think?"

"I suppose, but I can't dwell on it when I have more important matters to tend to."

Taken aback, Nancy said, "What could be more important than Mother?"

"My wedding plans, little sister. I loved Mother too, but I'm glad she can no longer oppose my marriage."

"That's the coldest thing I ever heard!"

"Truth is best," Judith declared stiffly.

Theo is right to be worried about his brother's marriage, Nancy thought as her sister walked away. "Poor Richard."

3

The Randolphs' legendary hospitality was celebrated in a number of majestic homes across Virginia. Matoax, Monticello, Varina, Dungeness and Turkey Island were designed to dazzle all who saw them. Tuckahoe wasn't the grandest, but it was the most welcoming courtesy of Anne Randolph's genteel maxim, "Tuckahoe belongs to its guests."

Commanding a bluff overlooking the James River, Tuckahoe was accessible via boat or hard-packed lane. Upon approach, visitors saw a simple, two-story clapboard house that appeared unworthy of a Randolph home until a walk around the side revealed a twin. Tuckahoe was shaped like the letter H with the verticals composed of two separate buildings, one reserved for family, the other for guests. The horizontal connecting the wings was a high-ceilinged great hall with arches at both ends and tall windows to capture light and, in summer, every available breeze. Rosewood and mahogany furnishings were simple but of the highest quality, but Tuckahoe was most famous for its elegant walnut paneling and sumptuously carved staircase, the finest in the Commonwealth.

On Christmas day, 1789, the house wore traditional holiday dress. From the evergreen wreath on the front door and swags of holly and ivy on bannisters and doorways to a single candle on each windowsill and the Yule log crackling away, Tuckahoe had never glowed more brightly. But this was no ordinary season. At noon, Judith Randolph of Tuckahoe would descend the famous staircase to become the bride of Richard Randolph of Matoax. The morning of the wedding, Nancy and Judith were roused by a servant girl who announced that the household was at breakfast, deposited a porcelain tray with cups of steaming coffee and quietly left.

"Wake up, sleepyhead!" Nancy dared give Judith a playful poke in the back. "Have you forgotten it's your wedding day?"

"Not with you around," Judith muttered groggily.

"Like you reminding me every day that I'm to become mistress of Tuckahoe?"

"Only because you need to be prepared. You'd better thank your lucky stars for Delilah."

"Oh, I do. I do."

With their mother deceased, older sisters Molly and Elizabeth married and gone and Judith set to leave, it now fell to Nancy to perform as plantation mistress. She would be responsible for the care of everyone at Tuckahoe, from her father and siblings to the house servants and lowliest field hand, along with an endless stream of guests. She would oversee meal planning and food preservation, supervise the cleaning, weaving, knitting, and soap-making and nurse the sick, Negro and white alike. Because she was so often incapacitated with pregnancy, Nancy's mother had relied on a slave woman named Delilah to augment her role. For the last twenty-four years, Delilah had kept Tuckahoe, a village unto itself, running like a well-oiled machine, and she would be Nancy's salvation.

"Richard has promised to find me someone like her," Judith said. "Until then, I'll have to manage. Thank goodness Matoax is smaller than Tuckahoe."

"Matoax is such a funny word. I wonder what it means."

"Don't you know anything about family history?" Judith's thin patience was easily eroded. "It comes from Pocahontas' Powhatan name, Matoaca. Now fetch me my coffee." Judith yawned and sat up. "I had such awful dreams."

"Did you? I didn't dream at all." Nancy pushed aside the dimity hangings and retrieved their coffee cups. She perched on the edge of the bed and burst out laughing when Judith pulled off her nightcap.

"What's so funny?"

"You slept on your hair wrong. You look like a porcupine!"

Judith grimaced. "Well, don't sit there like a fool. Get the brush and fix it."

Nancy struggled to pull the brush through Judith's snarled locks. "Mother always said you had more Powhatan blood than the rest of us which is why your hair is so thick. See? I did listen sometimes."

"I wish John Rolfe had never met Pocahontas," Judith groused. "Mingling our good English blood with a tribe of savages is…ouch! You're hurting me."

"I didn't mean to. It's such a tangled mess I can't do anything with it."

Judith grabbed a hand mirror. "Good heavens! I can't go to breakfast looking like this. Call Hanna. She'll have to dress my hair earlier than usual."

Nancy gave the bell pull a firm yank before dressing and heading for breakfast. She paused at the etched window to touch the glass and whisper a prayer for her mother. Her warm fingertips turned the window frost to water, and as it dripped and cleared the glass, she saw movement outside. A hasty wipe with her hand revealed a grand coach-and-four jangling up the drive. Nancy noted the Randolph coat-of-arms emblazed on the door.

"The governor himself!" she whispered, breath fogging the glass again. "This is going to be quite a day!"

The arrival of Governor Beverly Randolph, who had risen early for the drive from Richmond, was the first of many. By mid-morning, Tuckahoe's drive was a crush of coaches, landaus, phaetons and lone riders. While servants rushed to get vehicles parked and horses tended, the wedding guests went inside to exchange greetings, trade gossip and savor refreshments while waiting for the ceremony to begin. The grandfather clock in the great hall was striking noon when, Judith, hair tamed and perfectly coiffed, became the wife of Richard Randolph. Following the Anglican ceremony, the feasting began in earnest. Tables with fruit-laden crystal centerpieces groaned beneath heaps of oysters, venison, roast beef, chicken, pork, pheasant and abundant vegetable dishes. Following that course, guests left the tables so servants could change centerpieces and bring the first round of desserts. Afterwards, damask tablecloths were whisked away, and a second, much more elaborate dessert course was served on bare wood including gingerbread cakes, candied fruits, sugared nuts, bourbon balls, mince pies and plum puddings. Ladies sipped frothy syllabub and holiday wassail while gentlemen enjoyed wine, whiskey and brandy. After dessert, servants created a ballroom by removing the tables and lining chairs against the wall. Lively music from a Negro orchestra turned the room it into a kaleidoscope of color as dancers whirled with reels and jigs. The festivities would, Nancy knew, last well past midnight, and as she surveyed a knot of already unsteady young men, she hoped all would remain harmonious. She forgot about them when Judith and Richard began their good-byes before departing for Presqu'ile plantation to spend their wedding night. Nancy had never seen Judith, aglow in peach silk, look happier.

"Better get busy, Nancy. You're next, you know."

Nancy's hackles rose at the unwelcome voice. Her mother's youngest sister Mary rarely missed the opportunity to throw cold water on a pleasant moment.

"Hello, Aunt Mary."

Mary nodded at the cluster of lively young men. "Is one of those your intended?"

"I have no serious beaux at present."

"A pretty girl, like you?" Mary's mouth twisted into a sardonic simper. "I simply don't understand it."

"How unfortunate that you're bewildered by my romantic life, auntie. I do hope it doesn't keep you awake nights."

"Well, hardly!" Mary huffed.

"I'm so relieved."

Before Mary could respond to her sarcasm, Nancy threw John Randolph a helpless look. He rushed to whirl her onto the dance floor. Aunt Mary was left fuming while Nancy, without a backward glance, lost herself in an energetic Virginia reel. Moments later, both breathless, she and John inspected the remains of a tiered wedding cake draped in white paper fringe. It was flanked by crystal epergnes laden with candied flower petals, more fruits and sweetmeats.

"I've never seen so many different desserts." John popped a cookie into his mouth and chewed vigorously, oblivious when crumbs settled on his sleeve

"Our cook has been laboring for days. That cake is a work of art."

John, as was his nature, changed the subject. "I owe you an apology."

"Whatever for?"

"For my bad behavior on the day your poor mother died."

"I'd forgotten all about it."

"You're kind to say so, but it's caused me remorse and dismay. Theo too. Like most brothers, we love each other, but we also have our disagreements. Our sin was airing our differences at an inappropriate time."

"I appreciate your apology, John, but I promise the incident is forgotten."

"I'm glad."

"Now tell me where Theo is. I have been looking for him all day, but the house is so crowded that—"

"Were you looking for me too?"

Nancy wondered if John's scowl was real or for drama. "Of course, I was, and here you are!" She smiled. "And where's Theo?"

"At Matoax. He's fallen ill."

"Again? But I had a letter only yesterday saying he would be here."

John's eyebrows rose. "I didn't know you corresponded."

"It was a special occasion," Nancy demurred, hoping to maintain her secret.

"I see. Well, I suspect Theo fell ill the day he posted the letter. He was most vexed when the physician told him he couldn't attend his own brother's wedding."

"The poor dear. Do tell him I wish him a quick recovery."

"I will." Concern clouded John's face when he noticed the group of rowdies. "That arguing spells trouble."

"I was thinking the same thing." Nancy steered him toward the fireplace where a servant was stoking the Yule log. The heat felt good when flames crackled and sparks exploded up the chimney. Nancy noticed wayward tendrils of holly and ivy in the mantle centerpiece and tucked them back into place. "There. That's better."

"Dearest Nancy with an eye for perfection. I discover new and wonderful things about you every time we're together. What's more, you're one of the few young ladies of my acquaintance capable of—Hold there!"

John yanked Nancy aside when a youth reeled by, narrowly missing them before hitting the wall and crumbling to the floor. He laughed and struggled to rise, oblivious to shouts as Colonel Randolph and Tom Junior pushed through the crowd. Tom, scowling with rage, seized the offender and strong-armed him from the room. The young man's drunk companions hastily trailed, anxious to avoid Tom's notorious temper, and after a tense moment, things returned to normal.

"A close call." John said, releasing Nancy. "If your father and brother hadn't intervened, we might have had ourselves a duel."

"Papa doesn't miss much, and Tom has inherited his vigilance."

John turned puckish. "I must confess I look forward to my first duel. It's a rite of passage for college men, you know."

Nancy wasn't impressed. "If that's what college involves, I'm grateful I was educated here at home."

John wasn't expecting such a curt dismissal, but, as usual, remained fixed on his opinion. "You must understand that dueling is about defending one's honor."

"I see nothing honorable about men shooting at each other."

"You've been misled, cousin dear. Duels rarely materialize because the offense is reconciled to satisfy both parties. Those actually carried out seldom result in death. One in seven is the figure most often cited." When Nancy sniffed, he said, "It's part of growing up, like beatings in school. For boys, I mean."

"I'm not sure I approve of that either."

John grinned. "Then I assume you don't want to hear about the regular canings I received as an eight-year-old at the Maury School."

"I most certainly do not."

"Then I will say only that one good thing resulted, and that is my love and adulation for your new brother-in-law."

"Richard was there too?"

"Yes, indeed, and he was everything a little brother could hope for. He not only intervened when Master Maury sought to beat me, but often took the punishment in my place. He's been my hero ever since."

"What a sweet story." Nancy's mood brightened. "After Mama died, Richard spent a great deal of time here, and I share your admiration. My sister is a lucky girl."

John took her hand. "As are you."

"What do you mean?"

"You're now mistress of one of Virginia's most celebrated plantations. That's a very heady position for one so young."

"And not a little daunting," Nancy confessed.

"I know you'll make everyone proud." John squeezed her hand. "You're a Randolph, after all."

"I'll certainly do my best."

Nancy proved true to her word, but before the new year was out, her new position would be in serious jeopardy.

4

February of 1790 delivered tides of snow to Virginia, but none fierce enough to keep Tuckahoe from operating as usual. Most mornings dawned bright and clear, something Nancy welcomed when she visited "Mama's window." Sunshine lit the barren garden and fallow tobacco fields beyond, but was too weak to ward off the wintry chill inside the house. Nancy tightened her shawl and went downstairs to breakfast, eager for a cup of hot coffee. She found her father in the dining room, waiting to discuss the daily schedule. Too young to be assigned duties, her brother and three sisters were still asleep.

"Good morning, Papa."

Colonel Randolph grunted a reply, not looking up as he drizzled molasses over a bowl of steaming cornmeal mush. His flinty mood was not unusual, so Nancy poured coffee and made light conversation.

"It looks to be another sunny day," she began. "When I meet with Delilah, I think I'll suggest we spend it—"

"Tom Junior is getting married," Randolph announced.

"Wha…what?"

"To the Jefferson girl."

Nancy was both surprised and pleased. Because their fathers had grown up together at Tuckahoe and were longtime friends, she and Patsy Jefferson of Monticello were also close. They had enjoyed a lively correspondence when Patsy was in Paris while her father, Thomas, was America's Ambassador to France. Nancy had been enthralled by Patsy's exposure to the beau monde and envied her mastery of French. "I will seem like a country bumpkin when next we see one another," Nancy lamented in her letters. Patsy, generous as ever, assured her that was nonsense and that they were friends forever.

"Is that why he left Tuckahoe the morning after Judith's wedding?"

"Ran off is more like it." Randolph spooned more mush and washed it down with ale. "When your brother was at university in Edinburgh, we often argued about his extravagance. It was difficult paying his creditors because I've been hampered by poor crops and a bad economy. I wanted to save us the embarrassment of bringing him home, so I mortgaged more property." He leveled his gaze at Nancy. "Do you know what a mortgage is?"

"No, Papa."

"It's a legal agreement for borrowing money while using one's property as collateral. Most planters need mortgages to keep operating."

"Does that mean you're in debt?"

"All planters are in debt, child," Randolph said, annoyed by her naivete. "I own over eighteen thousand acres in four counties and almost four hundred slaves, all of them heavily taxed. When we first married, your mother and I lived quite well, but the war ruined the tobacco market, and I had to borrow money to stay afloat. I've had to rely on English firms to ship and market my tobacco and pay higher duties since we're no longer part of the British Empire. There are other factors but they're too complicated for someone like yourself." Randolph drained his mug and set it aside. "The night of the wedding, I informed Tom Junior that it was time he used that expensive education to become an asset to this family instead of a liability."

Uh-oh, Nancy thought. She knew criticism was anathema to her contentious older brother. "What did he say?"

"About the family debt? Nothing. Instead, he cavalierly announced that he'd promised to visit our Fleming cousins at Rock Castle during grouse season, and off he went. The ungrateful pup." Randolph muttered something unintelligible. "After Rock Castle, he traveled to Monticello, and this morning I received a letter declaring his intention to wed Patsy. With her father approving the union, of course I agreed."

Nancy's head was spinning. "When are they to marry?"

"The twenty-third, at Monticello."

"That's so soon!"

"I'm as surprised as yourself."

Nancy ate a few bites before saying, "I'm confused, Papa. If you have so many debts, why did you give Judith such a grand wedding?"

"Appearances, child. It's what we Randolphs do. We're not like other people, you know."

"I'm not certain I do."

"Then I'll tell you a sort of war story." He gestured at her plate. "Eat your breakfast before it gets cold."

Because Colonel Randolph was rarely warm, Nancy valued any inkling of paternal affection. "Yes, sir."

"Although I supported rebellion against Britain, I despised the egalitarianism that rose alongside the desire for independence. During the last years of the war, it was customary to receive captured British officers. I was entertaining four such gentlemen, whom I considered my equals, when three farmers arrived unannounced to discuss the use of Tuckahoe's mill. To my disgust, and that of my British guests, they tracked mud on your mother's carpets and spat on the floor while conducting business. That display of democratic discourtesy galls me to this day. I'd never encountered farmers or tradesmen who considered themselves my equal, and will never accept it. Ever! We Randolphs have been at the top of Virginia aristocracy for well over a century, and nothing matters more than maintaining that stature. Do you understand me, Nancy?"

"Yes, sir. I think so."

"Good girl. Now then. I want to explain your part in all this." Nancy wasn't so naive that she didn't know what was coming, and her heart sank when her dread was confirmed. "I know two fine gentlemen who would make excellent husbands."

"I'm only sixteen, Papa!" Nancy blurted.

"I know that, as you know that was your mother's age when we got married."

"But she made me promise not to marry until I was eighteen."

"Your mother's no longer here, young lady, so that promise is void." He waved a dismissive hand. "Now I'm particularly fond of Henry Lee, the one they call Lighthorse Harry for his feats as a cavalry officer in the war. I've known him for many years, and—"

"I know who he is, Papa. His wife Matilda just died."

"Which is why he urgently needs a mother for three young children. It's what we widowers are supposed to do."

"But he's twenty years older!"

"Eighteen to be exact, which is also of no consequence in our society."

"But you were only two years older than Mama!"

Her father was unhearing. "Benjamin Harrison is another admirable candidate."

Nancy bristled. "You make finding me a husband sound like an election."

"Don't be impertinent. Harrison comes from excellent stock."

"He's even older than Mr. Lee," Nancy protested, "and has a most unsavory history. He annulled his first wife to wed Susannah Randolph of Curles in hopes of increasing his fortune. When Susannah died childless, he had a son by his annulled wife. What gentleman does such a thing?"

"Where on earth did you hear such talk?!"

"Where I hear everything, Papa. At family gatherings. If there's one thing the Randolphs love, along with growing tobacco and marrying our cousins, it's gossip." Knowing she couldn't directly refuse her father's edicts, she tried to outflank him. "Wouldn't you prefer that I marry one?"

35

"Whom do you have in mind?" A flicker of recognition crossed his ruddy face. "Surely not one of the Matoax Randolphs!"

"Why not?"

"Because Theodorick is a wastrel, and there's something not right about John. I can't quite put my finger on it, but I'd welcome neither as a son-in-law."

"I'll admit John is peculiar, but you don't know Theo at all. He's going through a difficult period right now, trying to find his path in life."

"Nonsense."

"It's not nonsense," Nancy said, opting now for flattery. "He's only nineteen, and, unlike you, not every young man knows himself at that age."

Randolph considered his own youth. "When you're orphaned at age five, you learn to expect the unforeseen. Peter Jefferson, who raised me, lauded the public service of my father and grandfather and drummed into my young brain the importance of following in their footsteps. I became a vestryman at St. James when I was only three years older than Theodorick is now, and a county justice of the peace the following year. By age twenty-seven, I was elected to the Virginia House of Burgesses. Do you believe Theodorick capable of such achievements?"

"I've no notion of his capabilities, Papa, but please give me a little more time to find out." Uncertain of Theo's feelings toward her, Nancy gambled wildly in an attempt to avoid an arranged marriage. "If you're not pleased with Theo's progress in a year, I promise to wed a man of your choosing."

"Well, well," Randolph said, pleased in spite of himself. "Apparently you've inherited some of your old papa's negotiating skills."

"Have we an agreement then?" Nancy asked, hoping to press her advantage.

"I suppose so, now that Tom Junior will ally us with the Jeffersons. Next month, Patsy's father will become

America's first Secretary of State, and I shouldn't be surprised if he becomes president in a few more years. Such connections should prove highly beneficial for the Randolphs."

"Yes, Papa."

"Don't think I don't know you got around me, you little minx." Randolph gave Nancy a rare smile as he rose to leave. "Now I must be about the day's business."

Left alone to finish her breakfast, Nancy weighed her father's words about the duty of widowers with young children. Surely, he wasn't thinking of another wife with Tuckahoe being so well managed, thanks to her hard work and Delilah's deft hand. The notion was abhorrent, a hurtful insult to her mother's memory. She thought fast and came to a quick decision.

"I'll tell Papa I shouldn't marry anyone until Virginia and the others are grown," she told herself. "That way, he won't need to marry again."

Calm washed over Nancy as she convinced herself that she had found a solution to please everyone, including her father.

Fate had different ideas.

5

Hugged on both sides by a leafless forest of oak, hickory, dogwood and witch-hazel, the road to Monticello grew ever more torturous with its steep ascent. Visibility was fraught by dense fog, and wintry sleet the night before had rendered the track a muddy challenge. The coachman struggled to keep the beleaguered horses on course, but that didn't stop Colonel Randolph from rapping his cane against the coach roof and barking for him to be more careful.

"Unfortunately, the ride will get worse before it gets better," Tom Junior told Nancy. Even in the thin morning sunlight, she was pale with fright. "Every time I visit, I wonder why Mr. Jefferson chose to live in this wilderness."

"Because he played here as a child before he moved to Tuckahoe and loved this hill so much that he vowed to build a house at the top," the colonel explained. "I've heard him say it a hundred times."

"I'm glad he fulfilled his dream, but as a bridegroom I'd rather not tumble down a mountainside the day before my wedding." As if to underline Tom's concern, the carriage tilted precipitously when the horses rounded yet another precarious curve. "Good lord!"

With new dangers emerging around every turn and everyone's nerves on edge, the last leg of the journey transpired in silence. Nancy was too scared to speak, and sighed with relief when the fog thinned and the ground smoothed into a plateau. As the coach slowed and steadied, she found the courage to look out the window. A series of thickly wooded ridges undulated to the east, while westward a scattering of peaks poked through a blanket of clouds.

"How beautiful!"

"The Blue Ridge Mountains," Randolph said.

"They're glorious even in winter. I now understand why Mr. Jefferson loved this spot. Imagine seeing this every day."

"The view, I'm sorry to say, is far more impressive than the house."

"Papa's right," Tom said. "Patsy says Mr. Jefferson is forever tearing down walls or adding new rooms, and that when they were in Paris, he announced plans to knock most everything down and start over."

"I wonder why."

"Something about seeking perfection."

"I'm sure our host will be happy to explain," Randolph said as they drew up before a nondescript brick structure with construction materials strewn haphazardly about the yard. "Jefferson loves nothing more, not even politics, than talking about Monticello. Ah! There's the man himself."

Thomas Jefferson wrapped a heavy wool shawl around broad shoulders as he approached the coach with masterful strides. In her young life, Nancy had met many prominent planters and politicians, but none awed her more than the newly appointed Attorney General of the United States. Jefferson was strikingly handsome with blue gray eyes and dark red hair pulled back and tied with a black ribbon. His height of six feet, two inches, augmented by high-heeled boots, was imposing enough, but something Nancy couldn't identify proclaimed the presence of greatness. He shook hands with the Randolph men and gave Nancy a warm smile as she alit from the coach. Color rushed to her cheeks when Jefferson kissed each one in the French fashion and stepped back to observe her with an arresting gaze.

"Welcome to Monticello, Miss Randolph. Patsy has told me of your deep friendship and how dear you are to her. That's as it should be. My mother was a Randolph, so our blood is already mixed. And, like you, I grew up at Tuckahoe."

Nancy dropped a curtsy. "It's an honor to meet you, Mr. Jefferson."

"The honor is mine." He turned when Patsy called out and rushed from the house. She had inherited her father's red hair, blue eyes and engaging manner. "Here's our blushing bride."

"Darling Nancy!" Patsy cried, wrapping her friend in her arms. "I'm so happy you're here. I hope your journey wasn't dreadful. The road up the mountain can be a bit harrowing in winter."

Nancy's eyes widened. "A *bit* harrowing?! I've never been so frightened in my life."

"I do hope it was worth it."

"Every terrible moment!" The girls hugged again before Nancy nodded over her shoulder. "I believe there's someone even more excited than I to see you."

Patsy glowed as Tom dispensed a discreet embrace. His concern was unwarranted as Jefferson thoroughly approved his daughter's choice for a husband, and shepherded Colonel Randolph and Nancy toward the house to give the couple a moment alone. He paused when Nancy glanced back at the mountains.

"Do you like my view?"

"I told Papa I've never seen anything more beautiful." Jefferson beamed. "Thank you."

"The name Monticello has such a pretty ring to it."

"It means 'little mountain' in Italian." He pointed to a cobalt cone floating atop the clouds. "I own that peak too. It's taller than Monticello, so I call it Montalto, which means 'high mountain.' I plan to clear some of its trees so my view will include a meadow. I may even build an observation tower." His chest swelled with his own ambition as he took Nancy's arm and escorted her inside the house. "I seem destined to have a host of projects in progress at all times, which explains the chaos inside and out. I hope you'll forgive me."

"Everyone does," Patsy teased, following them inside. "And you'll forgive us if we excuse ourselves. We have catching up to do."

"Run along then. We gentlemen need our time as well."

Alone in Patsy's bedroom, Nancy marveled at Pompeiian red walls and matching, gold-fringed draperies. "How lovely!"

"Papa indulges me terribly." Patsy sat on a silk settee and palmed the seat in invitation. "His own quarters are as spartan as a soldier's, but he denies me nothing. It's been that way since Mama died. That reminds me. I must say again how sorry I was to learn of your mother's passing."

Nancy untied her bonnet and dropped it in her lap. "Your letters helped beyond measure."

"I was only ten when Mama died. I understood your grief."

"I don't think I could've borne losing her at that age, but let's speak of happier things. Tell me about the wedding plans. That's all I could think about on the drive from Tuckahoe. That, and falling off the mountain once we started up that awful hill."

"Father's in a frugal state of mind these days, so the wedding will be simple. Nothing like Tom's description of Judith's ceremony."

"May I see the dress?"

"It's not really a wedding gown, but at least I bought it in Paris."

Nancy watched, not without envy, as Patsy opened an armoire and retrieved a blue silk dress with a linen bodice bearing a crisp lustring finish. She clasped it to her body and spun around the room with an imaginary dance partner. Nancy clapped her hands. "I adore it. And it goes perfectly with your hair and eyes."

"Your brother likes me in blue, so he insisted that I wear it." Patsy fussed with a lacy cuff. "I love Tom with all my heart, but you know how much he likes getting his way."

"Oh, yes. He's not the easiest person to live with, but then a husband-and-wife relationship is nothing like that of a little girl and an older brother."

"I certainly hope not!" Patsy laughed and let Nancy stroke the smooth fabric before returning the dress to the armoire. "At first, I was nervous about marrying someone I barely know, but Papa approves. The two of them spend hours discussing science. It was Tom's favorite course at university and is one of Papa's passions."

"I'm sure it will be a wonderful match."

"Thank you, darling. Now tell me something. Not once in your letters have you mentioned a suitor. With that pretty face and figure, you must have no shortage of them."

Nancy took off her shoes and tucked stockinged feet beneath her. Having a female confidante her age, especially one as worldly and warm as Patsy, was a thrilling prospect and making herself comfortable added to the fun.

"The truth is, I didn't pay them much attention until Mama died. It was the strangest thing. One minute I was telling Judith that I wasn't old enough to think about romance, and the next minute I hung on Theo's every word."

"Theo?"

"Theodorick Randolph of Matoax. Judith married his older brother Richard."

"I've heard those names, but we've not met. Is it serious then, this spark with Theo?"

"I don't know yet. I haven't seen him since because he has recurring bouts of ill health, but we maintain a good correspondence. He's at Columbia, but he hates it, and I shouldn't be surprised if he resigns."

"To do what?"

Nancy pulled a face. "That's what Papa keeps asking. He's forever criticizing Theo and calling him a wastrel. He wants to match me with some ancient widowers, but I wiggled out of by saying that I preferred to marry a Randolph."

Patsy winked. "Don't we all!"

"I reminded him that I was mistress of the house and should remain as such until the little ones are married, but he wasn't convinced. The best I could do was wangle a year to determine if Theo is the one."

"What an exciting prospect!"

"I suppose so, but it also points up an awful inequity. Why do old men feel entitled to choose young brides? Our parents were close in age, and you're marrying someone your age. So did Judith, Molly and Elizabeth. Why shouldn't I be allowed the same choice?"

"Perhaps your father has other reasons for wanting you married."

Family or not, Nancy knew it was inappropriate to discuss her father's indebtedness or how he was hoping for a financial beneficial union with the Jefferson clan.

"Perhaps." A moment passed before Nancy said, "I hope I'm not prying, but why did your father never remarry?"

"Toward the end, when Mama was very sick, she told Papa she couldn't bear the idea of another woman raising her children. Papa agreed and has kept his promise."

"How considerate. Romantic too. You must be very proud of him."

"More than I can say."

The two chatted nonstop, thrilled to renew a friendship that was about more than longevity. As with her mother, Nancy found herself blissfully sharing confidences, and neither realized how long they had been sequestered until a servant announced dinner.

"Goodness! How did it get to be three-thirty?" Patsy looked at Nancy. "Shall we go?"

"Oh, no!" Nancy cried. "A moment more, if you please. It's so wonderful to see you. Letters are wonderful, but they don't let me say in person that I wish you and my brother every imaginable happiness."

"Thank you, dearest. I hope one day soon I'll be wishing you the same thing." The two began chattering anew until they were interrupted by a loud knock. It flew open before Patsy could respond. "Why, Tom! In my boudoir. Now you'll *have* to marry me lest my honor be compromised!"

She and Nancy giggled, but Tom was stone-faced. "Did you not hear a servant announce dinner?"

"Why, yes."

"Then why did you not respond?"

"I'm afraid your sister and I lost track of time."

"That's no excuse."

"There's no need to be cross, Tom," Nancy said. She'd seen that face before and hurriedly placated her brother. "We'll come right away."

"See that you do!"

6

Summer's arrival was sudden and intense. It clung to Virginia like a curse, searing crops and triggering tempers with an unholy mix of heat and humidity. By August, everyone at Tuckahoe was wearied by the torpor. Windows throughout the house were thrown wide, but with no breeze, it remained an oven.

Nancy was exhausted by more than heat as she sat in a shady side yard with Delilah and Bonnie, the cook, who was showing her how to shell field peas. The colonel's abrupt sale of two servants meant more responsibilities, but Nancy saw it as a chance to further prove her capabilities as mistress of the house and deter her father from considering remarriage. The matter had not resurfaced for weeks, not since Randolph began frequent business trips to Richmond. Nancy worried that this indicated more financial troubles, especially when he returned home in a sour mood and scolded her, without justification, for being slack in her duties. Knowing she and Delilah were an unbeatable team, Nancy wrote Patsy about her woes. She received sympathetic replies from her new sister-in-law, but they were all too infrequent because Patsy was expecting a child in January. She briefly considered confiding in Theo, who had gone back to Columbia and wrote tantalizing letters about his picaresque exploits in New York, but decided the subject was inappropriate. Judith was more distant than ever after her marriage, so Nancy was left to cope alone.

"You got to hold the shell just so," Bonnie said, "and pop the peas out like this. You see?"

The cook's demonstration drew Nancy's attention back to the task at hand. She tried hard to mirror Bonnie's deft actions, but was slow to catch on. "I'll never master this," she said, exasperated.

"Yes, you will," Delilah assured her. "Just takes a little practice."

Nancy drew a handkerchief from her sleeve and mopped her wet forehead. "I'm sure I could concentrate better if there were a breath of fresh air. We're in for another sticky day."

"I reckon when you stop wondering if a new season is ever gonna come is when it finally does," Delilah offered. "This summer's about worn itself out."

"And me with it," Bonnie added.

Nancy understood the cook's plight. While a fire was welcome in the cold months, it turned the kitchen outbuilding hellish in the long Virginia summers.

"Whoops! Well, at least it didn't break."

Everyone laughed when Nancy's clumsy efforts knocked her bowl into the yard. When she went to retrieve it, Delilah, whose hearing was keen, announced approaching hooves.

"You hear that, Miss Nancy?"

"Yes, I do, and it's much too hot to be receiving company."

"I'll go see who it is."

"I'll go. I'm fighting a losing battle with these silly peas."

Nancy left her empty bowl and went inside. Her plain daytime dress was hardly suitable for company, but she at least removed her apron and pushed some wayward locks into place before opening the front door. She saw her father alighting from a smart green carriage with bright red wheels, a vehicle for two that Richmonders called it a chariot. With his back to Nancy, Randolph blocked whoever was descending from the chariot, and when he turned around, she saw a young woman on his arm. A striking brunette, she resembled a tropical bird in her bright yellow traveling ensemble with matching ribbons trailing from a straw bonnet. Despite the heat, an icy frisson shot down Nancy's spine when she heard her father's rapturous introduction.

46

"Nancy, this is Gabriella Harvie of Richmond. I am blessed beyond measure that she has come into my life, and I do hope you two will become the best of friends."

"Miss Harvie," Nancy said, gamely masking her unease. "Welcome to Tuckahoe."

"Thank you." Gabriella's low, throaty voice belied her youth. She gave the house a cursory glance before turning back to Randolph. "It's lovely, Thomas. Just as you said."

"Thank you, my dear. Now come along. I'm even more anxious to show you inside." Randolph ignored Nancy as he ushered Gabriella into the hall and indicated the parlor. "Please make yourself comfortable while I excuse myself a moment. We'll have refreshments directly."

Gabriella smiled. "You're always so thoughtful, Thomas."

When her father blushed and bustled away, Nancy was tempted to follow and inquire about the visitor, but instead went into the parlor, dread deepening when Gabriella moved around the room as though taking inventory. She paused to touch the walnut paneling with a gloved fingertip.

"Thomas told me about this paneling. It's interesting enough, but far too gloomy for my taste."

"Tuckahoe is famous for it," Nancy replied, startled by the criticism. "My mother prized it. In fact, this was her favorite room." She watched, resentment mounting, when Gabriella picked up a porcelain figurine of Bacchus and examined it from all angles. "That was a wedding gift to my parents, another of my mother's favorites."

"How nice." Gabriella replaced the figurine and drew a lacy fan from her reticule. She opened it with a loud snap, and waved it fast. "Is it always so hot in the country?"

"I'm afraid so," Nancy picked up a palmetto fan. "That's why these are in every room."

"Thank goodness Richmond has river breezes," Gabriella said.

"I've never been there."

The expected response should have been an invitation to visit, but Gabriella said nothing. The two women sat wordlessly fanning themselves until Nancy broke the ponderous silence.

"May I ask how you and my father became acquainted?"

Gabriella drew herself up. "My father is John Harvie of Belmont plantation. He was a member of the Second Continental Congress and a signer of the Articles of the Confederation. He is also a former mayor of Richmond and one of its most prominent attorneys."

"How clever you are to recite all that," Nancy said with a little laugh. "Remembering such things are beyond me, but I suppose that's because the Randolphs have more governors and senators and lawyers and planters than any family in Virginia." When Gabriella only stared, Nancy said, "But never mind all that. Tell me how you met my father."

"Our fathers are old friends. I happened to be in my father's office one morning when the colonel came calling. What a happy occasion that was."

"No doubt." Nancy swallowed bile. "May I say what a lovely traveling costume that is."

"You're most kind. My Aunt Sibyl disapproves. She says I'm too young for such fashions."

"Nonsense. Given the opportunity, I'd wear it myself, and I suspect we're about the same age." When Gabriella said nothing, Nancy added, "I'm sixteen."

"I'm almost eighteen," Gabriella replied frostily.

Nancy was appalled when she tabulated the thirty-one-year difference between Gabriella and her father. "Goodness! You're younger than four of my siblings and the same age as my sister Judith."

"Is there a reason for your fascination with age, Miss Randolph?"

"Not really. I was merely curious."

"A rather peculiar thing to be curious about, I should think."

48

"Not for the Randolphs. We've been marrying our cousins for over a hundred years, you see, so banter about genealogy, especially people's ages, is something of a tradition."

Gabriella stiffened. "It's been my experience that some traditions are not worth maintaining,"

"If you say so."

The room went deathly silent until Randolph burst into the room to announce Delilah was bringing refreshments. He sat beside Gabriella and looked from her to Nancy and back again.

"Well, now. Have you two been getting acquainted?"

"Something more easily accomplished in your presence," Gabriella said.

Randolph was perplexed. "I'm not quite sure what you mean, but as I said before I hope you'll become friends."

"Oh?" Nancy asked with feigned innocence. "Is she to be a frequent visitor?"

"She's to be much more than that." Randolph beamed and took Gabriella's hand. "I'm honored to say that Miss Harvie has consented to become my wife."

So, there it is, Nancy thought. The mysterious dread that I experienced all summer is explained at last. Who imagined it would come wrapped in a bright yellow package with all the trimmings?

"I see," she managed. "And when is this to take place?"

"In two weeks. That's why I was so anxious for Gabriella to see Tuckahoe. She wants to be married here, so I assured her you'd be happy to arrange everything."

Nancy recoiled at the prospect. "A wedding takes a great deal of preparation, Papa. I'll need much more notice than—"

"The announcement was made yesterday in Richmond," Gabriella interrupted. "It cannot be changed."

Nancy could scarcely believe this monumental affront, that her father had not only secretly chosen a bride but told everyone in Richmond before his own children. His betrayal was so overwhelming that she rose to leave before losing her composure.

"Please excuse me."

"Not when there's much to be discussed," Randolph said.

"Sorry, Papa. I'm…I'm feeling a bit dizzy."

"Then go to your room and lie down, child!" he snapped, clearly nettled.

Nancy made her way upstairs. Even with the windows thrown wide, her room was stifling, and she found no relief when she went to the washstand and splashed tepid water on her face. She undressed and crawled into bed clad only in her sweat-dampened shift. Nancy closed her eyes and drifted to sleep, but the intense heat and distress triggered fever dreams that left her exhausted. She'd never felt so helpless and alone.

7

In the days that followed Randolph's stunning announcement, Tuckahoe walked on eggshells. Gabriella's ill-concealed acrimony quickly took root, and, within a week, was in full poisonous bloom. Miserable and distraught, Nancy made one last-ditch effort to dissuade her father from marrying the woman. The moment came in the Burnt Room, so name for a wall left scarred by a long-ago blaze, when Randolph finished inspecting the plantation books and praised her economizing.

"You've done very well indeed."

"Thank you, Papa. Now may I speak of something of a more personal nature?"

"Go on."

Aware of Gabriella's powerful spell, Nancy sought an approach that would not immediately antagonize him. "It's about the wedding."

"Ah." Randolph brightened as he leaned back in his chair and crossed his legs at the ankle. "If you're concerned about the expense, don't be. I want this to be as grand as Judith's wedding. Grander, even."

"It isn't that. I've been thinking the tradition of widowers remarrying because their children need a mother. I believe I've proven that such is not the case here as Delilah and I manage the little ones quite nicely. Is this not so?"

Randolph frowned but said nothing.

"I finally realized that my objections to a remarriage were selfish and that what matters most is your happiness."

"I'm glad you understand. I'm aware that you and Gabriella have had your differences, but they must cease once we're all living under the same roof."

"I have no objections to you remarrying, Papa."

"Then what are we talking about here?"

The moment of truth had arrived, and Nancy braced herself. "It's Gabriella to whom I object."

Randolph's face flooded with color. "What?!"

"Papa, please hear me out. If I don't say these things, I won't be able to live with myself. None of us will."

"What the devil does that mean?"

Nancy rushed to make her plea before the rumbling volcano erupted. "I've discussed the matter with Tom and Judith, Molly and Elizabeth too, and, because we love you, we're obliged to say Gabriella is not what she seems. Around you, she's all sweetness and light, but to the rest of us she's cold and calculating. She's rude to the servants and indifferent to the little ones. It all too apparent that she's marrying you not for love but—"

"Enough!" Randolph boomed. "I will hear no more slander!"

"Papa, please! This woman has blinded you to the truth, that you're nothing but a means to an end." She steadied herself and delivered the coup de grace. "She's made you the laughingstock of Henrico County."

The colonel's fist crashed onto the chair arm so fiercely that Nancy was surprised it didn't splinter. "If I hear one more bad word about Gabriella, you go out of this house. Do you understand me, girl?!"

Knowing her father did not make empty threats, Nancy fled the room and avoided him as the wedding day drew near. She was still smarting from his edict when Gabriella triggered another ugly confrontation. Resigned to maintaining the peace, Nancy had been on her best behavior, acquiescing quietly to the woman's endless demands. Her complacency ended when Gabriella summoned her to the parlor where she waited, hands on hips, staring at the walls.

"I cannot bear this hideous walnut paneling one more minute. It's dark and depressing and will ruin my wedding day."

Nancy was aghast. "You know very well that Tuckahoe is famous for its staircase and paneling."

"The staircase is fine but the paneling goes." Gabriella waved a hand airily. "There's no time to have it removed, so I'll have it painted." Pursed lips bloomed into a treacly smile. "White."

Nancy could not fathom this new horror. "Gabriella, please! I told you this was my mother's favorite room. It would be such an affront to her memory if—"

Gabriella's retort slashed to the quick. "Your mother is dead, Nancy."

Nancy fought for self-control. "You're going too far, Gabriella. This is simply unthinkable."

"Not for me, it isn't. Now, go find your father and tell him I want this room painted today."

Nancy had heard enough. "Tell him yourself."

Gabriella was furious. "Don't you dare walk away from me!"

Nancy was halfway across the room when the Bacchus figurine crashed into the fireplace. Gabriella drew herself up and gloated when Nancy saw the shattered shards of porcelain.

"You knew my mother loved that figurine," Nancy said.

"And you should know that I am bored senseless by hearing about your mother and her silly favorites. There is to be only one Mistress of Tuckahoe, Nancy Randolph, and she is neither you nor your mother!"

After that, Nancy avoided both villains in this ongoing tragedy. With Nancy out of sight, Gabriella found other targets. First, it was Bonnie who pleaded with Gabriella to scale back the wedding menu. There was no time, the cook insisted, to acquire all the foodstuffs Gabriella demanded, much less prepare them. Gabriella was unmoved. Next was Delilah, who listened with remarkable stoicism as Gabriella repeatedly changed her mind about everything from flower arrangements to dinner seating. Even the grooms assigned to care for the guests' horses felt Gabriella's sting, instructed to wear full livery. When one dared remind her that they wore abbreviated livery in the summer months, she declared that it was his dilemma, not hers.

On the day of the wedding, Nancy, her siblings and their spouses made little pretense that this was cause for celebration. After the dismal ceremony, they set themselves apart and watched with disdain while Gabriella's Richmond sycophants gushed congratulations. Nancy wondered if they were complicit in her machinations and knew that a viper lurked behind the syrupy facade. If so, they were blind to the disapproval in the Randolph camp, solidified when Nancy shared Gabriella's transgressions with Judith, their brother Tom, a very pregnant Patsy and the three Matoax brothers. All were appalled by the litany of ugly behavior and the colonel's resolve that his fiancée was perfection itself. Patsy was especially upset to hear about the mistreated children.

"Is she truly making them so miserable?"

"Judge for yourself." Nancy nodded at the two youngest Randolph children huddled in a corner, faces glum. "Gabriella has been so nasty, never in front of Papa of course, that Harriet and Virginia are too scared to leave their rooms. Yesterday when they were romping in the maze, she yelled at them to be quiet. What child plays quietly outdoors? Heaven knows, none of us ever did." She sighed with sadness. "They have been wretched since she moved in."

"You've surely tried to comfort them," Patsy said.

"Of course. Jane's fourteen and John's eleven, so they're old enough to understand the situation, but the little ones are terrified."

"What a virago," John declared.

"I still can't believe Papa let her paint the parlor white," Tom Junior said. "I can't bear to go in there now."

"You know Mama is spinning in her grave," Judith added.

"Please don't mention Mama," Nancy said. "I want to cry every time I think about her."

Theo, hoping to cheer everyone up with his New York adventures, offered his opinion of The Contrast, a new play by Royall Tyler. "I must say it takes some lively potshots at Americans consumed with British fashions, traditions and the like. The funniest character, and my personal favorite, is Billy Dimple. He woos three women at once, seeks money from each and ends up disgraced."

"As well he should be," Richard opined.

"I was fortunate to attend the theater in Paris," Patsy said. The Comédie-Italienne was my favorite. It was always so—"

Her words were lost beneath Colonel Randolph's call for quiet. With Gabriella at his side, all ruffles and dimples, he thanked everyone for being part of their special day and introduced John Harvie, father of the bride. Nancy was repulsed by the man's arrogant bearing and extravagantly twisted and beribboned plaits.

"In honor of this merging of our two families," Harvie announced, "Colonel Randolph has generously offered to sell me six hundred acres at Edgehill."

"And happy I am to do so, sir. As you said, since we are blending blood, why not blend land as well?"

The Richmond contingent cheered while the Randolphs remained deadly silent. If Colonel Randolph saw their glacial stares, he gave no notice as he proposed a series of toasts to his beaming bride.

As the eldest son, Tom was seething. "How dare he sell my patrimony!" he hissed. "That's almost a third of Edgehill's acreage!"

"After all Nancy has said," John ventured, "I should think an equally important question is how much our little Gabriella had to do with the sale."

"By God, she's not going to get away with it!" Tom swore. "Wedding day or not, Papa and I are going to have words. Now!"

Patsy seized his arm and urged him to wait until the guests were gone. "Surely a few hours won't matter."

"You're wrong!" Tom threw off her arm and stood. "Every minute counts when you're dealing with vultures like the Harvies. My fool of a father has taken the bait and swallowed it whole."

"Tom, please don't—!"

Tom ignored Patsy's plea and strode across the great hall, heedlessly jostling the Richmond crowd and leaving spilled drinks in his wake. He walked straight to his father and erased the older man's grin with a fierce demand.

"We need to talk, father, and we need to talk now!" he thundered.

Aware that all eyes were on him, Randolph leaned toward his angry son and whispered. "Remember yourself, young man! We have a houseful of guests and whatever it is, it can wait."

"No, it can't!" Tom hissed back. "I have something to say and I'm going to say it in public or in private. The choice is yours."

The colonel stepped back and addressed the crowd. "Please continue the celebration, everyone. I'll be back in a trice." He leaned down to reassure Gabriella who had suddenly gone ashen. "Don't worry, darling. I'm sure it's nothing."

Tom gave Gabriella a murderous glare. "Guess again, sir."

Randolph took his son's arm, but Tom yanked free. The colonel followed him into the Burnt Room and closed the door. He retrieved a handkerchief and wiped his sweaty brow.

"You'd better have a damned good reason for embarrassing me, boy."

"You're the embarrassment!" Tom shot back. "I don't know what kind of spell this witch has cast, but you've behaved like a fool since you met her."

"Careful," Randolph growled.

"You're blind and deaf to the truth. All it took was a wink and a smile and no doubt some promised paradise in the boudoir, and you throw your own flesh and blood to the dogs."

Randolph grunted and sank into a chair. "You don't know what you're talking about."

"To the contrary, I know exactly what I'm talking about. All us children do. We don't care if you remarry someone half your age or behave like a smitten schoolboy, but for God's sake don't give her what rightfully belongs to us. It's not enough that she turns Tuckahoe upside down to suit herself, but going after the family fortune too? I tell you it's not to be borne, Papa!"

"So that's it, eh? This business with Edgehill. That's what set you off."

"Can you blame me? Do you realize what you've done?"

"What if I told you I was setting aside the remainder of Edgehill for my children's patrimony?"

"Edgehill belongs to us intact, all two thousand acres."

"I didn't raise you to be greedy," his father retorted, anger rising to match that of his son.

"Greed is grabbing a bigger piece of the pie than you deserve, Papa. All I and the rest of us want is our due. You know it's only fair."

"What I know," Randolph replied, grim-faced and unmoved, "is that I've heard enough of your selfish drivel. I've made my decision, and it's final."

"Then what I'm about to do is final too. Patsy and I are leaving and you will see us no more."

"Go then, and good riddance!" Randolph snarled, getting to his feet. "You won't be missed."

"With that avaricious little tart warming your bed, I suspect not!"

"How dare you?!" Colonel Randolph lunged hard, but Tom deftly stepped aside so that his father crashed into the scorched wall. His head scraped the rough, crackled surface, and he reeled backwards into his chair. He sat hard, then touched his wet forehead and stared, confused, at the blood on his fingertips.

Tom was unmoved. "Good-bye, Papa."

He opened the door to find his family waiting outside. He grabbed Patsy's hand and, ignoring her pregnancy, roughly spirited her away. Gabriella pushed through and rushed to Randolph's side. After a moment, she looked up and screamed for everyone to go away. All obeyed except Nancy who refused to leave without a final salvo.

"I hope you're pleased with yourself, Papa. Today you've lost your namesake."

Gabriella glared, voice laden with vitriol. "That remains to be seen."

Part 2

"This above all: to thine own self be true,
And it must follow, as the night the day,
Thou canst not then be false to any man."
— William Shakespeare, *Hamlet*

8

Discord settled over Tuckahoe like a malignant cloud. Dissension with Gabriella, as Nancy wrote Theo and Patsy, was so pervasive you could set fire to it. Gabriella devoted herself to entertaining her Richmond coterie, forcing Nancy to add more duties atop her existing ones. She knew it was useless to complain to her father. More enmeshed than ever in Gabriella's web, Randolph told Nancy he was nullifying their agreement regarding Theo and resumed his campaign to marry her off. Nancy had no doubt that Gabriella fueled this plot to oust her so she might rule Tuckahoe alone.

The suitor chosen this time was another wealthy cousin, Archibald Randolph. He was at least close to her age, but Nancy found him hopelessly dull. He had none of Theo's wit and worldliness, and eroded her patience with long stretches of silence. When she told her father that Archibald was intolerable, he accused of her being ungrateful and ordered her out of his office. By spring, Nancy's discontent had grown exponentially and peaked one afternoon when she heard screams from the parlor. Hurrying to investigate, she found Gabriella shaking Virginia hard by the shoulders.

"Stop it!" Nancy pulled her tearful baby sister to safety and glared at Gabriella. "What in heaven's name were you doing?"

"Disciplining a willful, disobedient child," Gabriella calmly replied.

"What are you talking about?"

"I told Virginia to bring my tea, and she said that's what servants are for."

Nancy was incredulous. "You punished a child for telling the truth?"

"Children are meant to do as they're told," Gabriella retorted. "If the girl had done as I asked, none of this would've happened."

Nancy kissed her sister's forehead and sent her outside to play before turning angrily to Gabriella. "That was a monstrous thing to do!"

"May I remind you that I am the mistress of Tuckahoe, and that those living here are obliged to obey my rules?"

"I am sick to death of hearing you talk about being mistress of this house!" Nancy's voice rose along with her temper. "You have no idea what the title means. If you did, we would have peace and warmth, not rancor and unending chaos. You ought to be ashamed of yourself."

"How dare you speak to me in such a manner!"

"Because I am your equal and not some defenseless child or slave cowering before your tyranny. I'm not blind, Gabriella. I know you've mistreated everyone in this household, and this business with Virginia is the last straw."

"Precisely what do you propose to do about it? Tell your father?" Gabriella smirked. "We both know your complaints go unheard."

"Not when I tell him you hurt his youngest child."

"He gave me permission to discipline the youngest as I saw fit," Gabriella said coolly. "I was merely doing as I was told."

Nancy was livid. "You're the most heartless woman I've ever met. God forbid you ever have children of your own."

"If your father has his way, that will be soon enough." She waved a hand. "Now either see to my tea or run along."

Nancy's fury was so primal that she barely remembered going up to her room and slamming the door. She managed to collect herself by late afternoon when her father returned home, irritable as usual after dealing with the overseer's complaints. After a few private moments with Gabriella, he agreed to meet Nancy in the Burnt Room where, as Gabriella predicted, he was deaf to tales of her cruelty. He didn't even flinch when Nancy described Virginia's cries for help.

"Are you quite finished?" he asked.

Knees buckling, she sank into a chair, an accused criminal waiting to be sentenced. "Yes, Papa. I am."

"Then it's time to say what I should have said months ago." Nancy shrank from the finality in his voice. "Since you've made it quite clear that you're unhappy at Tuckahoe, the only solution is for you to live elsewhere."

The roaring in her ears made Nancy shake her head, as though she could dissolve the hateful words. "You…you would cast me out of my own home?!"

"You leave me no choice, daughter. This impasse is not of my doing."

His tone of finality told Nancy that further arguing was useless. "Then where shall I go?"

"Perhaps one of your brothers or sisters will take you in." Randolph read his desk clock. "I'm late for supper."

Nancy didn't know how long she remained alone in the Burnt Room, wishing she could fall through the floor and into oblivion. Somehow, she made her way upstairs to "Mama's window" where she kissed her fingertips and touched the pane. The glass was warm, but the April sunlight was fading fast, along with any remaining love for her father.

"Good-bye, Mama."

*

Nancy's first destination was Monticello. Tom and Patsy welcomed her, and she remained almost a month until Colonel Randolph summoned Tom to Tuckahoe, purportedly to make amends. It was, alas, another of Gabriella's ruses, and when Tom returned, he had the four youngest Randolph children in tow. Nancy was grateful to her brother for his generous rescue, but even with Mr. Jefferson mostly away in Washington City, Monticello was crowded beyond its limit. Realizing she had to move again, Nancy looked to Judith for help and mercifully her sister acquiesced. Because they had had little contact since their father's wedding, Nancy knew only that Judith and Richard were now at Bizarre plantation in a remote corner of Cumberland County. With seven hundred acres and sixty-seven slaves, it was considerably smaller than Matoax, which made Nancy wonder why they had moved. When she queried Tom, he muttered something about "poor Judith" and the "ineffectual Matoax boys" before changing the subject.

Since she and most of her siblings had visited there as children, Nancy had warm memories of Bizarre. When she arrived in spring of 1790, nothing appeared changed. The small, two-story house perched atop a high stone foundation overlooking the Appomattox River, with a gently sloping path leading to docks where tobacco hogsheads were loaded onto flat-bottomed boats for shipment to Petersburg. The place was rustic by Randolph standards and boasted none of Tuckahoe's luxuries, but Nancy had loved playing hide-and-seek in the thick forest and hunting for pottery shards at an ancient Indian mound. Her favorite pastime was climbing an ancient beech overhanging the river and watching her reflection in the brown water. The tree had since spawned a vast root system, and, upon her return, Nancy was delighted to find a comfortable natural bench. There was, however, little opportunity to laze there or dwell on memories. Life at Bizarre was far more demanding than at Tuckahoe, a reality that dawned the moment Nancy saw her sister. Judith had lost considerable weight, and her face was drawn. Her graceful hands, once much admired, were rough and red, and she seemed more distant than ever. When Nancy thanked her and Richard for taking her in, Judith's only response was that she could use the extra pair of hands. Nancy was distressed and bewildered by the dire circumstance but knew not to ask questions. Within a few days, however, Judith, made an unexpected confidence after Richard rode off to conduct business with a neighboring planter.

"We'll do our mending outside this morning." Judith picked up her sewing basket, and Nancy trailed her onto the front porch. Once they were settled in creaky wicker chairs, Judith began stitching a rip in one of Richard's waistcoats. "In case you're wondering about our sorrowful situation," she said, needle flashing in the sunlight, "you should know things will get worse before they get better. If indeed they ever do."

"You know I'll help any way I can," Nancy offered softly.

"I'm counting on it, little sister. Richard was no more cut out to be a planter than I was to be a farmer's wife." She grimaced at her calloused hands. "I've never worked so hard in my life, yet we barely manage to keep our heads above water."

Nancy started to say that her life at Tuckahoe had been continuous drudgery for the monstrous Gabriella, but knew Judith would see that as belittling her dilemma. She busied herself with a torn apron.

"I'm sure you're wondering why we left Matoax. It's embarrassing, but we're family so I suppose you deserve the truth." She sighed heavily. "When Richard was courting me, I deemed myself lucky because he was always generous. What I didn't know was that he never considered that things must be paid for when bills come due. I found Matoax quite comfortable, but we hadn't been there a week when he decided the worn carpets weren't good enough. We went Petersburg for new ones, very expensive of course, and after that came a new settee, a tea table and a dresser. He made other trips to buy livestock and harness leather and whatever struck his majesty's fancy. None were necessities, Nancy, and when the bills came, Richard requisitioned money from other Randolph plantations or sent his manservant to instruct the Randolph agent to pay for this, that or the other. He behaved as though we had an endless supply of funds until one of his largest creditors, a Petersburg merchant, confronted him in the street and demanded payment. Richard was of course humiliated. That was the last straw for his stepfather, Saint George Tucker. When word of the incident reached Mr. Tucker down in Williamsburg, he wrote Richard and demanded changes. The poor man has been endlessly patient and generous with Richard, with Theo and John as well, but this was too much. Mr. Tucker engaged an overseer and his family to run Matoax and dispatched us here, in the middle of nowhere."

"I thought you loved Bizarre."

"As a child, yes. As an adult, it's toil from sunrise to sunset." Judith stopped sewing and studied the sluggish river. "I'm almost at the end of my rope." She nodded as Shayla the cook strode across the yard. "It's only a matter of time before we sell her, but it's just as well. The trader lied about her cooking skills. The miserable woman either burns the food or serves it half-raw. I'm better in the kitchen than she is, and I'm all but helpless."

"Bonnie taught me a few basics about cooking, and I'm sure I could—"

"Good," Judith said. She resumed her mending. "I'll sell Shayla tomorrow."

9

Judith hadn't exaggerated about the constant toil, but, as promised, Nancy worked hard. She proved herself a fast learner in the kitchen and produced much better meals than the vanquished Shayla. Judith made no comment, but Richard was lavish with praise, and by late spring the three fell into a smooth routine. Without her father and Gabriella making her miserable, Nancy welcomed her first peace of mind in months, and was thrilled when Richard received a letter from Theo announcing that he was coming home. With Matoax now occupied by tenants, home meant Bizarre, and Nancy was so excited about a reunion she lowered her guard at dinner.

"Has Theo left Bermuda?"

Richard looked up from his plate. "How did you know about Bermuda?"

Rather than attempt some fanciful excuse, Nancy revealed the truth. "Your brother and I have been corresponding since Mama died. Papa disapproves of him, so we had to keep it a secret. Delilah and I cooked up a scheme to intercept Theo's letters." She savored the memory. "I was terrified of being caught, but I secretly enjoyed fooling Papa."

Richard couldn't resist a little teasing as he slathered another Johnny cake with butter. "So, a grand romance has been going on right under my nose, eh?"

"I'd hardly call it a romance, but I enjoy Theo's company and don't mind saying so."

"I noticed a spark between you two at Papa's wedding," Judith ventured. "No need to blush, Nancy. You know I have no objections to Theo's courtship."

"Nor I," Richard added. "Although his health is cause for concern."

Nancy shrugged. "He always jokes about it, so I never know if he's sugar-coating the truth."

Richard grew serious. "When we were children, Theo was often sickly. John too, although he often feigned illness with astonishing credibility. I worried about them both, especially when we went off to college. It didn't take Theo long to discover he enjoyed taverns and carousing far more than classrooms, and it finally caught up with him. He's dropped out of school before, but this time I don't believe he'll go back." He paused. "What did he tell you about Bermuda?"

"Only that New York was cold and snowy, and that he needed sunshine."

"Didn't you find it unusual for a university student to visit a tropical island in the middle of the school year?"

"Most everything Theo does is unusual."

"True enough, but, as you suspected, he was sugar-coating things. It was the doctors who sent him to Bermuda."

Nancy was alarmed. "Please don't tell me he's ill again."

"Yes, he is, and his prodigious drinking hasn't helped."

Nancy unhappily recalled her father calling Theo a wastrel, loath to accept that he might've been right. "Oh, dear!"

"Have faith, Nancy. Theo's habits will change when he's under my roof. As you know, everyone at Bizarre must pull their own weight, and my brother is no exception. Even John pitched in the last time he visited."

"Not without declaring that he considers it beneath his station," Judith added drily. "And that he was greatly inconvenienced."

Richard chuckled. "Something he's done since we were boys."

"When can we expect Theo?" Nancy asked.

"His letter was mailed from New York, so we should see him most any day."

Nancy was thrilled, but it in fact was another week before Theo completed the long ride from Richmond to

Bizarre. The morning of his arrival found her gathering wildflowers to brighten the inside of the house. She was adding bluebells to bloodroot when galloping hooves triggered a fuss of blue jays. She readjusted her bonnet to better shade her eyes and watched a dusty silhouette sharpen into a rider sitting very erect.

"Theo!" Nancy waved him over, and, as he drew up, admired a gray flannel coat over a white shirt and dark blue waistcoat. Buckskin breeches were tucked into top-boots, and the final, fashionable touch was a broad-brimmed beaver hat. She smiled. "You're as dashing as ever!"

"And you, my dear, are the picture of bucolic beauty." Theo reined his horse and dismounted with a flourish, hat sliding effortlessly into his hand before he opened his arms in invitation. He was pleased when Nancy rushed into his embrace. "You must forgive me for smelling like the road."

"All that matters is that you're home, Theo."

"Yes," he echoed. "Home." He wiped the back of his neck with a handkerchief. "It's not yet summer but it's already beastly."

"This is our first really hot day, and I'm afraid there's little breeze to be found."

"Bother all that. Let me get a better at you." Theo stepped back and nodded approval. "You're as lovely as ever."

"Even in my country bumpkin dress and my hair tucked inside a poke bonnet?"

"The smartest Manhattan belles could not compete," he avowed.

"Heaven loves a gallant liar," Nancy laughed. "But come along now. We must tell Richard and Judith that you're here."

"May we not have a moment alone?"

His request caught Nancy off-guard. "If you wish."

"I do wish, but first I must water my poor horse." Theo squinted against the glare. "Is the river that way?"

"You're turned around, dear." She pointed. "There, through those oak trees."

After ensuring that his horse had drunk his fill, Theo tethered the animal to a tree and inhaled deeply. "That old river smells wonderful."

Nancy indicated the beech tree on the riverbank. "You surely remember that shady place."

"Oh, yes. Especially the day John climbed too far out, showing off as usual, and the branch broke and dropped him into the river." Theo chuckled. "Its's one of my favorite childhood memories."

"See how much the tree has grown." Nancy led him to the seat formed by the roots. "I sometimes sit here with my sewing. If there's a breeze, this is where to catch it." As if by magic, a burst of wind rushed off the water. "There. You see?"

"Very nice." They sat together and dangled their feet in the air, admiring the canopy of leaves, undersides iridescent with water-reflected sunlight. "The first time I came here, we were fleeing the British."

"How awful!"

"Not really. I was only ten, so for me our flight from Matoax was more adventure than anything else. I was too naïve to understand the danger of enemy troops heading our way. Luckily, they didn't get this far and retreated after burning Richmond."

They sat in silence for a few moments, each weighing the upheaval bringing them to this particular place and time. Nancy was forever banished from Tuckahoe, and Theo's college days were finished. It was a landmark loss of innocence for both, and because neither knew what the future held, they sought contentment in the present. Nancy studied Theo while he gazed across the river. Long brown hair was pulled back and tied with a blue ribbon. With his smooth, clean-shaven face and a glow awarded by Bermuda's tropical clime, Nancy believed him the handsomest of men. He turned suddenly.

"What are you looking at, my pretty maid?"

Nancy blushed at being caught. "I didn't mean to stare. I only wanted to assure myself that you're truly here."

"Then let me assure you that I'm real." Theo took her hand and pressed it to his lips. "Do you believe me now?"

"I do."

"Then may I say something intimate?"

"If you wish."

"Since learning you and I were to be living under the same roof, I've thought of little else. I want to get to know you as no other man has done, and in return I will cherish you and share my deepest secrets." He kissed her hand again. "Am I reaching too high?"

"No more than I, Theo, because my hopes are the same."

10

Devoid of clouds, the September sky blazed white. Heat clung to Bizarre like a shroud, rising in thick waves to shimmer like a mirage. Nancy stood on the front porch and scanned the horizon until she spotted Richard and Theo working alongside the fieldhands. A few months ago, she could never have imagined such a sight, but with a rickety economy and ever declining tobacco prices, Virginia's planters were fighting for survival. Richard was no exception, and, as was his habit, turned to his stepfather for advice. Tucker was sympathetic until Richard admitted he'd left running Bizarre to its aged overseer and still knew little about tobacco.

Tucker shamed such lack of initiative and bluntly told him it was "time to get your hands dirty."

Toward those ends, Tucker recommended Daniel Moseley, an overseer with proven skills, and made Richard swear to learn from the man. Richard agreed, and a week later installed Moseley and wife Eula in the overseer's cottage. Moseley moved swiftly to analyze Bizarre's problems and showed Richard that the beds had not been properly cleared or prepared for planting. He explained how they must be closely monitored in summer for worms, beetles and suckers, those troublesome sprouts that drained the plant's energy. The curing process also required close attention as the mature plants were harvested and hung to dry in the barn. More care was needed while the leaves were stripped from their stalks, denuded of heavy veins and packed in hogsheads for shipment to market. Richard made good on his promise to Tucker by taking copious notes and following Moseley into the fields. The new overseer's skills revived an ailing crop, but a crisis arose at harvest time when some of his ablest field hands were felled by dysentery.

Richard proved his mettle by grabbing a blade and joining the crew in slashing the tall green plants to the ground. Mosely was further pleased when Theo followed Richard's example, and by the time the hogsheads were packed and shipped down the Appomattox River to Petersburg, the sun had turned the Randolph brothers brown as berries. Nancy admired Theo's deep tan and lean, sinewy physique, but remained troubled by his persistent cough. Theo pretended not to worry, but when Nancy expressed concern, he made two startling confessions.

After harvest, it had become their custom to take twilight strolls alongside the river to enjoy private moments and perhaps snare a random breeze. Richard and Judith were aware of these walks, but kept any romantic speculation to themselves. One evening, Theo took Nancy's hand as they passed the ancient river beech and led her to Sandy Ford, a spot where the Appomattox sometimes grew shallow enough to allow the passage of wagon traffic. The soft, grassy riverbank invited them to lie beneath a harvest moon and emergent star sparkle.

"I've something I must say to you." Theo locked his fingers behind his head and sighed, whether from fatigue or apprehension she couldn't tell. "Once again, I must ask to speak intimately."

"By now, you should know you may speak anyway you like."

"Good." Theo studied the sky, idly recalling a science course at Columbia teaching the name and locations of the constellations. He was pleased with himself when he identified Cassiopeia. "You know, dearest cousin, that my feelings for you grow stronger by the day."

"As mine do for you."

"That sweet truth compels me to share something that my brothers and Mr. Tucker don't know." Theo coughed softly, and Nancy was relieved when it didn't deteriorate into one of his frequent hacking spells. "When I was thirteen, I succumbed to such coughing fits that I was confined to bed for days at a time. I recall one such instance vividly because of a conversation between my mother and the doctor. They were outside my bedroom door and believed me sleeping, but I heard every word." Nancy's pulse quickened. "The doctor said in cases like mine, the patient rarely survived adolescence. From that day on, I counted each day as a blessing because every coughing bout might spell my end. Richard sometimes caught me crying, but I never told him why."

"Poor Theo. How dreadful!"

"It would be cowardly to blame my past bad behavior on ill health, but it's partly true. Since I doubted I'd live long enough to benefit from higher education, I devoted myself to dissolution. Richard went through a similar phase but knew when to curtail his carousing. I never did. People consider me debauched, and they're right." He drew a ragged breath. "I behaved so abominably last winter that I nearly died. I went on a drinking spree and woke up in a hospital after another student found me in a snowbank. I...I sometimes wish he hadn't."

"You mustn't say such things," Nancy whispered.

"When I couldn't stop coughing, the doctors insisted on a warm climate and sent me to Bermuda. They warned that I would die if I didn't swear off whiskey and the life of a libertine. I took their advice, but my future remains uncertain and not just because of my health. With my education ended, I have no means to support myself."

"Not so," she insisted. "These past few months are proof positive. You and Richard have both shown yourselves capable of meeting great challenges. Bizarre is recovering, and so are you. You look so much better than you did when you arrived a few months ago."

"I know. I see myself in the mirror and tell myself that the doctors were wrong, but, in my soul, I know it's only an illusion from laboring in the summer sun." He sighed. "That sun will soon be gone, and I fear the coming winter.

My cough always worsens in cold weather, and the older I get—"

"There are other physicians," Nancy insisted, "and other beneficial climates."

"I thought about that in Bermuda. I could thrive there, but with no funds to support myself—"

Nancy leaned close and rested a hand on his chest. "Then Charleston perhaps. Or Savannah. There are plantations there, and I've heard people speak of the mild winters."

"You've no idea how much I cherish your concern." Theo propped himself up on one elbow, and when Nancy's hand fell away, he pressed it back to his chest. "If I sought a warmer climate, I wouldn't want to be alone, and because I'm only half a man offering an uncertain future, I must speak from the heart." He looked into her eyes. "I have fallen in love with you, Nancy Randolph, and I want nothing more than to make you my wife. Will you do me the honor?"

"Yes!" she cried, throwing herself into his arms. "Oh, yes!"

They held each other close, lost in the moment before surrendering to a longing neither could deny. When the moment passed, they lay satisfied and still. The heard only the disharmony of croaking frogs and chirruping crickets until Theo touched Nancy's cheek.

"I've never known such happiness, my love."

"Nor I," she said. "Nor I."

He kissed her sweetly before helping her to her feet and took her hand again as they walked home. Lost in the memory of their newfound intimacy, they said nothing until they saw Bizarre's windows twinkling with candlelight. Richard and Judith were silhouettes moving inside.

Nancy was trembling with anticipation. "I can't wait to tell them our news."

"Not just yet, dearest."

"For what purpose?" Nancy asked, perplexed. "Aren't you eager to share our joy?"

"Of course, but remember those youthful years of exchanging letters and sharing thoughts and dreams with each other and no one else?'

"Yes, but—"

"I want that again, for a little while at least. Having our wonderful secret and exchanging glances that only we understand will prolong our joy. It would mean so much to me, Nancy." Theo squeezed her hand. "Might we do this?"

"Dearest Theo. By now you surely you know I can deny you nothing."

11

Nancy was grateful and relieved when Theo remained healthy through autumn and into the winter of 1792. Both believed it was due to abstinence from alcohol and good food on the table. Richard's collaboration with Moseley had produced a profitable tobacco crop enabling Judith to maintain a well-stocked larder and, to Nancy's relief, hire a skilled cook and even indulge in a few fripperies. Such bounty was fortuitous as Richard and Judith were expecting a baby in the spring. The Christmas holidays saw the couples socializing and calling on neighbors, most often at Glyntyvar, another family plantation where Mary and Randolph Harrisons were generous hosts.

At the end of January, Richard received a letter from John in Philadelphia where he'd been studying law for two years. It included mundane ramblings about school, his dislike of Philadelphia, a vague allusion to a failed romance and his waning interest in law. He also wrote that he missed his brothers dearly and hoped to visit to Bizarre in the summer. What John omitted was that he had been following in Theo's debauched footsteps with misbehavior noted by his mentor, Edmund Randolph, Attorney General of the United States. John escaped expulsion only because of high marks and an ability to debate with passion, a skill acquired by watching Patrick Henry's fiery speeches. In exchange for lenience, John promised Edmund that his drinking days were behind him.

Nancy also received a letter from John, unexpected since they had not corresponded in over a year. She was further surprised by his announcement that, when he visited Bizarre, he hoped they "might continue where they left off." Nancy liked John well enough but hoped the remark didn't mean he thought of her in romantic terms, especially with her secret engagement to his brother. Naturally she sought Theo's advice.

"The solution is simple enough," he said. "Tell him we're to be married."

"Which also means telling Richard and Judith."

Theo gave her a quick kiss. "We've had enough fun with our little secret, my love. Clearly the time has come to share it."

Richard and Judith welcomed the news, but after congratulations were offered, Nancy explained her dilemma with John. Richard volunteered to tell John the truth in his next letter and elevated everyone's mood by announcing that a celebratory dinner was in order. Corinna, the new cook, responded with peanut soup, veal chops with mushrooms cooked in port wine, sweet corn and cabbage, followed by a scrumptious apple tansy. It was such a memorable meal that Theo treated himself to a small glass of Madeira.

As was usual for country dwellers, families retired soon after dinner. With her engagement no longer a secret, Nancy anticipated a night of blissful dreams. Snuggled under a mound of quilts, she quickly fell asleep and slept soundly until Theo's ferocious coughing roused the entire household. She lay still, praying for the sound to cease, and when it worsened, she rushed to help. She burst into the hallway and collided with Richard, nearly knocking the candle from his hand.

"I've never heard him this bad," Richard said, grim-faced. "Maybe it's the wine and all that rich food."

"Maybe," Nancy said, voice timorous. "You don't think you should ride for the doctor?"

"I've been through this before, Nancy. There's nothing doctors can do."

Her heart dropped. "Nothing?!"

"They'll only prescribe rest and a healthy diet." Both turned toward Theo's door when they heard a particularly vicious paroxysm. "Dear God!"

Richard opened the door, and Nancy followed, horrified by what the candlelight revealed. Theo's nightshirt was splattered with blood, his face pinched with pain as he struggled for breath.

"Mercy!" Nancy cried.

"Help me get him into a sitting position," Richard urged. "That sometimes helps."

He set his candlestick aside and, with Nancy's assistance, propped Theo against the pillows. She brought water, but he couldn't stop coughing long enough to drink it. She could only watch, powerless, as the coughing rode agonizing waves before it finally slowed and stopped. Theo's breathing remained labored, but, with Nancy's help, he swallowed a little water. Richard helped his brother out of his blood-drenched nightshirt and into a fresh one. Nancy fetched a washbasin and towels, spreading one across Theo's chest in case there was more blood.

"I'm...I'm sorry to...disturb everyone," he rasped.

"Don't talk," Richard insisted.

"No," Nancy urged. "Just lie still." She wrung water from a cloth and wiped Theo's face, forehead and throat. "Go back to bed, Richard."

"Are you coming too?"

Nancy drew a chair alongside Theo's bed. "I'm staying here."

"You won't sleep a wink in that uncomfortable thing."

"I won't sleep in my bed either. I'll only lie there worrying."

"I'll leave an extra candle."

Richard squeezed Nancy's shoulder and was gone. She turned back to Theo, grateful that he had fallen asleep, exhausted. She drew a blanket around her shoulders and sat in silence, mindful of the regular rise and fall of Theo's chest. Sleep eased his pain and made him look peaceful beneath the flickering candlelight. Nancy kept her vigil until the spare candle sputtered and flickered out, but even in darkness she

78

did not abandon her love. Only when dawn worked its pale gray fingers into the room did fatigue lull her into a restless sleep.

Theo was better by morning, and by afternoon was able to eat something. He continued to improve, and life returned to normal for the remainder of January. He assured everyone that he was growing stronger every day, and, on the second of February, celebrated his twenty-first birthday with impressive gusto. Another two weeks passed without incident before the coughing returned. It was not nearly so severe as the last bout, but was enough to land Theo back in bed. Nancy remained at his side until the coughing subsided that evening.

"I'm alright now," he said. "Please go to bed."

"I'm afraid to leave you alone."

"Don't be. My lungs no longer ache, and that tells me I should pass the night without incident." He smiled. "But I won't sleep at all knowing you're stuck in that miserable chair."

"Are you sure?"

"I'm sure, my love."

Nancy kissed him and reluctantly left. She lay in bed, tingling with constant dread that Theo's coughing would return, but the house remained still. The next morning, she hurried to his room, relieved to find him awake, pale but peaceful. His greeting warmed her heart.

"Good morning, my love."

"Good morning, my love," she echoed. "How are you feeling?"

"Well enough for a sip of water."

Nancy filled a glass from a pitcher on the washstand and carefully helped him sit up, ever mindful of triggering a coughing spasm. She was elated when he drank without incident. "Do you think you might eat a biscuit?"

"Later perhaps. For now, sit beside me. I have a story for you."

To her surprise, the odd request made Nancy laugh. "A story?"

"Yes, dearest. Will you indulge me?"

"Of course." Nancy kissed Theo's cheek and sat on the edge of the bed. "Tell me."

Theo paused until the memory came home. "There was a tavern in Greenwich Village," he began. "On Ganesvoort Street, it was, and the tavernkeeper, Robert Patterson, lived upstairs. He'd been a sailor aboard the Hancock when it captured the British ship Fox, and my friends and I loved hearing his colorful sea stories. One evening, the barman said Patterson was ill, and, as fate dictated, he died that very night. As he was telling us the news, an old clock in the hall began to chime. The barkeep was shocked because it hadn't chimed in years, and we all sat silent while it chimed forty-seven times. When it finally stopped, the barman said that the number of chimes and Patterson's age were one and the same."

"Goodness! Can this be true?"

"Cross my heart." Theo's finger made an x across his thin chest and he mustered a smile. "I'm ready for that biscuit now, with lots of blackberry jam, if you please."

"Right away, my darling!"

Nancy kissed him again before grabbing a heavy shawl and rushing outside to the kitchen where Judith and Corinna were baking. As luck would have it, Corinna was taking a pan of biscuits from the fire. Judith gave Nancy a curious glance.

"You look like the cat that swallowed the canary."

"It's Theo," Nancy beamed. "He's sitting up and telling stories. He even asked for a biscuit with blackberry jam."

"Thank the Lord." Judith wrapped a hot biscuit in cloth and passed it to Nancy. "I'm afraid Richard ate the last of the jam, but there are peach preserves on the dinner table."

"Thank you!"

As Nancy hurried back to the house, she considered Theo's strange tale about the tavernkeeper's clock. She knew he had a remarkable repertoire of picaresque stories and wondered why he chose that particular one. She resolved to find out why, but when she delivered his still-warm biscuit and preserves, she found that her beloved Theo had left this earth.

12

Theo's sudden death crippled Bizarre with grief. While Judith sought comfort in her scriptures, Richard immersed himself in work with Daniel Moseley. Nancy, in pain and emotionally unmoored, suffered bouts of melancholia, and when it was accompanied by colic, she wrote Patsy for help. Because Patsy had inherited her father Thomas's interest in science and medicine, Nancy hoped she might have a cure. Patsy suggested gum guiacum used to treat colic, gout and rheumatism along with other maladies. Because the substance was available nowhere near Bizarre, Patsy sent a package along with advice to use it judiciously.

John expressed his anguish in letters. He made no mention of Theo's engagement to Nancy, but reiterated a desire to get home to Bizarre. He was especially anxious, he wrote, to meet his new nephew, John St. George Randolph, whom Judith delivered in May. All hoped that Saint, as the baby was called, would provide the much-needed beacon leading Bizarre back into the light. In June, another visitor arrived, Regina Dudley, a middle-aged, widowed cousin who had fallen on hard times. Richard, ever-generous, offered lodging until she found another Randolph relative to take her in. Judith reminded him that Mrs. Dudley was a meek, jittery sort sure to disrupt the household, but he refused to turn the poor woman away. Judith grudgingly conceded, but devoted herself to Saint and ignored Mrs. Dudley altogether.

One June evening after Judith had taken Saint upstairs to bed and Mrs. Dudley was reading in her room, Nancy and Richard sought a breeze on the front porch. Because it was a moonless night, Nancy brought a candle to illuminate the torn shirt she was mending for Richard. Bizarre's busy routine rarely allowed for time alone with her brother-in-law, so she welcomed the moment.

"Motherhood certainly sits well with Judith," she said. "When I see her with Saint, I yearn for a fraction of her joy and a child of my own." When Richard remained silent, Nancy added, "Please forgive my frankness."

Richard sipped his ale. "You need not apologize for wanting what every woman wants."

"I never gave it much thought until Saint arrived. These days it haunts my dreams."

"I presume you'll acquire a husband first," Richard chuckled. Nancy laughed too, but was grateful that the dark porch concealed her blush. The remark reminded her of Theo and the great joy, now lost, that he brought into her life. The thrum of nighttime insects also reminded her of the evenings she and Theo spent on the riverbank, alone and unseen. They were her most cherished memories of what might have been. "While we're being frank," Richard said after a pause, "what do you anticipate when John arrives?"

"I've no idea, especially since his letters never mentioned my engagement to Theo."

"That's my baby brother. Unfathomable and unpredictable." Richard contemplated a blackness speckled with lightning bugs. "I long ago ceased being surprised at his behavior."

"I hope there's no resentment on his part."

"Should there be?"

Nancy looked up from her work. "To my surprise, he flattered me quite lavishly on your wedding day. I never encouraged him and so I worry that he's fabricated romantic notions where none exist. That would explain his odd remark about continuing 'where we left off.'"

"With his wild imagination, those notions could be vivid indeed."

"That's what troubles me. I'm very fond of him, Richard, but there's something odd about your brother, something indefinable and unsettling. He seems much older than his years."

"He's always been like that. Mama said he was supernal, which could explain why he was reading Voltaire and Homer when he was only eleven."

"So he said." Nancy resumed work on the shirt. "Although I wondered at the time if he were exaggerating."

"Another of John's childhood traits, but one I considered harmless because it was never malicious. Time and again, he regaled Theo and me with fanciful tales we knew weren't true. When questioned, he revealed his true genius. The boy could debate both sides of an argument and occasionally did."

"You mean he debated with himself?"

"I've seen theatrical performances in Richmond not nearly so entertaining." Richard enjoyed a private memory before saying, "Let's not worry. John's excited about coming home and seeing his new nephew, and we should leave it at that."

"You're right. Sometimes my imagination takes me to dark places."

"A Randolph trait if I ever heard one." Richard drank the last of his ale and got to his feet. "Another long day tomorrow, so don't stay up too late." He leaned down and kissed the top of Nancy's head. "Good-night."

"Richard?"

"What is it?"

"Thank you for listening."

"What do you mean?"

"Theo and I bared our souls to one another, and since he was taken away, I've felt shut out and alone."

"I had no idea."

"There's no blame intended. Your time is consumed by the plantation and being a husband and a new father."

"Why did you not go to Judith?"

"I love my sister, but she's never been easy to talk to."

"I know," Richard said heavily. "You're not the only one feeling shut out. Sometimes I think I should never have—" His voice trailed off.

"Never have what?" she urged.

The mask that had so unexpectedly dropped was slipped back into place as Richard squeezed Nancy's shoulder and retired, leaving her to ponder his enigmatic remark. The revelation that he shared her loneliness and endured a difficult relationship with Judith was troubling, especially when she remembered her sister's fierce determination to marry Richard in spite of their mother's protests. Was he not all she believed, or was it the other way around? Or, Nancy considered unhappily, was it both? She saw only a man who loved his wife and baby and, after some hard reckoning, labored hard to provide for them and his poor relations as well. What more could a woman want in a husband?

Flickering candlelight danced on Richard's shirt where it lay in Nancy's lap. She pressed it to her chest, as if she might feel his familial caring and love. Heat flushed her face and throat when she was drawn to the shirt's raw scent. She was so unnerved that she put it away and went upstairs to bed. Sleep came easily, but not without forbidden dreams.

*

John never came. In July, Richard received a letter from a Richmond physician saying that John had been ill with scarlet fever for weeks. The doctor assured Richard that his brother would recover but forbade visitors. A few days later, a letter from John in very shaky handwriting declared that the disease had brought him "to the brink of death" but that he was slowly recovering and would arrive at Bizarre in September. As the time grew near, Theo's old room was aired out and made up with fresh linens, and Richard instructed Corinna to plan John's favorite dishes. Such preparations, Nancy remarked good-naturedly, suggested the return of the prodigal son.

"It will be good to have him home," Richard said one afternoon as the family gathered for dinner. "Yes, he can be petulant and unpredictable, but no one can say he's not colorful. He's been that way from the very beginning." He waved away a pesky fly. "The abracadabra story is one of my favorites."

"That's one I haven't heard," Nancy said.

"It happened after the war started. John was five or six years old when mother decided Matoax needed something to ward off the British. Her solution was to hang abracadabra over the front door." He chuckled. "As though they'd do any good. John was fascinated with the word 'abracadabra' which, for some reason, he had trouble saying. No one knew why because he was using big words long before Theo or I. He must've pronounced it half a dozen ways, and it didn't help that we teased him so mercilessly that he found a ladder and tore the charm from the front door. When Mother asked him why, he said nothing was useful if it couldn't be pronounced. He then made a great ceremony of burning the sign and invited everyone to watch." He grinned and said, "My little brother is nothing if not dramatic."

"And determined," Judith added.

Everyone but Mrs. Dudley enjoyed the strange tale. "Oh, I don't know," she fretted. "I think I'd best stay out of the man's way."

"No need for that," Richard laughed. "Of all John's unhappy targets, I've never known him to take aim at a lady."

As if the moment were preordained, the pounding of hooves announced a visitor. Expecting John, Richard threw open the door but gaped in confusion at the figure dismounting from his horse. It approached the front porch in great, long strides, a pale phantom clad in a white flannel coat with matching pantaloons and vest. The ghostly appearance was further enhanced by a beaver hat wrapped in white paper. Richard's confusion continued until he heard a high-pitched voice more appropriate for a pubescent boy than a grown man.

"What's the matter with you, Richard? Don't you recognize your own brother?"

13

While John surpassed his brothers mentally, a delayed puberty had rendered him physically inferior. As a boy, he had waited, confused and frightened, for the essentials of manhood to arrive, but lost all hope after scarlet fever cemented his symptoms. Physicians confirmed that John was doomed to remain beardless and to speak with a soprano voice, along with suffering other male deficits too devastating to contemplate. His tall, lanky frame was misshapen, leaving him with a concave chest and hunched shoulders. When he stretched to his full height of six feet two inches, he appeared to be on stilts, yet, with his shrunken torso, when seated he almost resembled a child. He was nineteen-years-old.

With no warning about the baffling transformation, Richard was stunned. "Dear God, John! What has happened?!"

"Fate, I suppose." John locked long arms around his brother and whispered in his ear. "I know you're shocked. So am I when I encounter an unexpected mirror."

Richard leaned back, still disbelieving. "The scarlet fever did this?"

John shrugged. "Well, I was never a Hercules, but the fever aggravated and advanced rather rapidly what already plagued this poor, wretched body. What stands before you is forever what the world will see. I now face a life of repulsing the ladies and petrifying small children." He grinned at Richard's worn trousers and homespun shirt. "Just look at you! Every inch the elegant planter."

Richard took the joke in stride. "Alas, my days as a gentleman of leisure are behind me. I've learned some hard lessons since coming to Bizarre."

John noted the lush rows of towering tobacco plants marching toward the horizon, along with the well-maintained kitchen and outbuildings and neat rows of slave quarters beyond. "It looks fine, much better than when I saw it last." He squeezed Richard's shoulders. "I'm proud of you, big brother."

"Thank you."

John doffed his hat when the others followed Richard onto the porch. "Judith, my dear. And Nancy. How lovely to see you both. I have been anticipating this happy moment for some time." He embraced his bewildered cousins before noticing the plump figure lurking inside the doorway. "And who might this be?"

"Our cousin Regina Dudley," Richard explained. "She's staying with us a while."

John gave her a polite nod. "Madam."

"Sir." Regina managed, barely.

Struggling like the others to mask her shock, Judith took John's arm and ushered him inside. "You've come at a good time. We were just about to sit down to dinner, and I'm sure you're famished after the long ride."

"Right you are. My, what tantalizing aromas!" John threw an appreciative glance at a table laden with food. "But am I not to see my nephew?"

"After dinner," she promised. "He's sleeping right now."

"A pastime I daresay he did not inherit from me," John said, hanging his hat by the door. "Richard will confirm that I loathed bedtime as a child because I was afraid I might miss something."

"So you did. Now take off your coat and sit here beside me."

"All the better to observe the exotic new me," John quipped.

Richard was embarrassed for him. "You must stop demeaning yourself."

"Nonsense, brother. We mustn't ignore the pig in the parlor." John's elongated fingers opened his napkin with a flourish and dropped it in his lap. "Except for cousin Regina, I know the ladies are wondering about my metamorphosis. It's only natural to be curious about such things, and I am not too aloof to explain. May I have a glass of wine before I commence? My illness erased my taste for ale."

"I'll get it," Nancy said.

John delivered a surprisingly offhand explanation of his physical transformation. With ladies present, he chose his words with discretion and studiously avoided the damning revelation that he was now impotent. After dinner, he asked again to see his nephew. Judith took him upstairs where he peered into Saint's crib, acting like any doting uncle until she asked if he wanted to hold the baby.

"No, no!" John jumped back as though scalded and folded arms across his chest. "A look will suffice."

"Good heavens, John. You're not frightened of babies, are you?"

"Certainly not, but handling them is women's work."

"Nonsense. Richard plays with Saint all the time."

"I'm not my brother, and I'll thank you to remember that!" John snapped. He glared at her briefly, then smiled, mood changing yet again. "And now, if you will excuse me, I shall indulge in another glass of wine."

Judith turned away, relieved that John's outburst hadn't awakened Saint as she scooped the baby into her arms and cooed softly. She knew John's behavior was erratic, but this unprovoked rudeness raised concerns about how his presence might affect Bizarre's status quo. Only time would tell.

Mrs. Dudley had retreated to her room, but John found Richard and Nancy on the porch. "Did you see my son?" Richard asked.

"I did, and he resembles you as much as a bundle of pink flesh could." He delivered a comical shudder. "I told Judith that I'm not one for dandling babies on my knee."

"Knowing you loathe children, I'm surprised that you wanted to see him."

"Of course, I did. He's a Randolph, after all."

"He is indeed." Richard indicated the rich green fields. "And if destiny plays fair, someday this will be his."

"Ah, yes. That fickle mistress, destiny." John perched his lanky frame on the porch railing and swung one foot back and forth. He sipped his wine and stared at Nancy. "We never know about her, do we?"

"No," she said resignedly. "We certainly don't."

"As one who was minding my own business only to be stricken and undone out of the blue, I'm only too aware of the vagaries of human existence. As poor Romeo lamented, 'O, I am fortune's fool!'"

Richard smiled. "Still quoting Shakespeare, are you?"

"Why not? Who penned more melodious lines or metaphors that strike like lightning and blind the mind?"

"I hope your question is metaphorical," Richard replied good-naturedly, awed anew by his brother's intellect. If John was already this erudite, he considered, what might he attain in adulthood? "After a long day in the fields, I haven't the strength for one of your debates."

"None invited. Nor was it my destiny or that of your son to which I referred. I assume you haven't heard the happy news from Tuckahoe."

"What news?" Nancy asked, wary at the mention of her lost home.

"It appears that Bizarre is not the only one with a new master-in-waiting." John sipped again and stared at the fields. "My, my. All that lovely tobacco."

"That's enough, John." This was the waggish, impossible side of John's persona, designed to prod and provoke, and Richard was having none of it. "Stop playing cat-and-mouse, and get the point."

"Very well." John faced them squarely and delivered his news with exaggerated drama. "Her Majesty Queen

Gabriella was delivered of a boy-child at Castle Tuckahoe two weeks ago."

Nancy did not mask her disgust. "I suppose we shouldn't be surprised."

"No indeed," John echoed, "although the baby's christening will surely raise a few eyebrows."

"Why is that?"

"They've named him Thomas Mann Randolph, Junior."

"How can that be?!" Nancy gasped. "That's my brother's name!"

"One designated for the heir to Tuckahoe," Richard added ominously.

"Precisely the point." John turned to Nancy. "The concerns you expressed about Gabriella at your father's wedding have indeed borne malevolent fruit. It's plain that she's sunk her talons into Tuckahoe with no intention of letting go." He took another sip of wine. "We already know that her father is part of the plan, after coaxing away all that acreage at Edgehill. The fact that he is one of Richmond's most powerful attorneys doesn't bode well for your brother's patrimony."

"I was a fool to believe that when Papa died Gabriella would allow Tom to assume his birthright as master of Tuckahoe." Nancy pulled her hands apart when she realized she was wringing them. "This will infuriate him, and believe me Tom's temper is something to be reckoned with."

"I wonder if he knows," Richard offered.

"I've little doubt. He and Patsy are still at Monticello, and since Papa and Mr. Jefferson are such good friends —"

"And the colonel is surely boasting about his new fatherhood," John finished. "We Randolphs are such colorful folks, *n'est-ce-pas?*

Nancy was not amused. "I'd hoped distance would insulate us from Gabriella's evil."

"This must cease at once!" John barked, startling everyone with a loud soprano cry. "I forbid anyone to mention that avaricious wench's name again and hereby demand a change of subject."

Despite the moment's gravity, Richard smiled. "One thing I'll say for our new John. He hasn't lost an ounce of the old flamboyance."

"You don't know the half of it," John laughed. "I have a fresh and most exhilarating pastime."

"Pray tell us what it is," Richard teased.

"You'll find out soon enough." John downed his wine and lofted the empty glass. "There's more grape, I trust."

"I'll open another bottle." Richard rose and stretched. "After hearing the news from Tuckahoe, I could use some strong spirits myself."

"I as well," Nancy said grimly.

14

It wasn't long before Nancy learned about John's new pastime. Because her bedroom was next to his, she heard heavy pacing accompanied by a muffled mantra.

"Macbeth hath murdered sleep!" John muttered over and over. "Macbeth hath murdered sleep!"

The intonation lasted nearly an hour, ending abruptly when John rushed to the stable to saddle his horse and thunder into the night. Dogged by insomnia, he rode until he exhausted himself and his steed, returning before dawn just as the hapless Mrs. Dudley was heading to the privy. Terrified by the phantom on horseback, she screamed and fled back into the house. John went back to bed for a few hours of badly needed sleep and went downstairs to discover Mrs. Dudley had departed for parts unknown. He apologized to everyone, but Judith thanked him for getting the woman out of the house.

"I'm sorry you couldn't sleep," she said, pouring his coffee, "but I've never met such a timid, bundle of nerves. She wouldn't say boo to a goose."

"I didn't mind her," Nancy said. "She reminded me a bit of Aunt Lucy."

"Aunt Lucy's fine, but deliver me from Aunt Mary. Whenever she visits, I count the hours until she's gone again." Judith grimaced. "Why was this family cursed with such a horrid woman?"

John's eyes twinkled with mischief. "Is she my aunt too? It's so difficult to remember who's who in this crazy family." He cackled. "Not to mention what's what."

"She's our mother's youngest sister," Judith explained. "Only a year older than me."

"How odd to have an aunt so close in age."

"That's not the only odd thing." Nancy said. "She's the nosiest person I've ever met."

"Indeed, she is, forever asking questions and poking her nose where it doesn't belong. When was the last time you talked to Molly? Haven't I seen that dress before? Someone didn't dust those shelves." Judith rolled her eyes. "I wish you'd been here to run her off too, John."

"I've had some strange requests, but never that one." John smiled and glanced out the window as Richard galloped by. "What kind of day do we have?"

"Chilly and windy. Richard and Mr. Moseley are packing the tobacco in hogsheads today if you'd like to keep them company."

"Alas, farm work is alien to my agenda, but I should fancy a walk if I had company."

"I've got my usual busy morning, but Nancy can go if she likes."

"I'll get my shawl." It wasn't like Judith to endorse any sort of leisure activity, so Nancy hurried John outside before her sister changed her mind. "Shall we walk along the river?"

"By all means."

By the end of September, the heaviest heat had vanished from central Virginia, and sharp night chills undid hopes for Indian summer. The oaks and maples in the forest surrounding Bizarre flirted with golds, scarlets and coppers, while the great overhanging beech was tinged purplish brown.

"I love this time of year," Nancy said. "All the colors."

"I must say that country living agrees with you. I've never seen you so radiant."

"You're very kind."

"And may I say you are plump as a pretty little partridge?"

"You may not," Nancy shot back, affronted. Then, softening, "But if that's the case, Corinna is to blame."

"Please don't think my words anything but friendly, dear cousin, and forgive my teasing. You're as lovely as ever."

"I don't know whether to be relieved or insulted."

"I hope you'll be relieved and allow me to speak frankly."

"I've never known you to do otherwise," Nancy said, steeling herself.

"Well done, my dear. As I said to you once before, you have the makings of a lawyer."

"Which, alas, do me no good at all." They paused while John picked up a piece of shiny quartz, examined it and tossed it into the river. "What is it you wished to say?"

"That I've been waiting for the right moment to apologize for presuming you might be attracted to me. That day at Tuckahoe I found you most sympathetic when I told you about myself and my adulation of Richard. Most young ladies are interested only in new bonnets and garden parties and pay scant attention to my conversation, but I believe you actually listened."

"If I listened, it was because I was interested. I'm also interested in new hats and garden parties, but they're quite out of reach these days."

"Because you're no longer luxuriating at Tuckahoe and are working hard at Bizarre?"

"My last months at Tuckahoe were far from luxurious, but you're right about Bizarre."

"Are you resentful?"

John was surprised by her quick response. "Resentment and regrets are a waste of time. Granted, there are things that upset me, but if I can't change them, I must accept them."

"Acceptance," he echoed as they passed the great beech, myriad leaves trembling in the river breeze. "An old word with new meaning for me."

"I'm sorry for your misfortune." Nancy was still adjusting to his altered appearance. John had been a child of

95

unearthly beauty, and she saw its loss as a tragedy. "No doubt it's an enormous burden, particularly for someone our age."

"But, as you say, if it can't be changed, it must be borne. You're wise beyond your years, Nancy."

"I don't know about that, but Mama said I was blessed with uncommonly good sense. All we sisters were, our brothers less so."

"You must miss him terribly." Before Nancy could ask what he meant, John said, "I loved Theo almost as much as Richard."

"I miss Theo beyond measure."

"I always wondered what path he might have chosen in life. Did you?"

"Oddly enough, Theo, like Richard, found satisfaction here at Bizarre. Considering their birthright, neither dreamed they'd end up working in the fields, but they proved their grit. Judith and I were so proud of them."

"Richard wrote me about that, but I couldn't envision either of them chopping tobacco, especially Theo. He was always in poor health."

"I wish you could've seen him last fall." Nancy drifted a moment, eye trailing to the now fallow acreage across the river. "He seemed to find himself in those fields, and they gave him good health in return. That's why his sudden passing was such a shock. One moment he was fine, and the next—"

"I know," John said gently. "I grieve for him too. For both of you."

"Thank you." Nancy felt a chill as they walked closer to the riverbank, and she changed the painful subject. "What about you, John? Are you still pursuing law?"

"No, not law. I thought Edmund would inspire me, but he's made the subject so bland and dry that I've lost interest. I'll return to Philadelphia this fall, but for what purpose I'm not certain." He paused when they reached Sandy Ford and noted the crisscross of wheel ruts. "Look there. The river's so low people have been driving wagons back and forth."

"It dries out at the end of summer, remember?"

John scanned the opposite bank. "It could use exploring."

"On one of your nighttime rides?"

He gave her a fixed look. "Do you find them peculiar?"

"Absolutely."

He roared with laughter. "I assumed that your good manners would compel you to profess otherwise."

"If I had done so, you would've seen right through me. Besides, who in their right mind gallops across the countryside in the dead of night?"

"Someone who can't sleep. Or someone who may be losing their mind."

"There's nothing wrong with your mind, John. In fact, Richard and I marvel at your genius."

"And what does Judith think?"

"I doubt she marvels at anything except her faith. And Saint, of course."

John cocked his head. "Not even her husband?"

"I didn't say that,"

"Which makes it that much more revelatory."

The reeds alongside the river swayed and rattled under a flurry of wind. Nancy rearranged her heavy shawl. "I'm getting cold, John."

"Come along home then."

"Will you be joining us tomorrow?" Nancy took John's arm when they reached the rocky stretch where he had picked up the stone. "We're visiting the Harrisons at Glyntyvar."

"Neither name is familiar."

"Mr. Harrison is another Randolph. In fact, his first name is Randolph. He and his wife Mary are always warm and welcoming. In fact, they're taking care of my baby sister Virginia these days."

"How far away are they?"

"The other end of the county."

"Perhaps I'll ride along and continue elsewhere."

"Where might you go?"

"I've no earthly idea. That's what makes it enticing."

Nancy squeezed the inside of John's arm. "I envy you, John Randolph."

"How so?"

"Because you can ride off into the great unknown and entertain all sorts of colorful adventures. Please don't think me ungrateful for Richard's hospitality, but some days I feel buried alive in the middle of nowhere. I despair of ever meeting anyone who might spirit me away to a different life. If only Papa hadn't met Gabriella. If only Theo hadn't died. If only—"

"Our lives are filled with 'if onlys,' cousin dear, and you and I have experienced, I'm sorry to say, more than our fair share."

John trembled inside with a profound rage that would have terrified Nancy if unleashed. If only I hadn't become a physical grotesque, he thought. If only I weren't doomed to a life of celibacy and solitude. If only I could know the love of a good woman and the joy of continuing our proud family name. If only.

"We seem destined to talk about fate tonight," he said finally. "I suppose discussing the unknowable is fascinating."

"I suppose." Nancy released John's arm and lifted her heavy skirts, clinging to the railing as she climbed the steps to the front porch. Although accustomed to walks, she was wearied by this one and welcomed the warmth inside the house. "I enjoyed our talk, cousin, and I hope you'll reconsider and stay a few days at Glyntyvar. I would welcome the excitement."

John smiled. "You find me exciting, do you?"

"After a fashion, yes, but if I may borrow your quote, 'Please don't think my words anything but friendly.'"

John leaned down to kiss her cheek. "Touché, madame."

Overwhelmed by fatigue, Nancy went upstairs to her room and sat on the edge of the bed, hoping the dizziness and colic troubling her all day would pass. When it persisted, she emptied a packet of powdered gum guaiacum into glass of water, drank it down and stretched out on the bed. Despite the early hour, she drifted right to sleep. Had she known what was coming, Nancy might have wished to sleep forever. Her visit to Glyntyvar was destined to unleash a scandal across the length and breadth of Virginia.

Part 3

"If he tries to transfer the stigma and evade blame, I will wash out the stain on my family honor with his blood."

- Tom Randolph

15

The morning of Monday, October 1, 1792, dawned cold and very damp. Clouds with dark underbellies shrouded the countryside as the Randolphs began a day's journey traversing the length of Cumberland County. Judith drove a one-horse buggy with Nancy, while Richard and John rose horseback. Because four-month-old Saint had a lingering cold, Judith left him with Eula Moseley who doted on the child. Richard and John chatted occasionally, but the women were quiet. Nancy, heavily bundled in coat, scarf and hat, suffered from a bad headache, while Judith, reins in hand, concentrated on the mud-slickened road. The monotonous drive threaded through hilly forests broken only by the occasional farm, lone cabin and small tobacco plantation. Dusk was descending when they reached the turn-off to Glyntyvar.

"Farewell, everyone!"

Without warning, John urged his horse into a gallop and disappeared down the darkening highway.

"Where on earth is he going?" Judith asked.

"Who knows?" Richard replied. "Surely by now you know John responds to siren calls us lesser mortals cannot hear."

"Good for him," Nancy muttered, more to herself than the others.

Judith turned to her sister. "I thought you were sleeping."

"Dozing off and on." She shifted positions to make herself more comfortable. "Are we almost there?"

"Another mile or so. How's your headache?"

"Still keeping me company."

Judith trailed Richard onto a narrow, badly rutted lane. After fifteen minutes of jouncing over potholes and rocky creek beds eliciting moans from Nancy, the road opened into a clearing. As they drew up before the unfinished, wood-frame house, Nancy wondered why the plantation bore such a high-flying Scottish name. Glyntyvar was far smaller than Bizarre, with only ten acres of tobacco and eleven slaves to work the fields. Even so, it provided a decent income for Randolph and Mary Harrison. Along with two young children, and for now Virginia, they occupied four large rooms, two upstairs and two down, connected by a central hallway and narrow staircase.

After greetings and embraces were exchanged, Mary explained that Judith and Richard would take one of the upstairs bedrooms while Nancy and six-year-old Virginia would share the other. Randolph offered to take her heavy coat, but Nancy said she had caught a chill and preferred to keep it on. She sat in a chair in a far corner and chatted with Virginia, but after a few moments she went to her bedroom to rest. She managed to come downstairs for dinner, but barely picked at the savory pork, greens and cornbread served by Mrs. Wood, the Harrisons' cook/housekeeper. The straightforward Mrs. Wood voiced what everyone else was thinking.

"You're looking a bit peaked, Miss Nancy. Shall I fetch you some laudanum in cinnamon water?"

"Thank you, no. I'm just wearied by the trip."

Richard helped her back upstairs. When they reached the bedroom, Nancy resisted his attempt to remove her coat. "I can't seem to get warm tonight."

"I'll give the fire a poke." Richard rearranged the logs until they crackled and blazed, all the while pondering Nancy's health. Because it had gone into decline after Theo's death, Richard naturally attributed it to grief, but when it persisted for months, accompanied by vacillating moods, he wondered if other factors were at play. Why, for instance, did she claim to be chilled in a room that was toasty warm? "I'm worried about you, Nancy."

102

"I'll be fine after a good night's rest." Nancy sat on the edge of the bed and managed a weak smile. "I'm sure I'll sleep well with Virginia in the same bed. I've missed her so, and she's such a comfort."

"Very well. If you need anything, Judith and I are across the hall."

Richard said good-night and went back downstairs. As soon as she was alone, Nancy undressed and took a dose of gum guiacum before slipping into bed. Cocooned by a pile of quilts and comforted by the drone of familiar voices downstairs, the warm room lulled her to sleep. She was only vaguely aware when Virginia slipped in beside her and snuggled close.

Outside Nancy's small window, the first frost of the season silvered the countryside. The clouds had dissipated, bequeathing a clear moonlit night that was eerily still. The residents of Glyntyvar slept well until the early morning hours when a scream, high-pitched and riddled with agony, tore through the house. In the slave quarters, Esau, Randolph's manservant, bolted upright in bed, waking his wife, Ruth. Downstairs in the main house, Randolph turned over and muttered to Mary.

"What in the name of God—?"

Before Mary could answer, they heard a louder, more agonizing scream, followed by footsteps overhead. Tracing the cries to Nancy's bedroom, Richard rushed across the hall to investigate. He pushed open the door and gasped in horror. Beneath the pale moonlight, Nancy writhed in pain while Virginia, whimpering and tearful, cowered in a corner. Lizzie, a young Negro girl, stood beside the bed. While Richard struggled to assess what was happening, Mary drew on a robe, lit a candle and hurried upstairs. Knowing Judith constantly complained of poor health, she went to her room first. She opened the door and called into the darkness.

"Judith? Are you well?"

"It's Nancy," Judith replied sleepily. "She's having one of her hysterical attacks."

Mary went to see for herself but the bedroom door was bolted. She called out and knocked hard. The door opened quickly, but Richard's large frame blocked her passage. "What has happened?" she cried.

"Nancy was having severe pain, so she sent Virginia for one of your girls. Lizzie brought laudanum."

"I'm...I'm alright," Nancy said weakly.

"May I come in?" Mary asked.

"Yes, but please extinguish that candle. Laudanum makes my eyes sensitive to light."

Mary blew out the candle and went inside. She saw four shadowy figures and smelled a sharp, acrid odor that she couldn't identify. She touched Nancy's forehead. "You have a fever."

"The laudanum should ease it," Richard said. "I'll stay with her, Mary. You go back to bed."

"Perhaps I should check on the children. I'm sure those screams scared them out of their wits."

"I'm...sorry," Nancy managed.

"No matter, my dear. I hope you'll be better by morning. Good-night."

"Good night."

Mary went back downstairs and, as she expected, found her children huddled with fright. She explained that their cousin Nancy had had a bad dream, and told them to go back to sleep. She slipped back into bed with Randolph and reported what she had seen.

"Are you sure Nancy is alright?"

"She said so." Mary slid closer to merge their body heat. "Both those sisters are prone to bad health. Judith has one malady after another, and poor Nancy has terrible colic attacks. Lizzie took her some laudanum."

"Do you think we should—?"

"What I think," Mary said wearily, "is that we should go back to sleep and see what tomorrow brings."

But Randolph could not sleep. Nancy's screams seemed too strong to be triggered by colic. He supposed it could be gastritis, but she had barely eaten dinner and there was nothing in Mrs. Wood's delicious supper to provoke an attack. He was still speculating when he heard footsteps traveling downstairs and a door opening and closing. Randolph assumed Lizzie was returning to the slave quarters, but when footsteps returned and traveled back upstairs, he changed his mind. Lizzie was a slender girl of fifteen with a light tread, while these footsteps were heavy. Something was wrong.

"Tomorrow," he mumbled, careful not to waken Mary snoring softly beside him. "I'll get answers tomorrow."

The house fell silent for the rest of the night.

Richard checked on Nancy early the next morning. She was weak and pale but whispered that she had no pain. Virginia, still fast asleep, made a small mound under the covers. The fire had gone out, and the room was cold. "I'll send someone to build a new fire," he said.

When Randolph insisted on laying the fire himself, Mary accompanied him. They found Nancy with the bedcovers pulled to her chin, voice riddled with embarrassment. "I'm so sorry I woke the household last night."

"No matter." Mary eased herself onto the edge of the bed. "Was it colic?"

"I believe so. The laudanum helped."

"Do you want something to eat?"

"Not right now. I just want to rest."

"As you wish. I'll check on you later." She turned toward the fireplace when Randolph's striker unleashed a bright spark to ignite the kindling. "The fire should take the chill off soon enough."

"Thank you."

Randolph nodded and left. Mary made to follow him, but Nancy motioned her close. After a whispered exchange, Mary went downstairs where she was confronted by a distraught housekeeper.

"What is it, Mrs. Wood?"

"This!" She showed Mary some damp bedclothes. "It's not my doing, ma'am. Someone tried to scrub away bloodstains and left me to finish the job. In case you didn't notice, there was blood on the stairs too."

"It's nothing to worry about. Nancy confided that it was only female trouble." She lowered her voice. "An especially vigorous menstrual period."

Mrs. Wood was instantly sympathetic. "The poor thing."

"She was mortified, naturally, so not a word to anyone."

"No, ma-am. Not a word."

Within the hour, the house came fully awake, and people began going about the business of the day. Concern for Nancy prompted Randolph to send for his mother Susanna at nearby Clifton plantation. Susanna, who knew nursing, spent the afternoon with Nancy and found her responsive and free of colic. Nancy remained in bed two more days, nourished by hearty soups, and by Friday was well enough to come downstairs. Her coloring was much improved, and she displayed a hearty appetite when she took a second helping of Mrs. Wood's pumpkin pudding.

"Leave some for me!" Virginia cried, giving everyone a much-needed laugh.

Assured by Nancy that she was well enough to travel, the Randolphs returned home the following day and resumed their usual routines. There was no further mention of the incident at Glyntyvar, for there was nothing to discuss, but within the week Nancy made a discovery that forever altered the peace at Bizarre.

16

Finished with chores one afternoon, Nancy went to her room to resume reading a popular sentimental novel by Lawrence Wilson. Written in epistolary form, The Plight of Sympathy told the sad tale of a young woman named Olivia, seduced and impregnated by her minister. Nancy had barely begun reading when Judith appeared with the baby.

"We're driving into Farmville for supplies. You'll watch Saint while we're gone."

"Of course." Nancy set the book on her bedside table and took the sleeping baby in her arms. "Will you be gone long?"

"A couple or three hours I suspect. Saint has been fed and changed, so he should sleep the whole time."

"Fine."

"That boy could sleep through a thunderstorm," Richard said from the doorway.

Left alone with the slumbering baby, Nancy held Saint close and studied his tiny face. It was still too soon to discern similarity to either parent, but Nancy liked to think he had her nose. She also let herself imagine if she and Theo had been blessed with a child, he might look like this. With the same mix of Randolph bloodlines, it was not an unreasonable fantasy.

Nancy cradled the child a bit longer before yielding to the lure of her book. Saint was sleeping so soundly he never flinched when she laid him on her bed. She sat again, and, reaching for her book, knocked a candlestick to the floor with a loud thud. She looked at the baby, fearing he would awaken, but Saint never stirred. Nancy was relieved until she recalled other instances when Saint was oblivious to sudden noises. When she remembered Richard's quip about the thunderstorm, the unthinkable flickered in her mind. She picked up the candlestick and tapped it on the floor. Saint didn't move. Urged on by dreadful suspicions, she clapped her hands hard. Nothing. The corners of her eyes burned when she leaned down to shout in the baby's face.

"Saint! Wake up!"

Nothing.

Tears streamed down her cheeks as Nancy backed away, devastated by the terrible truth that John St. George Randolph was deaf. She sat again and, not knowing what else to do, reached for her book. The sentences swam and blurred, and she could think of nothing except the afflicted innocent sleeping across the room. She laid down beside him and pondered how to tell Richard and Judith the awful news. When they returned from Farmville, she was so upset that she burst into tears and blurted her suspicions. Richard paled and rushed to pick up his son, but Judith was stoic.

"I've known for some time."

"You knew?!" Nancy gasped.

"I'm his mother. Of course, I knew."

"Why didn't you tell me?" Richard cried, tears brimming.

"Why does it matter? Nancy has done the job for me." Judith looked at the candlestick, as though it was to blame. "Another cross to bear."

"Why must you always say that?" Richard asked, face pained. "Bizarre is thriving. We have a good life here."

"Do we?"

Richard frowned. "Don't talk riddles, Judith. Are you unhappy? Discontent? Tell me."

"I've no time to talk about such things." Judith turned to go.

"For heaven's sake, Judith!" Nancy's heart broke when Richard's tears dropped onto Saint's tiny face. "We've all had our sorrows. Why should yours be any different?"

"You know why, sister."

Nancy turned to Richard, then back to her sister. "No, I don't."

"Mind the baby, Richard. I'm going out to the kitchen."

Left alone with Richard, Nancy fought anger and resentment. "The more time I spend with Judith, the less I know who she is. She was always distant, but she's now talking in riddles and seems intent on cutting herself off completely."

"From me as well," Richard said wearily. "I've tried to talk to her, but she walks away, just like now."

"Then what are we to do?"

Richard had no answer. Saint had finally awakened, and rekindled his father's tears when he looked up with dark, inquisitive eyes and smiled. "My poor son. What have I done to you?"

"It's not your fault," Nancy said, laying her hand on his arm as he jiggled the child. "It's no one's fault."

"I wish I could believe that."

The reality of Saint's deafness clung to everyone's thoughts, and while all remained civil, conversations were brief and guarded. Judith became ever more remote, prompting Richard to concentrate on outdoor chores and spending more time with Daniel Moseley. Nancy also kept to herself and drifted through her daily paces like a ghost. She wrote Patsy a tearful letter about her loneliness and isolation and begged to come live at Monticello. While Patsy sympathized, she replied that Tom was undergoing a trying period and was at present unapproachable. She encouraged Nancy as best she could and urged her to have patience. Nancy drew comfort, albeit scant, from her friend's words, and, as she had done before, sought escape through daydreaming and reading. One October afternoon, she began The Sorrows of Charlotte, another epistolary novel about an unjustly wronged young woman. She was immersed in poor Charlotte's travails when Richard shouted from below.

"We have visitors, Nancy!"

Company was cause for excitement, especially on a plantation as remote as Bizarre, and the Randolphs welcomed anyone who might interrupt the tedious routine. Nancy gave her hair a quick brushing and hurried downstairs, pleased to see Randolph and Mary Harrison. Her excitement waned when they regarded her with grim faces.

"What is it? Has something happened?"

"Yes, it has." Randolph helped Mary with her coat. "And it's most unpleasant."

"Let's all sit down," Richard suggested. "Judith, will you bring—?"

"Refreshments can wait," Randolph insisted. He started to continue but hesitated until the ticking of the longcase clock grew ponderous. Mary patted his arm.

"Go on, Randolph."

"Alright then. The day after you folks left Glyntyvar, Esau, my manservant, approached me to say that his daughter Lizzie had found something on a pile of shingles behind the smokehouse, something left there the night of Nancy's colic attack." Everyone glanced at Nancy before turning back to Randolph. When he didn't continue, Richard leaned forward.

"What did Esau say Lizzie found?"

"He said it was—" Randolph faltered, discomfort obvious.

"Was what?" Richard urged.

Randolph swallowed hard and spoke to the floor. "He said...he said she found the remains of a white infant."

Richard gasped. "You can't be serious!"

Amid the silence and shock that followed, Randolph held out his hands palms up. "Mary and I suspect it's nothing more than Negro foolishness, a rumor started when some slave heard Nancy's screams. Esau knows very well that gossip is forbidden at Glyntyvar, and he swore he would not repeat the story."

"And yet you chose to repeat the story to us," Judith said.

"Because we're old friends," Mary replied, affronted. "If your slaves were telling tales about us, we'd expect you to tell us and handle it appropriately."

"Has word spread off the plantation?"

"Esau came to me early on, so I'm hoping it's gone no further."

"We both do," Mary echoed. "Such stories can take a life of their own, especially when repeated often enough."

"But surely no one could believe such an outrageous claim," Richard declared. "The idea is beyond absurd."

"Of course, it is." Judith rose and smoothed her skirts. "Nancy, go out to the kitchen and tell Corinna we have two more for dinner. I'll set the table." When Nancy appeared lost in some personal reverie, Judith said, "Stop daydreaming and do as you're told."

Nancy rose slowly, retrieved her heavy coat from a peg by the door and slipped outside without a word.

The somber mood improved over Corinna's roasted potatoes, turnip ragout, corn pudding and Spanish fritters. Smoothed by a generous flow of wine and ale, the Harrisons' unpleasant news was pointedly avoided, thanks mostly to Randolph, the jokester of the family. His always amusing tales were turning the evening lively when Judith cited early morning chores and suggested the household retire. Nancy was the first to excuse herself, and as she climbed the stairs, her feet grew heavier with each step. She could barely muster the strength to undress before crawling into bed where the ugly events of the day finally took their toll. Sleep came quickly, but brought hideous nightmares about a burning smokehouse and the pungent smell of blood.

17

Richard and his Negro carpenter, Billy Ellis, were chopping firewood outside the stable when they heard approaching hoofbeats. Randolph Harrison dismounted and tossed his reins to Billy before jerking his head toward the house.

"Where are the women?" he barked.

"The kitchen," Richard replied, alarmed by the man's abruptness and grim face. "My God, man! You look as though someone died."

"I'm not so sure they haven't," Randolph grunted as they walked to the house. Once inside, he stepped to the fireplace and held his hands toward the flames. "Whiskey."

Richard poured whiskey for both. "Will you sit?"

"I've been sitting for hours," Randolph gulped half the liquor and turned his backside to the hearth. "And my behind is numb with cold."

Richard sank into a chair. "As you wish."

"No need to beat about the bush. Have you heard the rumors?"

"Rumors about what?"

"That nasty slave gossip I told you about when Mary and I last visited." Richard nodded, uneasiness growing. "It's worse, man. Much worse. I was in a tavern in Richmond day before yesterday when I overheard someone mention the Randolphs. Naturally I paid attention and was horrified when I heard Nancy's name."

"She was mentioned in a public house?!"

"You as well, Richard, but that's only part of it. The tale was not merely disgusting but related in the lowest of terms. The kind that provokes lewd laughter and scurrilous remarks." He drained his glass and replenished it without asking. "The more I heard, the angrier I became. I would've called the man out, but he and his thuggish cronies were drunk as lords and would've taken great pleasure in thrashing a planter, even a poor one like myself. It sickens me to think about it."

Richard swallowed hard. "Exactly what did the man say?"

Randolph grimaced. "He said that your sister-in-law bore your child and that the two of you murdered it and dumped the body behind the barn at Glyntyvar."

Randolph's face shimmered in and out of focus as Richard struggled to comprehend what he heard, to make sense of a world suddenly gone mad.

"But who...why—?"

"That damnable slave grapevine. Eight thousand people live in Cumberland County and more than half are ignorant Negroes who can't keep their mouths shut. If people are gossiping in Richmond, how long before word reaches Williamsburg and Fredericksburg? Perhaps even Washington City!"

Randolph did not exaggerate. With so few personal freedoms, slaves sought satisfaction in gossip about their owners. It was, after all, easy to acquire and share. Slaves attending church or visiting friends and relatives exchanged news, as did those hired out for work. Slave messengers traveling about the countryside were ever eager to swap stories with ferrymen, coachmen and other messengers, and to receive news in return. Such contact gave wings to rumors and dispersed them with alarming speed. Exaggeration and embellishment being human nature, tales inevitably changed when passed from one person to another, and if the story was salacious or demeaning to wealthy white people, it garnered special attention.

"I...I don't even know what to say, much less do," Richard groaned.

Now warmed by the fire, Randolph removed his heavy coat and sat. "I've had nothing else on my mind during that long, cold ride from Richmond. I kept telling myself that

113

such talk eventually plays out, that people forget things when they hear something more enticing. It's only been three months, so I suggest we wait and hope it confines itself to the taverns and lower elements."

"What if it doesn't? What it spreads to the gentry?"

"Then our family will rally behind you and close ranks as the Randolphs have done for a hundred years. It's not the first ugly rumor we've weathered, and it certainly won't be the last."

"It's no rumor, man. It's lies! There's absolutely no proof that—"

"Proof doesn't matter, Richard. The baser sorts, those people who wallow in gossip, only want something to disgrace the hated gentry, the high-and-mighty Randolphs. It's no surprise given their ignorance and—"

Randolph's words were interrupted by the boot scraper on the front porch. Richard opened the door and stepped aside as Moseley entered on a blast of icy air. The overseer's hat brim, pulled unusually low over his forehead, did not hide a black eye.

"My God, Daniel! What happened?"

Between gulps of whiskey, Moseley related a tale cut from the same cloth as Randolph's sordid report. While having his horse shod in Farmville, he overheard a pair of stable hands making ribald jokes about Nancy and Richard. Moseley had torn into the boys and launched a melee that sent them running, but he didn't leave unscathed.

"I wish I coulda done them much worse, sir," he told Richard. "They oughtn't be saying such terrible things about you and Miss Nancy."

"Thank you, Daniel." Richard clapped the man's shoulder. "Your loyalty is duly noted. Now you'd best get home so Eula can tend to that eye."

With Moseley gone, Richard turned a stricken face to Randolph. "So now the story's in my own back yard! Everyone we do business with in Farmville will hear those damned lies and see me as a monster ravishing his wife's virtuous sister. With my honor now impugned, I have no choice but to confront it, to fight a duel if need be." He trembled at the prospect. "Something at which I'll surely fail."

"You can hardly duel without a designated opponent," Randolph reminded him, "but if you feel obliged to address the issue, I'd look to your stepfather for help. Mr. Tucker is a General Court Judge, isn't he?"

Richard visibly brightened. "Yes, yes, he is. That's a splendid idea, Randolph. He can surely suggest some legal procedure to put this nasty business to rest. I'll ride down to Williamsburg straight away."

"You'd best take Nancy and Judith with you," Randolph said darkly. "With the rumors so close, you don't dare leave the women here alone. Moseley's a capable man, but I wouldn't saddle him with such a responsibility."

"You're right."

"And shield the women from the truth unless you want another of Nancy's hysterical fits." He took a parting slug of whiskey. "Now I must be on my way."

"Thanks for coming, Randolph. You're a good friend."

"We're blood, man, and I know you'd do the same for me."

Left alone, Richard couldn't stop thinking about Moseley's repulsive account of Nancy being called a harlot by common stable boys and himself labeled a fornicator and murderer. It was beyond comprehension that such calumny would be directed at a Randolph.

Richard turned toward rustling skirts and saw Nancy at the foot of the stairs. His heart clutched.

"I...I thought you were out in the kitchen."

She answered his question before he could pose it. "Yes, I overheard the conversation." When she stepped into the firelight, her eyes were red from weeping. An anguished wail emerged as she threw herself into his arms. "Oh, Richard! What are we to do?!"

He held her close, battling his own tears and struggling for self-control. "We'll go to Williamsburg tomorrow, and my stepfather will to sort this out."

"But what if he can't?" Nancy cried.

"He will," Richard asserted. "He has to."

The two were so absorbed by the moment that neither noticed the bitter face glowering through the window as Judith returned from the kitchen.

18

Nancy agreed when Randolph said that Judith must be told of the vicious gossip, at least in part. Judith sat in unreadable silence while he related a laundered version of Randolph's news. She said nothing until he mentioned his plans to strategize with St. George Tucker.

"How long do you reckon to be in Williamsburg?"

"As long as necessary. You and Nancy will come too. I'll not leave you here alone, but Saint will have to stay with the Moseleys again. He's too young to travel in this bitter cold."

"I'll talk to Eula." Judith pushed a wayward strand of hair from her forehead and left for the Mosely cottage.

"Unreadable as ever," Richard sighed miserably.

Nancy said nothing. She had other things to worry about.

The road to Williamsburg paralleled the Appomattox River to Petersburg and Matoax where Richard, Nancy and Judith rested for a day. A few miles below Matoax, they ferried across the much larger James River and continued along the Williamsburg highway. Despite the unpleasant circumstances of their journey, the travelers could not have had a more agreeable destination. Most Virginians regarded Williamsburg as the Commonwealth's most beautiful town. Designated the colonial capital almost a century ago, in 1699, it was laid out along a grid system divided by the grandly broad Duke of Gloucester Street. A market square, numerous neat gardens and a fenced meadow for farm animals created a refreshing pastoral ambiance. Homes, taverns and business emporiums were simple frame buildings, but a number of imposing Georgian brick homes faced Palace Green, a tree-filled park fronting the elegant Governor's Palace. Williamsburg had played its important role admirably, but in

1780, when it was menaced by the British Navy, Governor Thomas Jefferson moved the capital to Richmond. Resentment still simmered, but although Williamsburg lost its political status, it boasted far more charm than its unruly usurper.

St. George Tucker, as one of the town's most prominent citizens, occupied one of the larger homes on Palace Green. A handsome two-story clapboard structure flanked by twin wings and double chimneys, it radiated hospitality behind a white picket fence. When Richard drew up before it, Nancy and Judith watched in bewilderment when the front door opened and a crowd of young men spilled recklessly onto the green.

"What on earth?!"

"Judge Tucker is also Professor of Law at the College of William & Mary," Richard explained. "He teaches certain courses at home to provide students access to his vast legal library. We seem to have arrived as class is letting out." He stepped from the carriage and waved at the figure in the doorway. At age forty, Tucker was still handsome, with a patrician profile that a Roman emperor would envy. He grinned broadly when he saw his favorite stepson.

"My boy!" He hurried to the coach and dispensed a hearty embrace. "Why did you not write that you were coming?"

"It was a last-minute decision, and I apologize if we have come at an inopportune time."

"Not at all. Not at all. You're always welcome. I regret to say Leila is in Richmond indefinitely. Her mother is failing."

"I'm sorry to hear that." Leila Skipwith was the widow Tucker married three years after his beloved Francis, Richard's mother, died in childbirth. She had been a warm, caring stepmother whom Richard adored. "I'll miss seeing her."

"And she you." Tucker looked over Richard's shoulder. "And who have we here? Two Randolph lovelies I believe." He bowed low. "Welcome, ladies."

"Thank you, sir," Nancy said with a smile. Judith nodded but maintained the apathetic guise she'd worn since leaving Bizarre. If Tucker noticed her indifference, he gave no indication.

"Come along!" he called. "Let's get out of this biting cold."

Tucker dispatched servants to fetch luggage and ushered his guests inside. The ladies retired to their bedrooms to freshen up and warm themselves while Richard joined his stepfather in the library. Bookshelves rose on all four walls, broken only by a fireplace and two windows. Richard had enjoyed this room many times and relished the smell of paper, smoke and learning. He joined Tucker by the fire and explained the reason for his visit.

"I didn't know where else to turn, stepfather. You've always been there for us boys, and I've never needed your advice more than now. Can you help?"

"I will do anything in my power," Tucker assured him, "but first you must answer some crucial questions."

"Sir?"

"Was there a birth?"

Richard expelled the truth in a single breath. "Stillborn."

"The father?"

"Nancy has said nothing, but I've no doubt it was Theo."

"Then, my advice is to do nothing."

"But in the face of such damning lies—?"

Tucker raised a familiar silencing hand. "You and the women will remain here until this unfortunate talk dies down. To address it now, when it's the province of tavern drunks and stable hands, would be debasing, and I will not permit you to sink to their level."

"What if the talk reaches higher up?"

"Should that happen, and we must pray that it does not, a response from you is unavoidable."

Richard looked stricken. "I wouldn't know how to begin."

"Perhaps you won't have to, my boy. The public is fickle, and I'm guessing that this ugly business will evaporate when something more compelling comes along."

Tucker was a brilliant professor and an esteemed judge, but his assessment proved overly optimistic. Sordid rumors not only continued to thrive but gained gruesome new details. By February, tales reached John who wrote Richard that a Fredericksburg friend heard a tale about a battered infant corpse behind the slave quarters at Glyntyvar. By March, Tucker himself overheard something among his students. Conceding that the stories would not fade away of their own accord, he suggested Richard take Judith and Nancy to Tuckahoe where their father might offer perspective on the problem. Nancy flatly refused to be under the same roof as Gabriella, but Judith, despite discovering she was pregnant again, agreed to accompany Richard.

On the morning of their departure, while Judith was upstairs packing, Nancy stole a moment alone with Richard. She found him cleaning his pipe in the library and handed him an envelope. "You may need this at Tuckahoe." She grabbed his hand before he opened the envelope. "Don't! There's no time to read it now."

"But what—?"

"A signed confession that Theo fathered my child," she whispered. "I want you exonerated of any wrongdoing, and this is the only way to convince Papa."

"Your courage is admirable, Nancy, but such an admission declares that I was incapable of protecting you and adds to my shame and failure as a gentleman. Don't you understand? I have no choice."

"I understand only that I want to clear your name."

120

Richard threw his arms around her and spoke words that ransacked her soul. "We Randolphs do not live in a society where truth is best."

"But—"

He touched her lips with a fingertip smelling of tobacco. "And now, I must be on my way."

When they returned within the week, Richard gathered everyone in Tucker's parlor for a glum recounting of the events at Tuckahoe. "It's fair to say our hopes for support were dead on arrival. Gabriella announced that the colonel was ill and unable to see us."

"Ill from what?" Nancy asked.

"She never explained and brushed aside all questions," Judith replied. "Delilah reported that Gabriella has spun a poisonous cocoon around Papa and allows only her father and the servants access to him."

"As you can imagine," Richard continued, "Gabriella had plenty to say with her nasty little smirk. She said she'd heard the gossip about Glyntyvar, and by embellishing the rumors she brought Tom Junior and William into her camp. William blames me for the entire business and made certain that the rest of the family heard Gabriella's version. Tom now blames me for everything and says an admission of guilt is my only recourse. He also said that if I claim that Theo fathered the child, he would 'wash out the stain on his family with my blood.' Those, I regret to say are his exact words."

Nancy emitted a small cry.

Richard turned to his stepfather. "So much for my efforts to secure Randolph support. My standing as a gentleman is under siege by my own family as well as the community at large, and I am without a weapon."

"Not so," Tucker declared. "There is one route left for erasing the smears upon your good name, and that's a fair, open and judicial inquiry into the charges. In order for calumny to be obviated, it must be confronted."

"And how do I go about that?"

121

"You'll begin with a public notice which I will help you write."

19

Professor Tucker stole time from his law classes to carefully word Richard's defense. His plan to publish it in a newspaper was as bold as it was unprecedented. While politicians routinely used the press to issue or rebut insults, the elite plantation society never courted public opinion. It was time, Tucker decided, for this potentially powerful outlet to be exploited, and by the end of March, his work was polished like a fine diamond. He wrote Richard, now sequestered with Judith and Nancy at Matoax, that his open letter would appear in the April 17, 1793, edition of Richmond's *Virginia Gazette & General Advertiser,* the state's leading newspaper. And so it did.

To the Public
My character has lately been the subject of much conversation, blackened with the imputation of crimes at which humanity revolts, and which the laws of society have pronounced worthy of condign punishment. The charge against me was spread *far and wide* before I received the *smallest notice* of it—and whilst I have been endeavoring to trace it to its origins, has daily acquired strength in the minds of my fellow citizens.

To refute the calumnies which have been circulated, by a legal prosecution of the authors of them, must require a *length* of time, during which the weight of public odium would rest on the party *accused*, however *innocent*—I have, therefore, resolved on the method of presenting myself before the Bar of the public...

I do therefore give notice, that I will on the first day of the next April Cumberland Court appear there and render myself a prisoner before the *court*, or any

magistrate of the county there *present,* to answer in the due course of law*, any charge of crime which any person or persons whatsoever shall then and there think proper to allege against me.* Let not my accusers pretend an unwillingness to appear as prosecutors against me in a criminal court. The *only* favor I can ever receive at *their* hands is, for them to stand forth and exert themselves in order to (secure) my conviction.

Let not a pretended tenderness towards the supposed accomplice in the imputed guilt, shelter me. That person will meet the accusations with a fortitude of *which innocence alone is capable.*

If my accusers decline this invitation, there yet remains another mode of procedure which I am equally ready to meet. Let them state, with *precision* and *clearness* the *facts* which they lay to my charge and the *evidence* whether *direct* or *circumstantial* by which I am to be proved guilty, in any of the public papers. Let *no circumstance* of *time* or *place* nor the *names* of *any* witnesses against me, be omitted. The public shall then judge between me and them, according to other rules than the strict rules of legal evidence.

If neither of these methods be adopted in order to fix the stigma which has been imposed upon me, let candor and impartiality acquit me of crimes which my soul abhors, or suspend their opinions of my guilt until a decision thereon can be obtained in some other satisfactory mode.
Richard Randolph, jun.
March 29, 1793

The post created an immediate sensation across Virginia and was read as far away as Washington City, by no less than Thomas Jefferson, the United States Secretary of State. Knowing his daughter's concern for her friend Nancy, he strove to ease Patsy's concern by insisting that people were too rational to blame an entire family of Randolphs over

124

the actions of one person. To Patsy's relief, Jefferson stated that any guilt must fall upon Richard and urged her to be kind to Nancy "regardless of what the trifling or malignant may think or say." Jefferson's remarks prompted Patsy to reconsider Richard's audacious act and weigh what she personally knew about him. She was not alone.

Far from convincing the aristocracy of his innocence and strength of character, Richard's public declaration deepened concern for the erosion of their elite society. Unlike their revered patriarch, William Randolph, who carved an empire from a hostile wilderness, or the two ensuing generations who tripled William's wealth, secured powerful political positions, built glorious mansions and wielded extraordinary power, the fourth generation, was forged from lesser stuff. Societal change, a lack of toughening by war and continual intermarriage had sired one anemic soul after another, and the imperiled gentry agreed that Richard exemplified this deterioration. The shame of his debt defaults was resurrected, along with his banishment from Matoax to the smaller Bizarre and his debauched college days. There was renewed gossip about his dalliances with Betsy Taliaferro of Williamsburg and Kitty Ludlow of New York City, and speculation about other women who had succumbed to his appetites, including, of course, Nancy. Was Richard guilty of lusting after his own sister-in-law? Didn't his reference to the "supposed accomplice" subject Nancy to public scrutiny? How could a gentleman debase a well-born lady and then claim himself as the wronged party?

So many unanswered questions!

While the aristocracy deliberated, and working men continued their ribald jokes, no one person responded to Richard's provocative challenge. Instead, there arose a public outcry demanding he make good on his promise to appear at the Cumberland County Courthouse. In doing so, Richard finally found an adversary—the law itself.

On April 18, he surrendered to the Cumberland County sheriff and was taken into custody. Four days later he was brought before three judges who formally charged him "with feloniously murdering a child delivered of Nancy Randolph or being accessory to the same." He was then taken to the county jail and held without bail while awaiting a public examination.

Immediately upon hearing of Richard's arrest, Professor Tucker set about assembling a solid legal team to represent his stepson. This proved challenging. With the establishments of district courts four years earlier, Virginia's most skilled country lawyers abandoned their practices for the more lucrative rewards of city courts. Tucker well understood the professional disparity between county and district levels and knew Richard needed people at the top of their game. He chose no less than Patrick Henry, the renowned lawyer, former Governor of the Commonwealth and celebrated patriot whose immortal declaration, "Give me liberty or give me death!" had galvanized his countrymen to wage war against Great Britain. Henry's reputation was based on spellbinding oratory and a legal career spanning three decades. He was especially strong as counsel for the defense, so dazzling in his delivery that his courtroom appearances drew crowds just to watch the great man perform. The problem was that the fifty-seven-year-old Henry lived in seclusion at Long Island, his country house in Campbell County. Retirement notwithstanding, Tucker suspected that the old war horse could be lured from the pasture with the right fee. When Richard balked at more debt, Tucker insisted it was a battle to be waged at all costs. Henry received a generous offer, but although intrigued by the odd case, claimed he wasn't fit enough to make the journey to Cumberland County. Three days later, he informed Richard that he was available for twice the proposed fee. Tucker was appalled by Henry's greed, but a deal was struck.

Tucker's other choices were Richmond attorneys Alexander Campbell and John Marshall. Campbell was Tucker's cousin and boasted an impeccable record in civil litigation, and Marshall was famed for defending debt-ridden tobacco planters. Darkly handsome with flashing eyes, Marshall was also Virginia's fastest-rising legal star. The quintessence of veracity and gravitas, his logic yielded stunningly succinct arguments. This combination of Marshall's cool analytical mind, Campbell's professionalism and Henry's mesmeric speechifying produced the most potent legal team Virginia had ever seen. Tucker was confident that they could sway the sixteen justices of the peace sitting in judgment because they were hand-picked, not elected, and had scant legal training.

As he confided to Leila, "One might say I've done my best to load the dice in my stepson's favor."

But would it work?

20

Because the spring rains had failed to materialize, April 29, 1793, dawned abnormally hot, dry and dusty. Richard was awakened early by his jailors, fed a wretched breakfast and escorted to the courthouse by a gaggle of young toughs hired for his protection. He thought the measure unnecessary until he spotted the crush of elegant carriages and landaus mixed with modest shays, gigs and crude farm wagons jamming the green, all there to see him. While the gentry had quietly filed into the one-story frame courthouse, the rambunctious mix of townspeople and country folk was more appropriate for a carnival than a legal examination. Shopkeepers, blacksmiths, coopers, farmers, rowdies and rabble packed Copenhaver's Tavern and overflowed its wooden porch, jostling and joking in anticipation of seeing the famous Patrick Henry. Their high spirits turned vengeful when Richard approached. Jeering and screaming invectives, they rushed his phalanx of bodyguards before he was hustled to safety. Thwarted, the mob took their anger inside the courtroom, shouting and pointing at Richard, Nancy, Judith, John and a host of other Randolphs. Chaos reigned until the sheriff restored order and explained that the proceedings were an examination, not a trial, and that Virginia law barred Richard and Nancy from testifying. The fourteen justices serving as a jury were introduced along with the three defense attorneys. Loud applause erupted at the mention of Patrick Henry's name, until the distinguished barrister, clad in his trademark black suit, rust-colored duster and wig, raised a silencing hand. When the charge of infanticide against Richard was read, the courtroom went still as a tomb.

The first witness called was a stone-faced Randolph Harrison. Henry took his time before approaching, casually pacing back and forth until he knew every eye was on him. Only then did he pose his first question.

"Randolph Harrison!" he boomed. "On October first, seventeen ninety-two, you and your wife Mary welcomed Richard Randolph and his wife Judith and her sister Nancy Randolph to your home, Glyntyvar Plantation, in Cumberland County. The two families had dinner, after which time the household retired. Is that correct?"

"Yes, sir."

"Please tell the court what happened next."

"Mary and I were awakened by screams upstairs."

"Who was up there?"

"Our three visitors."

"Please clarify for the court."

"Richard and Judith Randolph and Nancy Randolph."

"Anyone else?"

"Judith and Nancy's little sister, Virginia, who was staying with us."

"How old is Virginia?"

"Almost seven, I believe."

"What did you do when you heard the screams?"

"I did nothing. Mary went upstairs to determine what had happened and to see if anyone needed help."

Henry faced the crowd. "According to your wife Mary's deposition, she believed Nancy had experienced a hysterical fit, and that when she went upstairs to investigate, she found that one of your Negro girls, Lizzie, had given Nancy laudanum. In addition to Lizzie, Mary stated that Richard Randolph was present in Nancy's bedroom along with the child, Virginia. Mary stated that she couldn't see clearly because Nancy asked her not bring a candle into the room since laudanum made her eyes sensitive to light. Mary said she felt Nancy's forehead and found it feverish, and then she went back to bed." Henry turned back to Randolph. "Was the household quiet after that?"

"No, sir. A short time later, I heard footsteps coming down the stairs. A bit later I heard them going back up."

"Do you know whose footsteps they were?"

"No, sir."

"Have you no idea?"

"Our servants use the stairs when we have guests."

"Did you hear any other unusual noises that night?"

"No, sir."

"What happened the next morning when the household awoke?"

"I went upstairs to build a fire in Nancy's room."

"And how did she appear?"

"She was very pale, but I can't say more than that. She had the covers pulled up to her neck."

"Did you converse?"

"I asked how she was, and she said she was a little better. I finished laying the fire and went back downstairs."

"Was the incident discussed further?"

"Only when my mother, Susannah Harrison, came over from Clifton plantation to check on Nancy. She has good nursing skills so I welcomed the idea."

"What did Mrs. Harrison say about Nancy?"

"She said Nancy had most likely had an attack of colic."

Henry let the crowd absorb that before continuing. "What happened after that?"

"My mother returned home, and the Randolphs stayed a few more days until Nancy improved, and they went back to Bizarre."

"The screaming was not discussed further?"

"No, sir."

"Was that the end of the matter?"

Randolph glanced around the courtroom. "Not exactly."

"Please explain, sir."

"After the Randolphs left, Lizzie's father, Esau, my manservant, told me that she'd seen something peculiar on a pile of shingles behind the barn."

"Could you be more specific?"

Randolph looked down at his hands. "He...that is, Esau said that Lizzie said it looked like the remains of a white infant."

Gasps rocked the courthouse.

"A literal case of 'he said, she said,'" Henry quipped. Then, "Did you go to investigate?"

"No, sir. Not straight away."

"What do you mean?"

"I mean that everyone knows Negroes are prone to story-telling and exaggerating the truth. I didn't believe Esau and told him as much. I also reminded him that he had been sternly warned about gossiping, and that I didn't want that ridiculous story repeated."

"By the phrase 'not straight away,' do you mean you eventually saw the shingles?"

"Yes, sir. Two months later I went out there to see for myself."

"And what did you find?"

"Nothing. The shingles were old and some were rotten. There were bird droppings and one of the shingles had a rust-colored stain."

"You saw no human remains?"

"No, sir."

"How long have you known Nancy and Richard Randolph?"

"Since we were children. We became close friends as adults and visit each other with some regularity."

"Please describe their relationship."

"They're fond of each other. There were the usual familiarities, but they're cousins, after all."

"Familiarities?"

"A friendly touch here and there. The occasional embrace and kiss."

"Nothing imprudent?"

"I never thought so, but others might not agree. The eye of the beholder I suppose."

Henry grew quiet and resumed his pacing. He kept his head down, chin against his chest, and after a moment returned to his witness. "One more question, Mr. Harrison. Given all that you have told me, about the relationship between the two defendants and what happened in your home, do you believe it possible that the Nancy and Richard Randolph were guilty of criminal correspondence?" There followed a flurry of whispers as the polite phrase for illicit sexual relations was explained to those unfamiliar with it.

"Absolutely not," Harrison declared. "Richard and Nancy Randolph are from the finest of families and would never engage in…that sort of thing. Never."

Henry faced the justices. "No more questions."

The courtroom hummed as Harrison stepped down and people swapped opinions and suspicions. The mounting heat and crush of bodies turned the small space into an inferno. Fluttering fans and waved newspapers were wan attempts at relief as seventeen more men and women took the stand, few of whom provided anything of importance.

John Randolph, who had accompanied Nancy from Bizarre to Glyntyvar, drew stares when he stood to unfold his tall, misshapen torso, strode bird-like to the witness stand and spoke in soprano tones. Describing Nancy during the trip, John said she was suffering from a headache. "Perhaps a portent of the terrible colic attack she suffered later that night." Asked he if believed Nancy to be pregnant, John glared angrily at Henry. "Never, sir! Nancy Randolph is one of the most innocent, sweet-natured young ladies I've ever known."

"Maybe a little too sweet-natured," one of the townies cracked. He sank in his seat when Henry shot him a withering glare.

"And you saw no inappropriate behavior between your brother Richard and Nancy Randolph?"

"Absolutely not. We're an affectionate family, Mr. Henry. And why shouldn't Richard be fond of a woman once destined to be his sister-in-law?"

132

Henry peered over his bifocals at the strange-looking youth. "Kindly explain, sir."

"Nancy was engaged to our late brother, Theodorick."

While the audience digested that revelation, Henry dismissed John and called other witnesses less forgiving in their assessments. Carter Page and Anne Randolph, a cousin from Powhatan County, were frequent guests at Bizarre. Page said little, but his wife claimed that Nancy and Richard were overly demonstrative with one another. Anne also said she questioned Nancy's sudden habit of wearing ill-fitting clothes which "hid a pretty figure" and cited the difference in Nancy's size before and after the incident at Glyntyvar. In fairness, she stressed that the change could be attributed to Nancy's troublesome health. Patsy Randolph concurred with Anne and stated that Nancy frequently suffered from colic and various female disorders and had her asked for advice on treatments. Henry quickly seized this new line of inquiry.

"Do you have any particular expertise in that area, Miss Randolph?"

"I share my father's interest and knowledge in scientific matters. He has taught me a great deal over the years."

"Your father?"

"Yes, sir," Patsy said, cheeks coloring.

Henry milked her response. "For the record and the elucidation of those ignorant of the fact, please identify your father by name and profession."

"Thomas Jefferson, Secretary of State of the United States."

As Henry intended, the courtroom buzzed at the mention of the illustrious Jefferson name which, he also knew, would add credibility to Patsy's testimony.

"Thank you, Mrs. Randolph. Now kindly tell us what you discussed with your friend, Nancy."

"A number of things." Patsy rattled off a list of ailments and treatments, none of which Henry found of special interest until she mentioned gum guaiacum. "She

133

asked if I could acquire some and send it to Bizarre as none was available in that area."

"What are the uses of gum guaiacum?"

"It's used to treat colic and rheumatism and various stomach disorders." Her color deepened when she added, "And to stimulate the menstrual flow."

"Anything else?" Henry pressed.

Eyebrows rose and fans quickened when Patsy replied, "It can also be used as an abortifacient."

"Is it your opinion that Nancy wanted the gum guaiacum for that purpose?"

"Absolutely not," Patsy replied coolly. "Had that had been the case, she would've sought it months earlier. Nancy told me it was for colic, and I've no reason to doubt her."

"Thank you, Mrs. Randolph. No more questions."

Henry returned to the table where he shed his wig and wiped his wet forehead while conferring with his colleagues. Many were disappointed that he hadn't unleashed his famous fireworks, but they were at least amused when he leaned back, propped his feet on the table and twirled his peruke on one finger. It was a trademark gesture suggesting he was either confident, bored or both.

After a short conference, John Marshall began reading depositions. The first was from Mrs. Wood, the Harrison's housekeeper. Mrs. Wood discussed the blood-stained sheets and said that, while they could've indicated a miscarriage, it was more likely menstrual-related. Susanna Harrison, Randolph's mother, reported that she had examined Nancy and found no signs of breast milk or anything else indicating pregnancy. Judith was Marshall's last deposition, and tension arose when her name was read aloud. She was, after all, the accused adulterer's wife, but those hoping for the words of a woman scorned were quickly disabused. Ever phlegmatic, Judith had stated that she remained awake after the first screams and that "no child could have been born in the next room or carried from it without my knowledge." Furthermore, she swore that Richard had returned to their bedroom after checking on Nancy and remained there the entire night, undermining suspicions that his were the footsteps on the stairs.

Depositions completed, Marshall and his legal team conferred briefly before Patrick Henry slipped his wig back in place and retook the helm of the examination. The witness he most eagerly anticipated was Mary Cary Page. She was the daughter of Archibald Cary, Speaker of the Virginia Senate, a fact that Mary took embarrassing steps to keep in everyone's mind. Mr. Cary was also Henry's oldest and most vociferous political adversary. He had every intention of treating Mary fairly, but meeting this small woman with tightly pursed lips and prissy demeanor gave him pause. His long career had taught him how to gauge people, and with a single glance he knew he was going to have a little fun. He might even give these yokels a glimpse of the old firebrand they would have paid admission to see.

21

Aware that Mary was itching to speak, Henry again took his time, fiddling with papers and delaying the moment solely to unnerve her. Finally, with tension soaring, he coughed loudly, cleared his throat and approached the witness. "State your name please."

"Mary Cary Page, sir. My father is Archibald Cary of Ampthill, the Speaker of the Virginia Senate, and my husband, whom you've already interrogated, is Carter Page, and he's sitting right over there. I'm Nancy's and Judith's aunt. Their mother Anne was my sister."

A nonstop talker, Henry noted. Good. He said nothing, knowing she would continue without prompting.

"I've known Nancy all her life and visited Bizarre many times which is why I can offer unique perspective on the case. That along with the fact that I'm a wife and a mother and know about such matters."

"What matters?"

She toyed with the fan in her lap. "Female matters, sir."

"Could you be more specific?"

Mary lowered her voice as though making a confidence. "Pregnancy," she whispered.

"Please speak up, Mrs. Page. This is a court of law, and we're all grown-ups after all."

Mary was visibly annoyed by the resulting laughter. She leaned her head back, scanned the sea of faces and all but shouted her response.

"Pregnancy!" This time the laughter pleased Mary, and as she preened and interacted with the spectators, Henry knew she could be a credible witness. Because she seemed eager to accuse Nancy, however, she could also be damaging. He steered her carefully.

"Please tell the court why you mentioned pregnancy, Mrs. Page."

"Because Nancy was pregnant, sir, and that's all there is to it. I knew it months ago when I visited Bizarre. It was no surprise considering how free she and Richard were with their affections. I frankly don't know how Judith endured it. Why, if my husband ever—"

"Please confine your remarks to the involved parties, Mrs. Page."

"Very well." Mary opened open her fan with a theatrical flourish. "I visited Bizarre twice last summer and noticed peculiar things about Nancy's clothes. When she lived at Tuckahoe, she was fastidious about her appearance, but, as Anne said earlier, she had taken to wearing loose fitting clothes. Rather slovenly and unfashionable too, if you don't mind my saying so."

"Not at all," Henry said, nodding at someone in the audience. "Pray continue."

"Well, when I asked Nancy about her appearance, she said her chores at Bizarre required comfortable clothes. I suppose that was a reasonable explanation, but it didn't sit well with me."

"What would you suggest she wear for gathering eggs, Mrs. Page? Surely not a ball gown."

"Of course not," she snapped, bristling at a loud guffaw from the back of the courtroom. "But as I said, it didn't sit right, so I suggested she undress to see for myself that nothing was wrong. Not only did she refuse, but her tone was dismissive. Some might say rude. When I attempted to discuss the matter with Judith, I was rebuffed, so I decided to get proof on my own."

"Why were you so compelled to pursue this matter, Mrs. Page? Indeed, why the need to inspect Nancy whenever you visited Bizarre?"

Mary drew herself up. "I was not prying, if that's your implication."

"That was your choice of words, madam. Not mine."

Mary ignored the implication. "It was a matter of duty, sir. I'm family, after all, and it's only natural that an aunt should see to her niece's well-being."

"Or lack thereof, it appears." More laughter. "This 'proof' you spoke of, Mrs. Page. Did you find it?"

"I did indeed!" She snapped the fan shut and leaned forward as though making a confidence instead of addressing a packed courtroom. "I followed Nancy around to familiarize myself with her daily routines. When I discovered that her bedroom door had a crack in it, one evening when I knew she would be undressing for bed, I knelt down by the crack and watched."

Mary's dramatic pause told Henry she wanted prompting, so he complied. "Please tell the court what you saw."

Mary shot Nancy a malicious glance. "I saw her standing naked before her mirror, and her belly was unmistakably swollen. There is no doubt in my mind that she was with child!"

The courtroom fell silent while Mary smirked and basked in her imagined triumph. Henry wasted not a moment before turning her fatal blunder to his advantage.

"You say you peeped through a crack in Nancy's door to find your proof?"

"Yes, sir, I did indeed," she announced proudly, unaware that she had tumbled into his trap.

Henry drew himself up and queried her in a loud, ridiculing tone. "If I may ask, madam, which eye did you peep with?"

The courtroom erupted with laughter as people anticipated the hoped-for fireworks.

"But, sir!" Mary cried, undone. "What I meant to say was that I—!"

"I daresay everyone present, young, old and in between, knows what you meant to say, Mrs. Page." Henry turned away and strode back and forth before the bench, eyes flashing mischief as he delivered his coup de grace. "Great God!" he thundered. "Pray, deliver us from eavesdroppers!"

Mary's face went crimson when whoops and applause acknowledged the eminent attorney's message. Under no circumstances did Virginia's strict code of honor allow gentlemen to eavesdrop. To do so was to employ unfair deception to expose someone performing in a manner contrary to their public persona. Only those operating outside the code, including women, the ill-bred and slaves, would stoop to such tactics, much less admit to them. Mary Page had accidentally proclaimed herself a busybody with less than honorable intentions.

"That will be all, Mrs. Page," Henry said with exaggerated politesse. "You may step down."

"But, sir, you have misunderstood what I—"

"That will be all!" Henry repeated firmly.

Mary's humiliation finished the interrogations, leaving Richard's three attorneys huddled in a corner and a courtroom humming with speculation. After a few moments, order was restored for John Marshall to make closing arguments. His keen sense of logic led him to an empirical presentation addressing—and dismissing—the five most crucial issues. First, the alleged closeness between Richard and Nancy was a natural occurrence for a family living together. "If they were trying to conceal a liaison," Marshall argued, "they would've been cautious in public, not careless, lest they arouse suspicion." Secondly, as for the alleged pregnancy, the Harrisons could scarcely have not noticed a woman ready to deliver. Thirdly, the use of gum guaiacum as an abortifacient was utterly illogical for someone, as Patsy Jefferson had suggested, far into a pregnancy. Fourth, the claim of miscarriage was "based on rumor initiated and spread by slaves for whom any suspicious appearance might be considered proof of criminal activity." Finally, there was Nancy's refusal to undress for her Aunt Mary which begged the question of what she might be hiding. "The most innocent person on earth might have acted in the same manner,"

Marshall averred, "because purity resents suspicion, and the resentment is stronger still when one is suspected by a friend." These powerful arguments, coupled with the absence of both corpse or weapon, directed the decision exactly where Marshall, Henry and Campbell wanted it. All fourteen judges concurred that while there had been an abundance of gossip and innuendo, there was no conclusive evidence of wrongdoing.

The verdict was read to the hushed courtroom. "On consideration whereof and of the circumstances relating to the fact, it is the opinion of the Court that the said Richard Randolph of Bizarre is not guilty of the felony wherewith he stands charged and that he be discharged out of custody and go hence thereof without delay."

While some spectators resented the verdict, others cheered. Many wondered if the accolades were for Richard, Henry's performance or Marshall's concluding arguments. No one weighed this conflict more carefully than John Randolph. His love for Richard was unwavering, but, despite his youth, John was no fool. He easily dismantled Marshall's defense, and could not dismiss the ghastly likelihood that his hero-brother had fallen from grace. That Richard and Nancy might not be who they seemed was a prospect that tortured him for years, even after he learned the truth.

John was not alone in his assessment. Richard's freedom and legal rights had been restored, but others wondered about his honor. Would his much-publicized victory silence the rumors about Nancy and himself, or, instead of sealing their Pandora's box, had they opened it ever wider? Indeed, it was only a matter of time before long-standing loves, hatreds and doubts emerged from shadows which no one knew existed.

Part 4

"Much of the domestic and even public discourse was produced by the mutilated and misconstructed repetition of free conversation at dinner tables by those mute but not inattentive listeners."

-Thomas Jefferson

22

In May, a second notice concerning the Glyntyvar rumors appeared in Richmond's venerable *Virginia Gazette & General Advertiser.* Again, the author was St. George Tucker who believed the public needed more convincing of Richard's innocence than his courtroom acquittal. In a skillful weave of legal and literary talents, Tucker took the unprecedented step of publishing private information in a public forum. His full-page broadside included a letter from himself to Richard and, more shockingly, letters from Judith and John revealing intimate Randolph information. Capitalizing on the calculated style of the day's wildly popular sentimental novels, the wily lawyer sought to seduce remaining doubters with a purely emotional approach.

Under the headline to "The Public," Tucker reminded the newspaper readership that he had reared and educated Richard Randolph since the age of eight, and that his former charge had been "tried by an examining court, at which *fourteen* magistrates presided, and *acquitted.*" It was followed by the evaluation of a "very respectable friend" present at the trial who said, "The charges against Mr. Randolph turned out to be the darkest and most unfounded a calumny that ever disgraced a country." In a letter to her sister Elizabeth, Judith wrote that the accusations that her husband ravaged her sister were "as false as the vile wretch in whom it originated, and that I have ever believed and positively known it to be so, as my conduct sufficiently proves." A second letter, to Tucker, stated, "Could I but convince the world of my poor husband's innocence, as perfectly as I myself am satisfied of it, I should be the happiest of human beings." In a third very brief missile to

Tucker, John Randolph confirmed the veracity of Judith's words.

Whether it was impacted by Tucker's bold broadside or eroded by time, gossip about the affair finally faded. Richard, Judith and Nancy returned to Bizarre and set about the business of rebuilding their lives, but the road was far from smooth. Judith suffered a miscarriage in late summer, and became ever more withdrawn, tending to Saint and devoting all free moments to reading the Scriptures. Her immersion into religion reminded Nancy and Richard of a nun who had taken a vow of silence, so they left her alone. It was no surprise when they turned to each other for solace.

One late November morning, smothered by the oppression clouding his life, Richard stood alone inside the barn. The cured tobacco leaves were gone, but their pungent aroma lingered in the crisp, cold air and melded with the mustiness of the old building. It was a familiar fusion that he found comforting, but now made his life feel as empty as the barn itself. The peace he prayed would come with public exoneration remained elusive. He believed himself still disgraced, and Judith's coldness augmented his pain. At age twenty-two, Richard was foundering.

The whickering of horses and loud creak of wagon wheels reminded him that Daniel Moseley was driving Judith into town that morning. When the wagon sounds faded, he went into the barren barnyard and stood alone, not knowing what to do next. The only movement was chimney smoke rising from the kitchen and house in a vertical plume. It grew mesmerizing until it was shattered by bitter gusts that drove Richard toward the warmth of the house. He found Nancy with Saint sleeping in her lap. He could not contain his despair.

"Nancy, I—"

"What is it, Richard?" she asked, alarmed.

"Judith," he sighed. "I don't know how much more I can endure."

"Nor I." She shifted the baby to make both more comfortable. "She's always been distant, but now she's a closed door. Every morning when I get up, I pray that she will return to us, that we can stop walking on eggshells."

"I pray the same thing." Richard sank into a chair and buried his face in his hands. "It's my fault. Everything is my fault."

"We both know that's not true. You did everything you could to right a terrible wrong. The public letter. Your trip to Tuckahoe. The trial. All of those were the deeds of a man with a good heart and a devoted husband. You need only consider how strongly Judith defended you in her deposition and those letters Professor Tucker published, and yet—"

"Richard looked up. "And yet?"

"She treats you abominably. There. I've said it."

"You sister has a side you haven't seen, Nancy."

"I thought I'd seen them all."

"A dark, difficult, vindictive side I discovered on our wedding night."

Nancy retreated. "I suspect this isn't something I should hear."

"Perhaps not, but considering what we've been through, the one thing this family doesn't need is more secrets."

"True enough."

"You remember how Judith became ill a few months after we married."

"She had la grippe, didn't she?"

"She had a miscarriage. She was pregnant when we were married."

"No!"

"You may remember we were to get married in February. Judith moved the wedding date to Christmas because she was pregnant." He sat heavily and took a ragged breath. "You'll think me a cad for saying so, but I was not the one who initiated the…intimacy. In truth, I originally resisted Judith's desires, but she was persistent."

Nancy was stunned into silence.

"It was because of that willingness that our wedding night was such a shock. As soon as we reached Presqu'ile, Judith locked herself in the bedroom and ordered me to spend the night elsewhere. I pleaded for her to tell me if I'd done something to displease her, but she refused to answer. My other unpleasant discovery that night was your sister's terrible temper."

Nancy stroked the hair on Saint's tiny head and smiled ruefully. "It runs in the family. Father has one and, heaven knows, so does Tom Junior. I have dreadful memories of Judith screaming and throwing things when she didn't get her way."

"At Presqu'ile, she was inexplicably rude to your sister Molly, and, for no apparent reason, mistreated the servant girl assigned to our quarters. It was hurtful and embarrassing." He untied the ribbon securing his hair and let it fall around his face. "I'm living with a stranger, Nancy. Trapped in an awful silence with no way out."

"Perhaps I can help," Nancy offered.

"But you're as powerless as myself."

"Not necessarily. The situation might improve if I moved away. In fact, it's been on my mind for some time. Last month I wrote Patsy about coming to live at Monticello, but they're filled to the rafters." She paused when Saint stirred and gurgled before falling back asleep. "I've even considered returning to Tuckahoe."

"As much as you despise Gabriella? You'll be absolutely miserable!"

"At least my differences with her are out in the open. With Judith, I don't even know where I stand."

"I can think of few things worse than no alternatives."

"Nor I."

The crackle and hiss from the fireplace grew louder as hopelessness weighed heavy. The walls seemed to close in, as though to crush these two unmoored souls along with the pitiful babe cursed to a life of silence. Time lapsed and spiraled aimlessly until footsteps on the front porch brought them back to earth. An explosion of arctic air blasted the toasty room before Judith slammed the door. Her usual steely visage was tinged with sadness as she handed an opened letter to Nancy.

"From Tom Junior." Judith hung her bonnet and coat on a peg by the door. "I'll take the baby now."

Nancy surrendered the sleeping Saint and began reading. Her face reflected a range of emotions, and there was a catch in her throat when she turned to Richard. "Papa died three days ago in Richmond."

"What happened?"

"Gout and gravel. Gabriella moved him to Richmond and summoned Tom when Papa's condition worsened. Tom says Papa wasn't making any sense and isn't even sure he recognized him."

"That doesn't bode well," Richard muttered.

"What do you mean?" Judith asked in an unexpected show of interest.

"I shouldn't be surprised if Gabriella and her lawyer father took full advantage of the colonel's vagueness."

"Oh, no!" Nancy cried. "The will!"

"When is the funeral?" Richard asked.

Nancy checked the letter. "Three days from now at Tuckahoe."

He stood heavily. "We'll leave first thing in the morning."

"The Moseleys will have to keep Saint," Judith said. "You'd best rest up for the long drive."

Nancy and Richard exchanged looks as Judith hurried to the overseer's cottage. Both were bewildered by the uncharacteristic thoughtfulness, and hoped it was a sign that Judith was thawing. All optimism faded the next morning when they climbed into the carriage and watched Judith's mood deteriorate along with the weather. Dark skies gravid with sleet turned the roads to mud and deviled the unhappy travelers. Jouncing over rough terrain and the constant tug of the reins ached Richard's arms and wearied the horse as well. An overnight at a James River roadhouse with robust fires and a cheerful innkeeper rejuvenated all except Judith who never reciprocated the man's good spirits. Morning brought more sleet and cold, but, when they finally arrived at Tuckahoe, they would find Colonel Randolph's funeral stormier than anything they endured on the road.

23

Despite the somber occasion, warmth prevailed as greetings were exchanged between siblings who hadn't seen each other in years. Neither Nancy nor Judith could remember when all ten Randolph children, from thirty-one-year-old Molly to eight-year-old Virginia, were together at Tuckahoe. After paying their respects to the colonel, laid out in the parlor, the men repaired to the Burnt Room for whiskey, cigars, and the usual talk of politics, taxes and tobacco, while their wives and sisters gathered in the great hall to swap family stories and child-rearing advice. With no mention made of Richard's trial, the mood was that of a family reunion, but talk soon turned to their inexplicably absent hostess. All arriving guests had been greeted by Delilah who said only that Gabriella and her son were sequestered upstairs.

"It's hardly the first time she's been inhospitable," Nancy told Patsy. "One of the first things she did after marrying Papa was to throw us out of the house. Thank heavens you and Tom Junior took in the little ones."

"We always wanted to do more, but with Papa constantly remodeling Monticello, rooms appear and disappear as if by magic. Things will be different when Tom and I move here to Tuckahoe, and I hope you'll join us. Gabriella has made it clear that she prefers living in Richmond, and with the colonel gone now, I assume—"

"Assume nothing where that harpy is concerned," Nancy said. "Deception is her middle name."

"Papa would agree," Patsy laughed. "He said I should avoid her like a bad note on my harpsichord."

"Mr. Jefferson is ever the diplomat," Judith said. "God forgive me for saying so, but Gabriella was unforgivably mean to Richard the last time we visited."

The room buzzed with ladies asking for details, but before Judith could respond, Tom Junior entered from the Burnt Room with the other men in tow. Weary of waiting and a little drunk, he raised his hands for quiet.

"Everyone here knows Papa hated procrastination!" he said, glaring at the ceiling. "The funeral was set for an hour ago, yet that woman upstairs has kept us waiting without reason and—"

"We're quite ready." Gabriella materialized beneath the arched doorway alongside her father. There were scattered gasps at the black silk dress emphasizing rather than concealing her curves, and a voice without a hint of gravitas. "If everyone will follow me into the parlor, Father Alexander is waiting."

Per Gabriella's strict instructions, the eulogy was brief, after which the mourners donned coats and headed to the family cemetery. The dark cloudbank threatening snow had blown over Chesapeake Bay, leaving behind a clear sky with blinding sunshine. Eager for a moment of solitary reflection, Nancy hurried ahead, intent on a quick prayer at her mother's graves before the others arrived. She drew up in horror.

"Have mercy!"

Anne Cary Randolph's tombstone was obscured by vines, her gravesite overgrown with weeds. When she saw this willful desecration, Nancy's loathing of Gabriella metamorphosed into pure hatred. Her eyes stung with tears as she dropped to the ground, and tore at the overgrowth like a wild animal. The approaching mourners watched, horrified, as she continued her furious task until her mother's name was visible and the plot was free of weeds. Richard helped her to her feet and offered a handkerchief to wipe away the dirt.

"No!" Nancy waved him away and held out her filthy gloves. "I want everyone to see evidence of Gabriella's crime."

Richard steered her away and positioned her between himself and Judith. Nancy fell silent, so consumed with rage that she heard nothing of the priest's eulogy, but she did not miss the sound of dirt shoveled onto the casket.

"No straw," she murmured.

"What's that?" Richard asked, leaning close.

"Nothing. Nothing at all."

Back in the house, the family took a light lunch in the Great Room with Gabriella presiding at the head of the table. It was lost on no one that her father took the seat ordinarily occupied by the colonel, or that she pointedly ignored the filthy gloves on the pristine tablecloth beside Nancy's plate. Conversation was minimal and strained until dessert was finished and Gabriella told Tom Junior to join her in the Burnt Room. When her lawyer father followed and closed the door, everyone knew it meant the reading of the colonel's will.

"I'm worried," Patsy told Nancy when they retreated to the parlor.

"So am I."

Along with the others, they huddled and waited, looking warily toward the Burnt Room when they heard Tom's raised voice. An uneasy calm followed before it too was interrupted by a noisy outburst.

"I feel like I'm going to jump out of my skin!" Nancy whispered.

Tom's voice soared again, louder this time, before the door to the Burnt Room flew open, slamming the wall so hard the hinges barely held. He was apoplectic when he reached the parlor.

"They've ruined me, Patsy!" he shouted. "Ruined me!"

"What has happened?"

"It's worse than I feared! Far worse!"

Nancy made room on the settee. "Please sit down and tell us what happened."

"If only I'd been there when Papa died," Tom lamented as he sank between them. "If only I'd known how far that brazen bitch and her thieving father would go to take control!"

"Tom!" Patsy gasped, shocked by his language.

"The time for politeness is gone, Patsy, and my patrimony with it. The week before Papa died, Gabriella and her father convinced him to draw up a new will. How simple it was for a mendacious wife and her attorney father to manipulate someone not of sound mind." He leaned forward and pressed the heels of his hands against his eyes. "Papa left bequests for all the children except me and appointed John Harvie the guardian of John, Harriet and Virginia. By naming himself steward, Harvie is the unquestioned master of Tuckahoe and will remain so until his grandson comes of age. When Harvie and Gabriella stole my stewardship, they also stole my right to inherit Tuckahoe."

"No!" Patsy gasped.

"That's not the worst of it. Papa's new will named William and me as executors. That means Papa not only gave away my birthright but saddled me with his debts!" He faced Nancy. "We've been roundly cheated sister. You, me, Judith and all the rest."

News of their father's will struck the older Randolph children like a thunderbolt. Disinherited and disgusted, they departed for their scattered homes. Tom lingered to down more whiskey, and by the time Patsy gathered the children to leave, he was drunk and belligerent. He staggered outside and was arguing with the coachman when Nancy came to say good-bye.

"I'm so sorry about all this, big brother."

"What have you got to be sorry about?" he snarled. "You're not the one Papa saddled with debt."

"For heaven's sake, Tom!" Patsy gasped.

"No one asked you!"

"But your sister was only trying to—"

Tom's hand caught Patsy squarely across the cheek and knocked her to the ground. He leaned against the carriage, feet wide apart, glowering as though he dared her to get up. Strangely, he didn't resist when the coachman steered him inside the coach where he crumpled against the seat and began to sob.

"Patsy!" Nancy wailed, helping her to her feet. "Are you alright?"

"It's nothing." Patsy pecked Nancy's cheek. "I'll be fine."

"Please don't tell me my brother has struck you before."

"Alright then. I won't tell you."

Patsy herded the children into the coach, climbed in after them and lowered the shade. While Nancy stood dumbfounded, the driver clucked to the horse and the carriage lurched away.

"Good-bye, dear friend," she whispered.

When the coach disappeared, shock and outrage writhed inside Nancy like an angry serpent, an unholy mix propelling her back inside the house. With the last visitors gone, Gabriella was in the parlor sipping sherry with her father. Gabriella lofted her glass at Nancy's approach.

"Look who's here, Papa," she said with a cheeky smile. "The Jezebel of the Old Dominion." Nancy noted that John Harvie did not rise when she entered the room. "I trust you've come to say good-bye."

"And more besides."

"Then make it quick. I'm not in the habit of conversing with adulterers."

"May I ask what proof you have to support such an accusation?"

"Proof is not needed for what is common knowledge."

"Common gossip, you mean. The sort that you've been all too eager to spread about Richard and me."

Clearly rankled, Gabriella said, "This is tiresome, Nancy. Say what you came to say and begone. You're not welcome here."

"You made that plain when you stole my brother Tom's patrimony and Tuckahoe along with it."

The stinging accusation brought Harvie to his feet. "I'd advise you to watch your tongue, young woman. Unless you want to face accusations of slander, let me remind you that I'm a lawyer who wields considerable—"

"I'm all too familiar with what you wield!" Nancy shot back. "Your case for slander is as absurd as your ethics are reprehensible. My entire family has witnessed your lying and thieving and manipulation of a sick man for material gain and your total disrespect for the Randolph name. As for you, Gabriella, today you showed your true self, a selfish, conniving gorgon who desecrated our mother's grave. It will be no surprise when you do the same to our father."

Gabriella's eyes narrowed to slits. "How dare you?!"

"How dare I what? Tell the truth? You're the one guilty of slander, and it won't take long before everyone in Richmond knows what happened today. No doubt you have a coterie of rich, like-minded rabble, but there is no room among decent people for larcenous parvenus such as yourself."

"Get out, you trollop!" Gabriella screamed. "Get out!!"

"Best mind your language, my dear, lest someone think you ill-bred."

"Out!"

Nancy bobbed a mocking curtsy. "With the greatest of pleasure."

24

The loss of Tuckahoe was only a harbinger of the woes befalling the Randolphs of Bizarre. Even with Daniel Moseley's expertise, the plantation failed three years in a row, and Richard's financial problems worsened with a dunning by Patrick Henry for unpaid legal fees. Desperate for money, he acquired a certificate to practice law in neighboring Prince Edward County, but his gamble failed after landing no cases. This confluence of calamities eroded Richard's health and triggered sporadic fevers that baffled Dr. Phelps, the physician in Farmville. Richard would recover enough to go back to work only to be felled again. Judith stocked a battery of medicines and dosed him regularly.

The only bright note came in September, 1795, when she gave birth to a healthy baby whom she named Tudor. Vivacious and endlessly curious, Tudor was a much-needed diversion from the demands of his poor deaf brother, Saint. Another addition to the household came in the spring of 1796 when John announced that he was returning to Bizarre. Richard and Judith were amenable, but Nancy was uneasy. Since Theo's death, she and John had corresponded regularly, and while his letters were mostly genteel, unprovoked barbs occasionally surfaced. Nancy did her best to ignore them, but when he arrived in May, his coolness warned that battle lines had been drawn. At twenty-two, John had metamorphosed yet again, a persona more mercurial than ever.

Somehow, the family fell into a tolerable routine with the best moments coming when everyone gathered on the front porch after dinner. One June twilight, with the babies asleep, Judith and Nancy caught up on their sewing while Richard and John discussed politics and enjoyed a bowl of tobacco. Spirits remained high enough for John to regale everyone with tales of his colorful escapades, and while Nancy remained nettled by his superior attitude, she couldn't deny he was entertaining.

"Who would like to hear about my college duel?"

"It will only be my thousandth time," Richard laughed, "but perhaps the ladies will oblige."

"Not I," Nancy declared.

"Pray tell why not," John said, feigning disappointment.

"You already know I disapprove of dueling," Nancy replied, deftly threading a needle. "My opinion hasn't changed."

"For heaven's sake, let him tell his story," Judith grumbled.

"Thank you, cousin dear." John crossed his long legs and continued while mist rose and swarmed across the river. "All Virginia gentlemen know the importance of honor, but I scarcely imagined I'd be defending mine at age sixteen, much less that it would involve my closest friend. Robert Taylor was his name. Our professors called us 'fiery spirits,' and one afternoon those spirits got out of hand when we debated opposing sides of a political question. I relished the feisty exchange, but Robert took it to heart and challenged me to a duel. The next morning, accompanied by our seconds bearing pistols, we met on a foggy field outside the city."

Nancy was appalled. "Who on earth gives guns to schoolboys?"

Richard tapped his pipe against a boot heel and flushed out the ashes. "John has a way of skirting rules and regulations created for us ordinary folk,"

"Well-said, big brother," John enthused. "So, there we were, two nervous lads playing at being adults. When the countdown ended, our volleys went wide of the mark, but I found success with the second shot."

"You didn't kill the poor boy!" Judith gasped.

"No, no. My bullet struck his hip."

"But why on earth would you want to shoot your best friend?"

"I didn't *want* to shoot him, Judith, and I certainly didn't want to kill him. Kindly remember that I neither issued the challenge nor created the rules of chivalry. I was, however, obliged to play by them. I'm pleased to say Robert and I were reconciled on the spot, and he promised to carry my bullet in eternal memory of our friendship. Isn't that splendid?"

"The word I would choose is peculiar," Richard chuckled. "Now let's change the subject."

"As you wish," John conceded. He indicated the rag bag between Nancy and Judith. "What are you ladies so diligently working on."

"Mending clothes for the field hands." Judith shook out a large homespun shirt. "Those poor souls wear them out as fast as we mend them."

"That's no surprise considering how hard they work." John glanced at the lush fields, gleaming gold in the fast-fleeing sunlight. They were empty of workers now, but breezes stirred the tobacco leaves to life. His thin face darkened. "How deceptive those fields are."

"What do you mean?" Richard asked.

"Sometimes I see lush green beauty. Other times I see a prison. I don't know what's more disturbing about slavery, its inhumanity or the gnawing shame which no one dares mention."

"Both are things we can lay at the feet of our colonial founders." Richard's wooden chair creaked as he shifted his weight and relit his pipe. Between puffs, he said, "No doubt you know about stepfather's new dissertation for abolishing it."

"Indeed, I do. He plans to present it to the General Assembly this fall. He always taught us on to follow our conscience on unpopular matters, so it will be good to see him practice what he preaches."

"How do you envision the reaction in Washington City?"

"I wish I could be optimistic, but the subject couldn't be more contentious."

"What exactly does Mr. Tucker propose?" Nancy ventured.

"His opening argument is that slavery is incompatible with the underpinnings of our revolution against Great Britain, and that it's time to admit and accept its moral wrongness. He proposes gradual emancipation, such as they used in Massachusetts, and cites Haiti as a warning against it coming too quickly."

"Haiti?" Richard asked.

"A French colony in the Caribbean and an ongoing bloodbath," John replied. "Five years ago, the slaves rose up and slaughtered thousands of French planters and their families."

Judith gasped. "Lord have mercy!"

"The country declared its independence, but even with emancipation, Haiti remains lawless and mired in chaos. Our fledgling country cannot afford such catastrophe."

"No, we cannot."

"May we not talk of something less disturbing?" Judith asked.

"Of course, we may," John stood and stretched. "What a fresh, sweet smell rising from the river."

"It's especially nice this time of year," Nancy offered. "When it's high and in a hurry."

"What a poetic way of putting it." John extended a hand. "Shall we have a walk before it gets dark?"

Nancy was leery of his olive branch, but reconsidered since it offered a break from the hated sewing. "Alright."

The two wandered awhile without speaking, each lost in the velvety Virginia dusk. Enough sunlight remained to glow on the lingering blooms of spring. Red bleeding heart and orange butterfly weed did colorful battle with yellow and blue indigo and vivid bluebell. By the time John suggested they turn around and follow the path to the wharves, the sun had assigned elongated shadows to the docks. Nancy pointed toward a bench facing the water.

"Mr. Moseley built that for me last summer. It's much more comfortable than that old beech tree." She sat and inhaled the fragrance of wild phlox, thick along the bank. More silvery mist shimmered atop the racing river. "Here's another of your deceptive tableaux, John. Everything about this view says beauty and serenity, and yet slave cabins lie beyond those oaks."

"I apologize for mentioning slavery. It's not a fit topic for ladies."

"It's not a fit topic for anyone."

"I didn't realize you had an opinion on the matter."

"Because I'm a woman?"

He held out his hands, palms up. "Well—"

Nancy was vexed by his glibness. "That attitude is as archaic and absurd as dueling, John. Of course, I have an opinion on slavery. Are we women supposed to ignore the injustice we see every day?"

"I only meant that—"

"I know exactly what you meant," Nancy said, cutting him off again. "But never mind because for once, you and I are in agreement. Slavery is shameful and evil and I pray to God that Mr. Tucker's proposal falls on the right ears."

"As do I." John gave her a wry look. "Do we truly disagree that much?"

"We do."

"Why do you suppose that is?"

"There's no supposition involved. It's because you believe you alone have all the answers. That was quite evident in your letters."

John's eyebrows rose. "Might you cite an example?"

"Your worst offense was your claim that I could never fathom your bonds with your brothers. Theo and I were closer than you could imagine, and I'm close to Richard as well. How could you be so hurtful?"

"It was not my intention."

"I think you mean every word you say, John. How often I've heard you tout their power. You once said a clever tongue could destroy the sturdiest of souls." Seeing John momentarily flummoxed, Nancy pressed her advantage. "What you see as clever, others see as sad and supercilious."

Her calculated arrow found its mark.

"That doesn't bother me one whit!" John shot back, anger rising in his thin chest. "I'm an aristocrat. I love justice and I hate equality."

Nancy feigned admiration. "I couldn't have described you better myself."

"Do you mock me, madam?"

"No need when you do it so well yourself."

John's soprano voice soared higher. "I'm sorry if my frankness offends you!"

Nancy fluttered a hand as though brushing aside a pesky mosquito. "You confuse frankness with condescension, but continue if you wish."

Her sarcasm kindled John's temper. He leapt to his feet and paced the wooden dock. The click of his heels echoed across the river, growing ever more ominous until he halted to wave a finger in Nancy's face.

"If you were truly close to my brothers, then please justify the evils you inflicted upon them."

The back of Nancy's neck blazed. "I've no idea what you're talking about."

John drew himself up and expelled his poison like a cobra. "My poor Theo is dead, and Richard's honor and reputation have been destroyed. Tell me, cousin dear, how you live with that?"

25

"How dare you?!" Nancy sprang to her feet. "You of all people know the truth, John Randolph. You even swore to it at Richard's examination."

"I swore what I was expected to swear, thanks to that gentry protocol you find so archaic. Without the illustrious Randolph name and social standing between you and the real world, where do you think you'd be right now?"

"I...I don't understand," Nancy stammered.

"Then let me help. You can begin by telling me what actually happened between you and Theo." He swung an arm wide. "There's no better time or place, just you, me and this foggy old river. We're family and I deserve to know."

Nancy's legs turned to jelly, and she sat hard on the bench, swallowed by a darkness devoid of time and place. She closed her eyes and drifted.

"Theo is the only man I've loved," she said slowly, "and I know he loved me too. You think I'm the reason he's gone? Richard himself said Theo would've died months before if I hadn't cared for him. Knowing that enabled me to endure the terrible times that followed. Yes, John. I bore Theo's child whom God saw fit to take, as he had taken your brother." Nancy took a deep breath to continue a confession she could not stop. "Richard and Judith knew about the stillbirth at Glyntyvar, and the truth would have died too had the slaves not begun their evil gossip. Once that happened, Richard and I were helpless to stop it. Gentleman that he is, he did everything in his power to put the incident behind us, even risked his life by testifying at the examination. Had he been found guilty of murder, he would've been hanged, you know."

Nancy smelled the wine on John's breath and opened her eyes to find him in her face.

"I know the risk my brother took to save your hide," he spat. "It begs the question why you did nothing to save his."

"Not so, John."

"Tell me."

"When we were in Williamsburg, your stepfather suggested Richard take our case to Tuckahoe and ask my father for help. Before Richard left, I wrote a letter naming Theo as the baby's father and asked him to give it to Papa. He refused, saying that such a confession asserted that he couldn't protect his family and would further demean him as a gentleman."

"Bah!" John scoffed. "He'd never make such a choice."

"Perhaps you don't know him as well as you thought."

"Show me the letter!"

"I destroyed it."

"Why should I believe you?"

"Since you clearly don't believe anything I say, go ask Richard." When John remained in her face, her anger boiled over. She grabbed his shoulders and pushed him away. "Go on!" she cried. "Ask him!!"

"So I shall!" John shouted.

Both realized dusk had turned to nightfall when Richard's voice floated through a blackness alive with lightning bugs. "What's all the shouting down there?"

John glared at Nancy before stomping off the dock. She remained there until the thunder of hooves announced he was gone. Exhausted by the terrible exchange, she climbed the stairs to find Richard and Judith waiting on the porch.

"What was all that yelling?" Richard asked.

"Nothing important. We had a spirited discussion about slavery, that's all."

"Apparently spirited enough to drive John off on one of his night rides."

"Oh, you know how dramatic he can be."

"Better than anyone."

Richard's next words were lost beneath a noisy chorus of frogs along the riverbank, loud enough to worry Judith that it might wake Tudor. She went upstairs to investigate, leaving Nancy and Richard alone on the small porch. Richard leaned close to be heard over the cacophony.

"You and John weren't discussing slavery, were you?"

"No." Nancy sank tiredly into a chair. "An ordinary conversation escalated into a war of words, and I was suddenly under attack."

"How he loves to blindside people." Richard sucked on his pipe and set it aside when he realized it had gone out again. "What was he talking about?"

"You. Me. And Theo."

"Go on."

Nancy was loath to reiterate John's ugly accusations but told Richard the truth. "He didn't believe me about the letter I gave you in Williamsburg, so I told him you would confirm its existence. He must have been afraid of the truth because he fled into the night."

"What he feared was not the truth but that you would win the argument." Richard reached through the darkness and squeezed her hand. "For now, we must put this latest unpleasantness behind us and get on with our lives."

"Why must he make things so difficult?"

"It's just John being John, my dear." Richard withdrew his hand. "Interestingly enough, something good has come from tonight."

"I could use some good news."

"Our discussion about slavery has given me impetus to act on something I should have done years ago. Upon my death, Bizarre's slaves will be freed."

"Dearest Richard." Now it was Nancy's turn to show affection. She rose and leaned down to kiss Richard's forehead. "This isn't the first time you've been my hero."

"I'm honored."

162

"Thank you. Oh!" Nancy covered her mouth too late to hide a yawn. "I'm suddenly worn out."

Richard laughed. "My lunatic brother has that effect on people."

"Indeed, he does."

True to his word, the following day Richard wrote St. George Tucker of his wishes, and by mid-June, he received a revised will with a codicil granting manumission to the slaves of Bizarre upon their owner's death. After a ride into Farmville to have his will witnessed and notarized, Richard headed home beneath threatening skies. He'd scarcely left town when the heavens unleashed thunderstorms that rocked the countryside. By the time he reached Bizarre, he was soaked to the flesh and went to his room to change into dry clothes. Startled by a loud crash, Judith and Nancy rushed upstairs to find him on the floor, naked except for his breeches and shaking hard with fever. Together they got him into bed, and Nancy dispatched Moseley for Dr. Phelps. The storms grew worse, savaging the county with sheets of rain so powerful that the doctor didn't arrive until nightfall. Judith and Nancy stood at the foot of the bed, helpless as the elderly physician attempted to quell Richard's chills. Nothing worked, but exhaustion finally lulled Richard into a fitful sleep beneath a mound of blankets.

"Well?" Judith asked.

"I wish I had answers, Mrs. Randolph. I've treated Richard's fevers before, but these are the worst I've seen. All I can do is leave a variety of medicines and hope that one or a combination will help. Have you paper?" Nancy raced to retrieve foolscap, ink and quill, and watched over the doctor's shoulder as he scratched out recommended dosages for calomel, tartar emetic, quinine jalap, and laudanum. "I'll try to come back tomorrow, but the Appomattox is rising fast and, if these storms continue, you may have to do without me."

With Dr. Phelps gone and Judith minding the babies, Nancy sat on the edge of Richard's bed and studied his pale face. She flinched every time the bedroom blazed white with lightning and thunder boomed overhead. One especially loud thunderclap prompted Richard to open his eyes, only to gaze unseeing at the ceiling before falling back to sleep. Occasionally he lapsed into delirium.

"Theo!" he gasped. "John! Where are you boys?!"

Temperature soaring, Richard threw back the covers to bare a torso shiny with sweat. Nancy wiped his chest until his skin, to her horror, turned clammy and cold. She was further alarmed when he began shivering until his teeth chattered. She called for Judith, and the two commenced a vigil of maddening ups and downs. One minute Richard slept, and the next he flailed so violently that it took them both to keep him from pitching off the bed. He burned up with fever, then shuddered with cold before succumbing to more delirium. He muttered incoherently and called for people whose names neither sister recognized. Nancy and Judith tried one combination of medicines after another, and shortly before dawn, Richard fell into a deep sleep. When his breathing became smooth and steady, Nancy told Judith told to go to her room and rest. She drew her chair close to the bed and was beginning to drowse when she heard a low murmur. His eyes fluttered open and he began mumbling.

"What is it, Richard?"

"Nan...Nancy?"

"I'm here."

She leaned close when his lips struggled to form words. "You and Tucker," he breathed.

"What about us?" she urged.

"The only true friends I ever had."

The eyes closed, and the voice was stilled. Nancy screamed.

"No! No! Please God, no!"

Judith fled back to the sickroom, drawing up hard when she saw Nancy's ghostly face. Her sister's voice was otherworldly as she confirmed the worst.

"He's gone, Judith. Richard is gone."

26

Nancy nerves turned raw whenever she heard an approaching rider. She knew it was only a matter of time before John learned of Richard's death and came to Bizarre. She feared his return because their disastrous last encounter had driven him to flee and because the loss of his beloved older brother would surely ignite new rage. On the afternoon of June 17, two days after Richard was buried, the dreaded hoofbeats arrived. Nancy braced herself when she and Judith went into the front porch and saw John leap from his horse and yell up to them.

"Where is he?"

"By...by the grape arbor," Judith managed in a wavering voice. She pointed, and, along with Nancy, watched John's ungainly stride to the grave. Judith's hand rose to her throat when he dropped to his knees, touched his forehead to the ground and shook with sobs. She and Nancy retreated into the house to wait uneasily, but when John came inside, he quietly hung up his hat and sat. His long fingers curled like talons on the arms of the chair, and, after bowing his head for a long moment, he looked at Judith.

"Please forgive me," he said softly. "Losing another brother has left me quite undone. Kindly tell me what happened."

"As you know, Richard had been in poor health for some time. He went into Farmville on some personal business and was caught in a thunderstorm on the ride back. When he got home, he collapsed with a fever which Dr. Phelps was unable to diagnose."

Judith realized they were in the eye of a hurricane when John's mercurial temper reignited.

"Some time, you say?! Oh, come now! Surely you can be more precise than that! My brother's health began to decline the day he was dragged through that kangaroo court." John glowered at Nancy. "We have you to thank for that!"

166

"That's enough, John!" Judith said, coming unexpectedly to Nancy's defense. "When that awful ordeal was over, Richard said we were to never discuss it again."

John's frown deepened, then disappeared as he nodded acquiescence. "Out of respect to you and Richard, I will abide by his decision."

Both women noticed he had not deferred to Nancy.

As John calmed further, he toyed with his watch ribbon. "Why did you refer to Richard's business as 'personal'?"

"Because that's what he said before he left for town."

"He went to get his new will notarized," Nancy said.

"New will?" John and Judith chimed.

"He decided to make a change the last night you were here, John. In fact, it was our discussion of slavery that inspired it."

"What sort of change?" John asked.

"His slaves are to be freed upon his death."

"What?!" Judith cried.

Nancy was surprised. "You didn't know?"

Judith trembled with rage. "Clearly there are things husbands share with parties other than their wives!"

"Hold up!" John raised a silencing hand. "Are you saying you haven't read the will?"

"Richard told me years ago that I was his sole heir. He added something after the boys were born, but I never read anything. He said I wouldn't understand it."

Appalled by the potential consequences of such a codicil, John struggled to remain calm. "Where is the will?"

"I suppose it's in that desk with the rest of his documents," Judith replied, voice trembling as the truth deepened. "Bizarre cannot function without workers! I'll be ruined!"

"Hush, now," John said. "There are a number of ways to affect manumission, and there's no point in speculating until we know the terms of the will." He went to Richard's desk and rifled the drawers until he found the will and began a careful perusal. Judith clung to his every word when he read aloud.

"He excoriates our ancestors for what he calls 'usurping and exercising the most monstrous tyranny over black slaves' whom he considers 'equally entitled with ourselves to the enjoyment of life, liberty and the pursuit of happiness.' He sought to impress upon Saint and Tudor what he calls 'a just horror of slavery.' He wants some four hundred acres across the river distributed among the male slaves to work for themselves and 'begs their forgiveness for the manifold injuries I have too often inhumanely, unjustly and mercilessly inflicted on them.'" John grimaced. "To be honest, I don't disagree with him, but this condemnation of slavery is certain to alienate our family and the neighboring planters as well."

"Never mind all that." Judith was far more concerned for her own wellbeing. "What are the terms for manumission you mentioned?"

John continued to read, stern face brightening when he found good news. "Manumission will come only after the plantation's mortgage is paid off. That will buy us valuable time."

"Us?"

"Since Richard is no longer able to protect his family, it's my duty to take charge." John set the will aside and retrieved a bottle of whiskey from the sideboard. He poured a shot and lifted his glass high. "To my courageous big brother in admiration for freeing his workers from bondage and inspiring me to do the same." He downed the whiskey. "When the time is right of course."

Judith, grateful to feel Bizarre's onerous burden shift to someone else's shoulders, refilled his glass. "I've never needed anyone so much, John. You're all that stands between me and calamity."

"I do this for your boys' legacy as well. With poor Theo gone and no likelihood that I will produce an heir, they are all we have to carry on the family name. It's in their best interests that I make Bizarre productive and erase its debts so it can be sold for a good profit, and I promise to commit myself to those ends."

"For which I will be eternally grateful."

Nancy, appalled by the idea of living with this unpredictable madman, said nothing. Her mind was racing with possible escapes when John's mood vacillated again. "Since we're going to be living together, I must apologize for abusing you, Nancy. I was upset."

Still chary, she managed a soft, "It's forgotten."

"Good." John smiled and lifted his glass, "Cheers."

While Nancy sought escape through one of her sentimental novels, Judith went to check on the two slave women boiling oak galls to make more black dye. Knowing her one mourning dress could not withstand the rigors of farm work, she set about dying all her clothing. As she watched the iron kettle's roiling, noxious blackness, she weighed the fragility of life and recalled John's remark about not siring sons of his own. Richard had alluded to his brother's impotence, but Judith never pursued a subject too indelicate even for husband and wife. She assumed, correctly, that John's misfortune had to do with the bout of scarlet fever.

"Poor man," she murmured. "Another cross to bear."

The next morning, despite suffering a monstrous hangover, John gathered Richard's will, deeds and plantation records and left for Williamsburg to confer with St. George Tucker about putting Bizarre's finances in order. His stepfather perused the documents and drafted a workable plan, and although John praised its logic and manageability, he balked at the recommendation to sell Matoax.

"Impossible," he declared.

"Not so," Tucker countered. "Such a sale will provide the much-needed revenue for whittling away Bizarre's debts."

"But—"

169

"But what?"

"A few years after you married Mama, she took us boys down to an old plantation called Roanoke where we all slept in a log cabin. I was only nine years old, but I distinctly remember her promising that it would one day be mine. 'When you become a man,' she said, 'you must hold onto the place with a tight fist. A boy's first step toward ruination is to sell his father's inheritance. If you keep your land, your land will keep you.' It's her voice which I hear now."

"Your mother was a wise woman." Tucker rarely spoke of the gentle soul who made him a widower eight years ago, and loss was evident in his voice. "She gave you excellent advice, but it cannot always be followed. I know you grew up at Matoax and that your parents are buried there, but clinging to it will prove calamitous. If you weigh the hard facts, you'll understand and agree."

"I suppose so," John conceded at length. "But why must change be so difficult?"

"Because it's as inevitable as growing old, my boy, and it's human nature to shun things we can't control."

When he heard those words, something unanticipated coursed through John's body, then fled with a jolt. He straightened in his chair and wondered if the disturbing sensation was the loss of youth. Up until the moment he read Richard's will, John still considered himself a lounger and dabbler whose time was best spent carousing in taverns, attending racetracks and debating politics with his youthful cronies. Without warning, at only twenty-three, he found himself cast as a patriarch responsible for his widowed sister-in-law and her sister and surrogate father to his two nephews. Adding to that was the challenge of freeing Bizarre from debt while providing for the plantation's sixty-seven slaves. Yes, John thought. My youth is up the waterspout.

Part 5

"Despair is the damp of hell, as joy is the serenity of heaven."

-John Donne

27

In the year following Richard's death, Bizarre was blessed with much-needed tranquility, all save John. His fluctuating moods continued, as did his night rides. After a midnight robbery near Sandy Fork, he brandished two pistols, which, coupled with his fame as an excellent marksman, kept highwaymen at bay. At home, he remained plagued with insomnia. Once again, Nancy heard his leaden pacing and Shakespearean mantra. "Macbeth hath murdered sleep. Macbeth hath murdered sleep." John's presence was otherwise welcome, especially since he kept his promise to bury the saga of Glyntyvar. Nor was mention made of his terrible accusations toward Nancy. Although barely tolerating Judith's ponderous religiosity, he otherwise enjoyed company of the two very different sisters. He even spent a little playtime with his nephews.

Most surprising of all was John's business acumen. By following Tucker's advice to sell Matoax and ramp up production at Roanoke, he secured the money to pay off much of Bizarre's mortgage and put the troubled plantation on solid footing. Like Richard, he respected Moseley's knowledge and heeded the man's warning that tobacco leached key nutrients from the soil and that exhausted fields were must be left fallow for three years or replanted with corn with long roots to reach new earth. Moseley enriched the soil with composted manure provided by cattle, sheep and hogs, delighting Nancy and Judith with fresh milk, cream and butter. Judith turned up her nose at milking, but Nancy was a dutiful student for Eula Moseley who knew as much about livestock as her husband did agriculture. Saint and baby Tudor benefitted too, giggling gleefully when Nancy let them pet her favorite pig, a sow named Gabriella.

By summer of 1798, with the plantation prospering and spirits improved, Nancy treated herself to a bit of travel, staying a few weeks with Patsy and Tom at Monticello, where things were mercifully peaceful. Judith also ventured out, and took her sons on a riverboat cruise down the Appomattox to Petersburg. Travel for both ended when January and February buried Bizarre under a succession of snowstorms making roads and rivers impassable, but when skies finally cleared, John rode off to see friends in Richmond, and the sisters accepted an invitation from St. George Tucker and his wife Leila to visit Williamsburg. By happy coincidence, Daniel Moseley had a sister there who "needs visiting," so he offered to drive them. The childless Eula was delighted to take care of the boys, having developed a special rapport with the deaf Saint.

Nancy and Judith were warmly welcomed in Williamsburg where Leila made certain they were well entertained. She had been away during the sisters' visit seven years ago when Richard sought legal counsel from Tucker. Nancy adored Leila's vivacity and enjoyed herself for the first time in years. The ladies were enjoying tea in the parlor when Leila announced that they'd been invited to a ball.

"At Bassett Hall, no less. You'll get to see one of the most beautiful homes in Williamsburg."

"But I have nothing to wear!" Nancy said.

"You're welcome to borrow one of my gowns," Leila offered. "If you won't mind something a bit matronly."

"Not at all! Oh, thank you, Leila."

Judith, however, demurred. Three years after Richard's death, she remained swathed in widow's weeds and announced she couldn't possibly attend a public function. Leila, who shared her husband's diplomatic skills, encouraged Judith to indulge in a little amusement.

"Perhaps you might wear one of my garnet brooches," Leila suggested. "It would discreetly announce your wish to return to society."

"Oh, I don't know," Judith said, fussing with a black cuff.

"I assure you no one will disapprove, and it will do you good to get out."

"She's right," Nancy said.

"I have all I need right here." Judith brandished a prayer book before retreating to a far corner to read it.

Nancy ignored her and smiled at Leila. "May I see the dress?"

"Of course."

The gown was a cream-colored muslin creation with balloon sleeves. Nancy held it up to her throat and studied her reflection in a mirror. "It's perfect, Leila. Just perfect."

"You certainly wear it better than I, and there are shoes to match. I daresay you'll be the belle of the ball, my dear."

"I'm afraid at twenty-five, my days as a belle are long gone."

"Nonsense. You're a very pretty girl and Williamsburg loves new faces. There will be plenty of dashing young officers to whirl you around the dance floor and shower you with—"

"Dancing!" Nancy cried. "I don't know any new steps."

"I shouldn't worry. You may see them in Richmond and Washington City, but Williamsburg's dancing feet are planted firmly in the past." She laughed. "This isn't to say they still dance the minuet, but I'm sure whatever steps you know will be fine."

"I do hope so," Nancy sighed. "It's been ages since I've been out in society or worn anything pretty."

"Then it's high time for a change," Leila declared.

The evening of the ball, Judith again declared that she was staying home and resisted all entreaties to change her mind. Nancy was frankly relieved to be free of her sister's sour moods, but kept her feelings to herself. With Leila's encouragement and Tucker's flattery, her self-confidence blossomed, and by the time they climbed into the coach, Nancy was in another world. She reveled in the lively townscape as they rode alongside the Palace Green and turned onto Duke of Gloucester Street. Despite the winter cold, the sidewalks bustled with people going about their evening chores, congregating in taverns and patronizing the cobblers, butchers, candle-makers, drapers and other merchants lining the broad boulevard. The street itself was even busier with regular traffic thickened by a stream of coaches and carriages and single riders heading for the ball. Directly ahead, Nancy spied a sumptuous coach-and-four with lively horses exhaling clouds of steam as they zigzagged down Blair Street onto Francis Street. The Tuckers' coach trailed it through the gates of Bassett Hall, and Nancy was further enchanted by an allée of oaks illuminated by torchlight. Even leafless silhouettes, they were memorable. Another surprise came with the house itself.

"My goodness! It reminds me of Tuckahoe!"

It was no exaggeration. Both houses were white, two-storied frame structures with chimneys at both ends and a small roofed porch in the center. They even had the same number of windows, four on the first floor and five at the top. In front, liveried servants, cloaks billowing, worked frantically to keep the long line of coaches moving. Nancy was reminded of the throng of carriages when Judith and Richard were married at Tuckahoe. Was that really ten years ago?

"There's Colonel Gibbes," Leila said as a tall, uniformed man alit from the glamorous coach-and-four. "In case you're wondering, the beautiful redhead taking his arm is his sister."

"Where's his wife?" Nancy blurted.

Tucker chuckled at her boldness. "He's a widower, you little minx. I'll arrange an introduction as soon as we get inside."

"For heaven's sakes, husband!" Leila nudged him good-naturedly. "Let the poor girl catch her breath first."

The interior of Bassett Hall was as lavish as the outside was restrained. A spacious entry hall boasted white paneling and wainscoting and an unusually wide staircase.

Candelabra blazed everywhere, showering light on the richly dressed crowd. Nancy was fascinated by two young women in flowing gowns with waists under their half-bared bosoms, but most were dressed like herself. Men sported jackets of superfine woolen broadcloth and high-collared waistcoats or cobalt blue army uniforms with white trousers and well-varnished black boots. Only a handful of older guests wore the hated powdered wigs. Amid exuberant conversations and the comforting rustle of silks and satins, Nancy and the Tuckers fell into a receiving line to meet their host, Philip Johnson, and once formalities were exchanged, she found herself in a spacious parlor with furniture removed to provide dancing space. Tucker brought her a glass of sherry which she barely sipped before uniformed twin brothers approached.

"Professor Tucker," they chimed, executing crisp bows to him and Leila. "And Mrs. Tucker."

"Nancy," Tucker said, "may I present Lieutenants James and Joel Fletcher?"

Nancy dropped a curtsey. "Gentlemen."

Before she could ask who was who, one brother asked her to dance, and suddenly she was on the gleaming floor, caught up in a spirited country dance. She was scarcely escorted back before the other twin swept her away. It continued in this fashion for half an hour until Nancy, exhilarated but short of breath, begged to sit down. The brothers secured an empty divan and, flanking her like guards, regaled her with local gossip which, to her amusement, included finishing each other's sentence. The room, chilly when Nancy first entered, was now hot and humid with the crush of dancers, and she found herself needing fresh air. She was about to excuse herself when Colonel Gibbes emerged from the throng, introduced himself and asked her to dance.

"I confess, sir, that I am momentarily exhausted, but I would be grateful for some fresh air."

"Your servant, madam." Gibbes bowed and offered his arm.

She turned to the Fletcher brothers. "Will you gentlemen excuse me?"

"Certainly," they chorused, disappointment evident at being outranked.

A big man with a soldier's physique, Colonel Gibbes easily blazed a trail through the crowd and found a room with an open window. She joined other overheated guests seeking relief from the cold, crisp air.

"Better, Miss Randolph?"

"Much better." Nancy nodded at the window. "It seems our host has thought of everything,"

"Indeed, he has," Gibbes agreed with a smile. "Including comely guests."

"You're too kind, sir."

"Not at all." He smiled for the first time. "You are, I believe, a guest of Professor Tucker."

"I am."

"I had the privilege of being one of his students some years ago, when I entertained the notion of being an attorney. Destiny intervened when I discovered a love for the military." He flicked a near-invisible piece of lint from his uniform sleeve. "May I ask how you know him?"

"My sister Judith married one of his stepsons. I was engaged to another." When Gibbes' eyebrows rose, she added, "He died before we were wed."

"My sympathies, madam. I know what it's like to lose someone young."

Nancy remembered Tucker saying Gibbes was a widower. "I'm sorry."

"How long you will remain in Williamsburg?"

"The decision rests with my older sister," Nancy replied. "I live with her at Bizarre plantation."

"Did you say Bizarre?"

"Yes, I did." Panic flooded Nancy when Gibbes fell silent, as though weighing her reply. She had come to the ball ebullient and optimistic, but could not stop worrying that the scandal in her past might undo everything. Had this stranger heard the tales and would he recoil in disgust when he guessed her identity? She retrieved a lacy handkerchief when beads of sweat bloomed on her brow. "Is something wrong, colonel?"

Gibbes shook his head. "Not at all. I was just thinking that I've never heard a more peculiar name for a plantation."

The fear in Nancy's heart dissolved. "Nor have I. No one knows who named it or what may have been their inspiration." She decided to test her luck by revealing a bit more about herself. "I grew up on a plantation named Tuckahoe after an Indian creek."

"Tuckahoe is quite famous." Gibbes said, eyes brightening. "Why, you're one of the late Colonel Randolph's daughters. I had the honor of meeting him some years ago in Richmond. He was a member of the House of Burgesses, was he not?"

"And the state legislature." Despite their differences and dreadful final moments, Nancy remained proud of her father's achievements.

Colonel Gibbes looked pleased. "Miss Randolph, may I have the privilege of calling upon you tomorrow afternoon?"

"You may indeed, sir." Nancy glowed, heartily relieved that the gossip dragon had been slain. "I should enjoy that dance now, colonel."

Gibbes beamed. "Splendid."

28

Nancy was still floating on blissful memories when she and the Tuckers returned home. She secured a lit candle and stole upstairs, hoping not to wake Judith who was sharing her bedroom. To her surprise, Judith was sitting up in bed, a sheaf of religious leaflets in her lap.

"Goodness!" Nancy whispered. "I expected you to be asleep."

"You know I have trouble sleeping in strange houses."

"I guess I forgot." As Nancy sat to remove her shoes, she felt Judith's gaze. "Is everything alright?"

"I was about to ask you the same thing."

"If you're wondering if I had a good time, the answer is yes. The ball was lovely. I met some very nice people, and I danced and danced and then danced some more." Judith said nothing as Nancy removed Leila's ballgown and hung it carefully in an armoire. "The house was beautiful. It reminded me of Tuckahoe. There was even a mahogany case clock like Mama's."

Judith was silent until Nancy donned her nightgown and cap and slipped into bed. "You know they were ridiculing you, don't you?"

"Who? What are you talking about?"

"The people at the ball knew about you and were laughing behind your back."

"Stop it, Judith."

"That's why I don't want to go out in public and be humiliated for my sister's sins."

Nancy angrily turned away, facing the wall. "If that's what you believe, then add it to your list of crosses to bear."

"Don't you dare mock me!"

"You're mocking yourself and you don't even know it." Nancy retorted. "You weren't there tonight, so you have no idea what happened."

"Tell me about it then. Spin another of those rosy tales that fill your imaginary world."

"I'll tell you only that a certain Colonel Samuel Gibbes will be calling for me tomorrow afternoon. He's handsome and intelligent and a wonderful dancer. Best of all, he appears to be very fond of me."

"I hope he has a fast horse," Judith said.

"What do you mean?"

"I mean that by tomorrow afternoon we should be near Petersburg."

Nancy sat up and turned toward her sister. "Since when?"

"Since I told Moseley we're leaving tomorrow. I don't like cities, and we've been away from Bizarre long enough."

Nancy held her temper in hopes of changing Judith's mind. "Surely one more day won't matter, Judith. If you're missing the boys, you know what good care Eula takes of them."

"My word is final."

"Then I'll stay on by myself."

"I'd advise against it," Judith muttered. "Unless you want this man to learn the truth."

"What truth?"

"Don't make me say something we agreed to never mention again."

"Then why are you alluding to it?"

"Military men love to talk, and this officer of yours is bound to hear the stories. When he does, you'll face more disgrace, so take my advice and get away while you can."

"No!" Nancy snapped. "I won't surrender the one chance I have to—"

"To what? Abandon your duties at Bizarre? Leave those who took you in when no one else cared?"

180

"Admit it, Judith. You're no happier with the arrangement than I am."

"I admit nothing."

"And therein lies the problem."

Judith ignored the accusation. "We both know you can't afford to pay passage home, Nancy, and I can only pray that you won't humiliate us further by begging Mr. Tucker for money."

"I wouldn't dream of it. I'll just tell Mr. Moseley we're staying another day."

"He won't do it because I won't let him."

"Why should our overseer do your bidding over mine?"

Judith reached for the snuffer and trimmed her candlewick. Her voice, vengeful and hard, burned through the darkness. "Because I pay his salary."

After an exhausting, mostly sleepless night, Nancy could think of nothing but Colonel Gibbes as Moseley's wagon jounced along the road north. Before leaving Williamsburg, she wrote a note for the Tuckers to give to Gibbes when he came calling. She apologized for an abrupt departure not of her doing, and invited Gibbes to visit Bizarre. Despite this effort, she suspected she would never see him again and wondered if she could forgive Judith for crushing this potential courtship. Her sister had done ugly things before, but this was the worst and, sadly, it was only the beginning. Back at Bizarre, Judith's character underwent another, more troublesome transformation. Instead of keeping silent, she maintained a litany of health complaints as wearisome as her religious doggerel. She grew ever more consumed by her faith and, when not praying or reading Bible verses aloud, buried herself in devotional reading. When Nancy, exasperated, asked Judith to stop proselytizing, she was soundly berated.

"You're just like Richard!" Judith snapped. "He never understood that a powerful, abiding faith is our only weapon against the hand of affliction, and look what happened to him. To both of you!"

Nancy's only peace came on Sundays when Judith drove across the river to the Old Briery Church. The Randolphs had been Anglicans for centuries, but, as the Presbyterians were the only nearby congregation, Judith became an ardent member. Having remade herself, Judith decided to alter Bizarre as well. Nancy learned of her sister's misbegotten plans one sunny March afternoon while she was gathering a sheaf of yellow and blue indigo. She was lost in the amusing sights and sounds of a squirrel chasing his mate around and around a pine tree, chittering merrily, when Judith's gruff declaration ruined the moment.

"I'm fed up with people traipsing across our land!"

Hoping to skirt a brewing storm, Nancy continued picking flowers. "What people?"

"Don't tell me you haven't notice the endless stream of beggars asking for food and lodging."

"No more than usual."

"Then you've been off in another of your dreamworlds," Judith scoffed. "Every wagon driving across Sandy Ford or heading to Carter's Sawmill thinks it's their duty to stop here first." She pointed. "No doubt that open gate is the perfect invitation."

"Then close the gate, sister."

"Don't be frivolous. You know that won't solve the problem."

Nancy completed her bouquet and stood. "Isn't this indigo pretty? It should be quite cheerful in the—"

"A waste of time better spent elsewhere!" Judith shot back. "And don't try changing the subject."

"Alright then. It would be inhospitable to turn those people away. Richard once remarked that a traveler could venture from Farmville to Williamsburg without spending a cent on inns, that there were enough farms and plantations along the way to provide free food and a bed."

"Bah! More of Richard's foolishness! If he'd had his way, this house would be filled to the rafters with homeless relatives. First that stupid Mrs. Dudley, and then his cousin Anna Darden and her two brats. They drove me to distraction, always yammering, always underfoot."

The ugly scene, not long after Richard's death, was an unimaginable breach of hospitality. Despite Anna's pleas that she had no funds and nowhere else to go, Judith had ordered the Dardens from the house. Nancy had pressed a few coins in Anna's hands without Judith's knowledge, and it troubled her to this day that the poor woman and her children had not been heard from since.

"Virginia hospitality is famous, not foolish," Nancy countered, tucking the flowers in a basket and walking away with Judith close behind.

"I'm fed up with freeloaders and with visiting neighbors too. I had a talk with Mr. Moseley. Right now, he's on his way to Carter's Sawmill for lumber to fence off the house and dependencies."

"A fence?!"

"Yes, a fence. And a high one too."

"But what will people think?"

"I don't care what they think. It will provide us peace and quiet and cut household expenses. I'm more interested in putting food in my son's bellies than coddling some stranger, and that's final."

Nancy was speechless as Judith stalked away, leaving her with Richard's long-ago plaint that he lived with a stranger. "So do I, my darling," she sighed. She thought of him again a week later when Moseley and his men finished constructing what was more wall than fence. Bizarre now resembled a medieval fortress with a drawbridge permanently raised, Judith's declaration that the world was unwelcome. She knew Richard would've hated it and couldn't imagine what John would say when he returned home.

29

John had been in Cumberland County since early March, commiserating with Senator Creed Taylor. His furtive interest in politics had been whetted the previous summer when Taylor, much to John's surprise, suggested he run for Congress. Believing he was, at twenty-six, too young and inexperienced, John demurred until the senator cited his qualifications.

"Your success in turning Bizarre around has proven you a capable businessman and earned you the respect of our neighbors," Taylor insisted. "Your law studies in Philadelphia taught you policies of concern to our fellow planters, and your debating is as powerful as your oratory." While John weighed the praise, Taylor added, "The Seventh District seat is coming available next year. I believe it's yours for the taking."

Unbeknownst to Taylor, John's interest in politics began in Philadelphia when he accompanied his cousin Edmund to a dinner attended by the finest political minds of the day. John was enthralled by their conversations, and when he dared to engage, shock at his high-pitched voice was erased by his provocative questions and cogent commentary. Invitations to more dinners followed, during which he gained the admiration of many of his superiors.

"People want new blood in congress," Taylor continued. You can deliver that, and plenty more besides."

Vanity stroked, John agreed, but for the time-being told no one at Bizarre of his plans. His first political debate came on Court Day in March. He knew there would be enormous crowds at Charlotte Courthouse because the first speaker was none other than Patrick Henry. Awed by the famed orator, John was grateful that they weren't running for the same office. In Henry's honor, a specially painted red, white and blue platform was erected before the courthouse, but Henry didn't ascend it. Like everyone else, John was shocked when the frail, sixty-one-year-old legend appeared on the porch of the White Horse Tavern and spoke in a quavering voice inaudible to all except those closest. People nudged each other, asking what the great man had said, further distressed when Henry had to be helped inside the tavern. A few lucky souls managed to squeeze inside the White Horse, but most milled about in disappointment until a tall, slender young man ascended the empty platform and challenged Henry's speech. Startled by the strange soprano voice and wondering what presumptuous upstart would dare debate Patrick Henry, the curious crowd surged forward. Few had heard the name John Randolph, but the more people listened, the more captivated they became. When John finished speaking over two hours later, he received a thunderous ovation. He recollected little of what he said and was jolted from his odd oblivion by Taylor's slap on the back.

"Where in God's name did that come from, boy?" Taylor exclaimed.

"I...I don't know." John broke into a wide grin as men lined up to shake his hand and well-wishers promised their votes. "Once I started speaking, everything else faded away."

Taylor was overwhelmed. "I expected good things, lad, but this?! All I can say is congratulations!"

Senator Taylor and those at Charlotte Courthouse were not the only ones awed by John's speech. A week later, the *Virginia Gazette & General Advertiser* chronicled the phenomenon. "At the conclusion of Patrick Henry's speech, John Randolph, a mere stripling and first-time congressional candidate, had the audacity to respond. Those who heard Henry's eloquence were indignant that anyone should attempt to answer him. Yet, they were arrested and enchanted by the music of a strange voice. Oh, that was a glorious scene, and Charlotte Courthouse deserves to be eternally enshrined, for it was there that one sun set in all its glory and another of equal splendor rose on exactly the same spot."

Other newspapers also reported the event, although with less hyperbole, and four weeks later, the Seventh District went to the polls to choose between John Randolph, Powhatan Bolling and Clem Carrington. Carrington quickly fell to the wayside, and for a time it appeared that Bolling was the victor, but when the final votes trickled in from the district's far reaches, John's numbers soared. At the end of the day, he topped Bolling by five votes and, to the surprise of many, including himself, John Randolph secured himself a seat in congress.

John's campaigning had kept him away from Bizarre, but news of his victory preceded his return. He appreciated Nancy's sincere congratulations and compliments on his robust appearance, but was annoyed by Judith's unsightly fence and her demand to know how his new position might benefit the plantation.

"I won't be sworn in until December," he explained. "Besides, Moseley is doing a splendid job. You don't need me here."

Judith frowned. "Does that mean you're off again?"

"Day after tomorrow. I want to travel the Seventh District and meet my constituents. I also need to spend more time with Creed Taylor. There's much he can teach me about the political ropes."

Like a whirlwind, John vanished as fast as he'd appeared and remained away until July. His second homecoming was far less triumphant, beginning with a clumsy dismount Nancy and Judith watched from the porch. His dissolute condition was further apparent when he weaved unsteadily up the steps and presented a red face shiny with sweat.

"Ladies."

"Hello, John," Nancy said.

"You're drunk," Judith snapped.

"Drunk I am, and drunker I shall become," he muttered as he reached the porch. "And not without good reason."

"What might that be?"

"Patrick Henry is dead."

"Is that what brought you home?" Judith asked. "To tell us that old lawyer died?"

John shot her a murderous glance. "An old lawyer who saved this family from doom, woman!"

"What happened?" Nancy asked as he pushed past her and into the house.

"Most folks consider it a terrible tale, but I see it as heroic." John tossed off his stained, dusty jacket and poured a whiskey before folding his lanky body into the closest chair. "Doctors diagnosed acute digestive disorder but they couldn't help and the old firebrand remained in terrible pain. There was but one choice, one to either cure him or kill him."

Judith grimaced. "Mercury."

John took a sip of whiskey and nodded. "Right you are!"

"And he made that choice?"

"Right again. He took a chair, said a prayer and drank the mercury. He then sat staring at his fingernails, waiting to see if they would turn blue. When they did…well, he now belongs to the ages."

"How can you consider such behavior heroic?" Judith asked. "The Bible clearly states that—"

John silenced her with a withering glare. "Woman, deliver me from your pious proselytizing! The great man chose to leave this earth and his personal agony on his own terms. I call that courageous, and I don't give a continental damn what you think."

"There's no need for coarse language," Judith huffed. Her lack of conviction revealed she was in no mood to argue, especially with John in a drunken state. "I'll set the table for dinner."

John ignored her and turned to Nancy. "I noticed that the river was dangerously low when I rode in from town, and the heat is all anyone is talking about. How is the crop?"

"Moseley said that unless the heat breaks and we get rain to quell the drought that production will be small."

"That's what I was afraid of." He drained his glass and held it toward Nancy. "If you please."

Nancy refilled his glass and watched him dribble whiskey on his white waistcoat. He studied her for a long moment, then watched Judith quietly setting the table. For no apparent reason, he cackled loudly, a hideous sound unnerving both women. Then, as it often did, John's mood switched from benign to belligerent.

"Judith!" he boomed, throwing one long leg over the arm of the chair and swinging it back and forth.

"What...what is it, John?"

"How do you know so much about medicine?"

"What do you mean?"

"I mean, dear sister-in-law, that you were very quick to suggest it was mercury that killed Patrick Henry."

"It was speculation, not a suggestion."

"You sounded very sure of yourself. Were you so sure of yourself when you dosed my brother?"

Judith was stung by the implication but remained composed. "We told you how terrible that night was. It was absolute chaos with Richard in agony and us trying to make sense of all those things Dr. Phelps left with us."

"What sort of things?"

"Medicines, John. Tartar emetic, calomel, quinine jalap and, oh, I can't remember what else."

"Laudanum," Nancy added.

"Yes. Laudanum. I mixed them according to Dr. Phelps's instructions, and Nancy administered the dose. We did the best we could but—"

"Clearly your best wasn't good enough."

"John!" Judith gasped.

He ignored her and aimed his scowl at Nancy. "Nor yours, my pretty maid. Everyone knows about your medical skills, especially your vaunted knowledge of gum guaiacum. Did you employ that knowledge when you concocted that fatal dose for my brother?" When Nancy stared in shock, he shouted, "Answer me!"

"Stop it!" Nancy yelled back. "You're drunk and rude and your accusations are ridiculous!"

"You're right that I'm drunk and rude, but the jury is still out on my accusations." He leered at Nancy. "We know all about juries, don't we, cousin dear?"

Nancy refused to endure more insults, veiled or otherwise. She started for the stairs, but, even drunk, John was quick. He leapt to his feet with startling speed and grabbed her wrist.

"Do you think you can walk away from me like you walked away from the courtroom, believing your precious honor intact? Do you think you fooled me like everyone else? Don't you think I know you killed my brother?"

John was too drunk to notice, but Judith watched Nancy's face undergo a disturbing transformation. Hurt was replaced by resentment which, in turn, became rage. She broke free of John and flung her arm wide as she took aim. Her open palm caught him off-guard, striking his cheek with such force that he was hurled to the floor. He lay still, stunned into silence.

"I will hear to more of your drunken raving!" Nancy shouted. "No more!!"

John's raucous laughter followed her up the stairs, where, shaking badly, Nancy grabbed the railing for support. She had never struck anyone in her life, but instead of shame, she felt satisfaction. The sensation deepened when John clambered to his feet and reeled from the house. When hoofbeats faded away, Nancy went back downstairs where Judith waited with rare praise.

"You did the right thing, little sister."

Nancy's knees went weak and she sank onto the bottom step. "You think so?"

"I do indeed. John's insane, you know." Judith pulled a handkerchief from her apron pocket and wiped the back of her neck before joining Nancy. "It wasn't just his body that the scarlet fever left twisted and deformed. It was his mind, too. You know about the pacing and voices in the middle of the night. Those crazy horseback rides to heaven know where and wild accusations that swoop out of nowhere and now this." She shook her head. "Accusing you of murdering Richard."

"I'm not surprised," Nancy said tiredly. "John said years ago that he blamed me for Theo's death, too."

"What?!"

"It was one evening when we went walking together. The conversation took an unpleasant twist and he turned like a viper. You and Ricard were on the front porch and heard the shouting. I knew he was no longer fond of me, but I never imagined he would launch a personal attack." She waved a hand. "Nor do I imagine we've heard the last of it."

"Probably not." Judith stood and smoothed her skirts. "For now, I'm thinking John's new career as a congressman may be more of a blessing than we thought."

"How so?"

"It should keep him away from Bizarre."

30

Despite his drunkenness, John made his way forty miles south to Roanoke Plantation where he found peace and contentment in the old log cabin, with only his books and servants for company. He lingered until early December when he departed for Washington City which he wanted to explore before being sworn into office at year's end. What he saw of the fledgling capital wrenched into keen perspective the task of forging a new nation.

In 1791, Congress passed the Residence Act establishing a capital on the north bank of the Potomac River east of Georgetown, Maryland. The federal district had been dubbed Columbia, and its confines named for America's first President. The city itself, designed by Pierre L'Enfant, a French-American military engineer, was carved from a dense hardwood forest and dominated by the President's House and the Capitol building atop Jenkin's Hill, described by L'Enfant as "a pedestal awaiting a monument." Diagonal avenues radiating from those two buildings created handsome squares and plazas that spun off lesser streets. John admired the ambitious plan, but precious little had materialized. The extraordinarily wide thoroughfare called Pennsylvania Avenue was, depending on the season, a dusty, rutted path or sea of muck, and dotted with unfinished, shoddily built federal buildings. Surrounding the Capitol was a scattering of shops, taverns, stables, and oyster and vegetable markets. A brewery was the town's sole industry, and in a nearby swamp, slaves worked a gravel pit in the ongoing crusade to make muddy streets passable. Hovering over all, along with scavenging seagulls, was the pervasive odor of tar, fish, rot and privies. The few accommodations for legislators were shacks with only the most basic amenities, so limited that senators and congressmen often slept two to a bed.

Taking the crudeness and inconvenience in stride, John drew pride from this raw little settlement with big dreams. He embraced it, identified with it, and was excited to call it home. It inspired him to approach his new position with equal parts enthusiasm and determination, and on December 19, 1799, he climbed the steps to the small, unfinished Capitol building to be sworn in. He was directed to Thomas Sedgwick, Speaker of the House of Representatives, whom he found in the North Wing. John introduced himself and waited politely for acknowledgment. Sedgwick, a Massachusetts Federalist in fierce opposition to John's Democratic-Republican views, feigned ignorance of the tall, gawky Virginian, and gave him a long stare over the rim of his bifocals.

"How might I be of service, young man?"

"I'm here to be sworn into office, sir," John politely replied.

Knowing he had an audience of like-minded colleagues and eager to play the situation for humor, Sedgwick lobbed an unwise volley. "Are you quite certain you're old enough?"

John's retort was quick and loud. "Ask my constituents!"

Thus, the stage was set for a career destined to keep the nation's capital entertained for years. Like him or loathe him, John Randolph of Roanoke Plantation was a man whose rapier-sharp wit, strong opinions and lack of inhibition would make him one of the most memorable and controversial politicians of the new century.

Aside from sporadic correspondence with Daniel Moseley, John had no contact with Bizarre. He stayed away at Christmas, and by the time spring arrived, Nancy and Judith wondered if they would ever see him again. With a failed crop, creditors pressing for payment, the demands of two young sons, and no husband, Judith's mood grew ever gloomier, and the atmosphere at Bizarre was charged with bitterness. She visited her frustrations on Nancy with treatment more stringent than before. Judith assigned her sister a back-breaking load of chores and forbade her from visiting the neighbors or entertaining guests who might consume costly food and drink. Despite endless claims of poverty, Judith insisted that her poor health required repeated visits to Sweet Springs in western Virginia and left Nancy to care for Saint and Tudor. Nancy adored her nephews and dutifully nursed Tudor, who seemed to have inherited his Uncle Theo's poor health, through a string of illnesses, and exhibited great patience with Saint's deafness. She knew airing her grievances would only earn Judith's wrath and more rejoinders of crosses to bear, so she wrote her siblings, begging for help. Learning that they too faced financial disaster awoke her to the unfathomable reality that the Randolphs, once the most influential family in Virginia, were toppling like dominoes. Nancy's younger sister Jane and her husband Thomas Eston Randolph were fighting to hold on to his ancestral home, Dungeness, while sister Molly and husband David Meade Randolph had lost Presqu'ile plantation with its grand house staffed by forty servants, and, more recently, their fine Richmond home, Moldavia. They now occupied a tenement which Molly, once one of Virginia's most celebrated hostesses, operated as a boarding house. Tom Junior was struggling too, and once again refused her request for sanctuary with the reminder that his father-in-law was now President of the United States and that Monticello was required for higher purposes. With all options extinguished, Nancy faced a life of unending drudgery.

The first years of the new century dragged on in endless repetition, each day as empty as the last. One bleak December dawn, 1806, Nancy awoke to find herself more exhausted than when she went to bed. She looked through her lone window at a pallid sky as grave as her mood and began trembling with the bleakness of her life. Soft whimpering became painful sobs, and she lay paralyzed by wave after wave of despair until Judith called up, ordering her to be about her chores.

"I...I can't do this," Nancy said to herself. "I don't know what I'm going to do, but it's not this. Not anymore."

She forced herself from bed and drew on her wrapper, waiting for the trembling to stop before going downstairs. She found Judith stringing dried apples and cranberries, while Saint, now twelve, and eight-year-old Tudor sat by the fire, engaged in garbled talk only they understood.

"What do you mean, sleeping so late?" Judith demanded. "And why aren't you dressed?"

Nancy sank into a chair and pointed her feet toward the crackling flames. "We have to talk, sister."

"Talk is a waste of time when there's work to be done." When Nancy continued staring at the fireplace, Judith said, "Well? I'm waiting."

"I feel trapped, Judith. I'm like a mule tethered to a millstone, walking in endless circles and going nowhere."

"Bah. You're no more trapped than I."

"But you have a plantation and two sons. I have nothing."

"A lot of good Bizarre's doing me with more failed crops and debts piled to the ceiling." Judith jabbed a needle through an apple and reached for another. "As I've said before, my faith gets me through difficult times. If you came to church with me or read my periodicals, you'd find help too."

"It's not that easy."

"It's as easy as opening your heart to our Lord and Savior Jesus Christ. Have you forgotten our Christian teachings?"

"Of course not, but they're not what I need right now."

"Which is what?"

"Hope. A kind word. Change. Anything to keep me from feeling like I'm buried alive."

"What are you giving the children for Christmas?"

The brusque change of subject was Judith's way of announcing the subject was closed. Nancy sighed and tugged her wrapper more tightly around her. The house felt unusually cold.

"How do you suppose I could pay for a present?"

"It doesn't have to be store-bought, Missy. You've got two good hands."

"With fingers worked to the bone."

Judith ignored the remark. "Why not pass on one of those little things my husband gave you."

"What are you talking about?"

"Those fripperies and gewgaws stashed in your room."

"Richard delighted in surprising us both with little things, Judith. You make it sound like a naughty secret." She paused before asking, "What were you doing in my room?"

"I'm mistress of the house. That entitles me to go anywhere I wish."

"Including my room?" Judith silently kept threading, but Nancy would not be ignored. "Answer me!"

"This conversation is tiresome." Judith glanced out the window and noted the growing sunlight. "Get dressed, Nancy. It's way past time for you to gather the eggs."

"Gather them yourself."

"What?!"

"You heard me."

Judith appeared calm but Nancy noticed her fingers trembled as she continued her work. "What I hear," Judith said bitterly, "are the words of an ungrateful wretch who has no consideration for the one person on God's earth who has taken care of her."

"If that were true, you wouldn't work me like a slave from sunup to sundown. For heaven's sake, why did you assign me so many chores?"

Judith shrugged. "Because my girls have better things to do."

"That's not true. I'm in the slave quarters every day and see your girls idling about."

"I'm aware of how much time you spend in the quarters, especially with Billy Ellis. You've become far too approachable for him, Nancy. You know how wrong that is, and I want it stopped immediately!"

Nancy was stunned by the accusations of impropriety between herself and the Negro carpenter. Billy was a gentle soul who balanced his ugly fate with admirable dignity and always had a sympathetic ear. The two shared what confidences they could under Virginia's strict racial code, and as their friendship deepened, Nancy dared violate one of the most ironclad taboos by teaching him how to read. Billy answered her kindness with his craftsmanship. One of her most cherished possessions was a wooden bird carved especially for her after she admired the clever toy wagons he made, unasked, for Saint and Tudor.

"What on earth is inappropriate about sharing a few kindly words with someone even more trapped than myself? Heaven knows he's been a better friend than you."

"How dare you make such an odious comparison!" Judith ordered Tudor to take his brother upstairs, and when the boys were gone, she glared at Nancy. "Have you forgotten that slaves are the cause of all our troubles? That malicious Negro grapevine is precisely what destroyed Richard's reputation and—"

"Stop it, Judith! You know that subject is not to be mentioned!"

"How can I remain silent when your presence is a constant reminder of the unthinkable, unforgivable sin of my husband and my own sister—"

"The baby was Theo's, and you know it!"

"I know nothing of the sort. You both lied about it."

"You insufferable hypocrite!" Nancy drew herself up and delivered the coup de grace. "I'm not the only one who lied about a dead baby!"

Color drained from Judith's face as she struggled to speak. Only a hoarse croak emerged and she watched in silence as Nancy began to pace.

"Perhaps you're right." Nancy said slowly. "Perhaps it's time we ended our dance around the truth." She moved to the fireplace and caressed the spill vase atop the mantle. She toyed with the tapers for transferring fire, arranging and rearranging them with peculiar calm while weighing her next words. "For years I've listened to you harp on my sins and assign blame for a single act of love which would've gone unpunished if my poor Theo hadn't died. What's never been mentioned is that your part in committing the very same sin." Judith remained mute as Nancy unleashed more truths. "Not long before he died, Richard told me that you were intimate well before you wed, and that pregnancy was why you chose an earlier wedding date."

"That's a lie!" Judith gasped, finally finding her voice.

"He said what you claimed was la grippe three months after your marriage was the miscarriage of a fetus five months old."

Judith shook terribly, voice an octave higher than usual. "Stop it!"

"Richard also told me how you locked him out on your wedding night, and at other times for no reason. Forever afterwards, he believed he had married a stranger. A selfish, unemotional stranger. He didn't seek satisfaction elsewhere, but by all that's holy he would've been justified in doing so."

"Lies!" Judith screamed again. "All lies."

Nancy approached her sister slowly, voice steady as she leaned close. "No, Judith. It's not lies. For years you've accused me of living in a dream world and losing myself in sentimental novels, but in truth you're the one shunning reality. Everything I've said now is God's truth, and I hope you won't destroy what little love and respect I have for you by denying it."

Judith tried to rise but lost her balance and fell back into the chair. With some effort she managed to stand and deliver her ugly ultimatum.

"I'm done with sheltering liars and adulterers and fornicators and ungrateful wretches under my roof. You're to leave here tomorrow morning, sister, and that's absolutely final!"

Part 6

Nil admirari

("Be overwhelmed by nothing")

- Randolph family motto

31

Daniel Moseley's wagon edged slowly along the approach road to Tuckahoe. The drive was rutted and littered with tree limbs felled by autumn winds and winter snows. Because the plantation had always been well-maintained, such neglect deepened Nancy's dread of what lay ahead. Empty houses age much faster than those occupied, and Tuckahoe was proof positive. Four years after Thomas Randolph's death, Gabriella married a banker and moved to Richmond after selling Tuckahoe's slaves and hiring a caretaker to protect her son's ill-gotten legacy. As the wagon drew closer, Nancy saw peeling paint, broken shutters, weeds sprouting on the roof and an overall feeling of gloom.

"Place looks like a ghost town," Moseley muttered.

"Sounds like one too." Nancy sighed when Moseley reined the horse and an eerie hush enveloped them. The din of a working plantation was absent, and Nancy missed the familiar clang of the blacksmith's hammer, animal noises, people shouting, wheels creaking, and the squeals of children playing by the slave quarters. "This is the sort of quiet one can hear."

Moseley was appalled. "You can't stay here, Miss Nancy."

"It's only until I determine what to do next." When she saw the worry on his face, she said, "I appreciate your concern, but you know I have nowhere else to go."

"How will you get in?"

"There should be a caretaker in the overseer's house."

Moseley leapt down and assisted Nancy from the wagon. As she squared her thin shoulders and marched alone across the cold, cracked earth, he thought it the most courageous sight he'd ever seen. She returned with a middle-aged black man named Jack Lassiter who nodded politely to Moseley before unlocking the front door. He gave it a push and stepped aside as it swung back with a painful creak. Nancy's heart thumped when she entered a monument to desuetude. Cobwebs shrouded the chandeliers, and everything was cloaked in dust. The air was thick and dead, and the floor was dotted with animal droppings. There was no furniture. Moseley came through the door with her few belongings, and stopped short.

"I meant what I said, Miss Nancy. You'll freeze to death if you stay here."

Undaunted, she said, "I was hoping Jack might build a fire in my old bedroom."

"Right away." The caretaker headed for the woodpile but not before giving this strange white woman a look that questioned her sanity.

Realizing she would not be dissuaded, Mosely said, "Shall I carry your things upstairs?"

"I'll manage. It's a long drive back to Bizarre. You should be on your way."

Mosely started to go, paused and spoke what had nettled him all day. "It ain't right, Miss Judith throwing you out like this. Your own sister. It just ain't right, and I know Mr. Richard...well, he would hate knowing that—"

Nancy touched his shoulder. "Right or wrong, it was inevitable."

The overseer made one last attempt at reasoning. "What are you going to eat, Miss Nancy?"

"Don't tell anyone, but I made an early morning raid on the larder." She gave him a sly smile. "Judith will be most upset when she discovers a shortage of ham, biscuits and a few other things."

"And after that's gone?"

"My other sisters send a little money now and then, and I'm sure Jack Lassiter will share his source for provender." When Moseley didn't move, Nancy said, "Please run along now. The longer you stand there, the harder it is for me to…to do what must be done."

"As you say, Miss Nancy. Good luck to you."

"One more thing, Daniel."

"Ma'am?"

"From the bottom of my heart, I thank you and Eula for your years of hard work and devotion. I will miss you both dearly."

Moseley touched the brim of his hat and walked away, but not before Nancy glimpsed his tears. She retrieved her carpetbag and portmanteau and climbed the stairs to find more desolation on the second floor. Her old room was barren except for her grandfather's trunk containing a few old books and some half-burned candles. Considering what she had seen so far, Nancy deemed it a treasure trove. She set down her belongings and felt a heart flutter when she was drawn to the hall window where she had etched her mother's death date. She resisted the urge to touch the glass, instead stepped away and whispered to herself.

"I'm glad you're not here to see this, Mama." She jumped when her name was shouted from downstairs. "I'm up here!"

Jack Lassiter turned out to be a godsend. He not only built a roaring fire and stacked surplus logs, but brought a pitcher of water, a washbowl and an argand lamp so Nancy didn't have to rely on the small candles. He even dragged in a pallet from his cottage along with extra blankets to provide a makeshift bed. That done, he told Nancy to find him if she had other needs and left her alone. At the sound of tiny scurrying feet, Nancy stashed her food inside the trunk, dragged it closer to the fireplace and wrapped herself in a blanket. She sat on the floor and rested her back against the trunk, for a while losing herself in the dancing, crackling flames. She was unaware that the room was darkening until flash of fire in the window pane revealed the sun sinking across the James River. It was one of the most beautiful sunsets Nancy had ever seen, but it melted into a blur of reds and oranges when she wept the bitterest tears of her life. Her family was ruined, her dreams erased. She was alone, destitute and with a future as empty as the old house she once called home.

She was thirty-one years old.

Nancy fought gamely, but after two days, even with Lassiter's help, it was obvious that Tuckahoe was too primitive for her to remain longer. Grim inventory reminded her of her one remaining option. The last letter from her sister Molly stated that, while their Richmond home was packed with boarders, she and her husband David would help her find lodgings elsewhere. Resigned, Nancy sought out Lassiter who explained that the easiest and cheapest way to get to Richmond was the river.

"Just stand on the river bank down there and wave," he said. "One of those bateaux will stop for you."

Nancy was dubious. "But what if they don't?"

"They will. It may take a while, but they will."

Flat-bottomed boats called bateaux were the workhorses of Virginia's waterways. They plied the James with regularity and were accustomed to travelers seeking passage. Lassiter helped carry Nancy's belongings down the hill to Tuckahoe's forlorn docks, and helpful as always, offered to flag a boat. Nancy didn't relish being left alone, but, when she saw that the man was shivering, she thanked him and sent him on his way. She rewrapped her woolen neck scarf against the wet chill fixed her gaze up the ice-riddled James and thought about Richmond. Nancy was, at heart, a country girl and viewed city life with trepidation. She would have been even more concerned had she known the town's past was as turbulent as her own. After being named the state capital, the nondescript hamlet had barely realized its lofty designation when turncoat general Benedict Arnold burned it to the ground in 1786. Within months, another conflagration consumed more than fifty houses, but the scrappy little town determinedly rebuilt. To cement its status,

Thomas Jefferson designed a capitol building modeled on an ancient Roman temple. The imposing, pillared structure, completed in 1788, dominated the city from atop Shockoe Hill. The four-tiered steeple of St. John's Episcopal Church was another landmark for those who got lost in a townscape riddled with hills, gulches, boot-gulping swamps and dirt roads to nowhere. While it primarily remained a rough-and-tumble riverport of brawling taverns and busy bordellos, prominent residents pointed with pride to the enormous Gallego Flour Mill and the docks along the James River which, come summer, would be jammed with square-riggers, coastwise schooners and bateaux. The wharves would thunder with the din of Negro stevedores loading flour barrels and hogsheads of tobacco and roustabouts unloading French wines, English woolens, Caribbean spices and coffee from Jamaica. This muscular hurly-burly was visible proof of Richmond's determination to become Virginia's foremost entrepôt, and, to even the most skeptical observer, it seemed well on its way.

After an hour's wait, a heavily laden bateau rounded an upriver bend and veered to port when its navigator spotted the woman waving from the bank. As the boat drew to shore, Nancy shrank from the fierce-looking, black-bearded frontiersman, but a wrinkled old woman in a poke bonnet smiled warmly and beckoned her aboard. That smile eased Nancy's fears, and she took the boatman's outstretched hand and climbed aboard.

"I reckon them pelts oughta be comfortable enough," he said once Nancy told him her destination. "Richmond ain't much farther."

Nancy found warmth between tall stacks of deer and bear pelts, grateful that they blocked the gusty wind. She was no longer fearful, but watched warily while the trapper navigated a jam of ice chunks, some as large as the boat, before entering the Kanawha Canal. Considered an engineering wonder when it opened in 1790, the two-hundred-foot-long canal bypassed the Great Falls of the

James with three locks lowering boats over thirty feet. Another mile and a half of river linked to a second canal ending at Shockoe Bottom.

"This is Richmond, ma'am!" the man shouted, negotiating a berth between two identical bateaux. "Tie us up, Maw!" While the old woman secured the lines with impressive nimbleness, her son helped Nancy ashore where he waved away her offer of money. "Weren't no trouble, ma'am. Me and my maw know a lady in distress when we see one. You'd best take care. Town can be dangerous if you don't keep your eyes and ears open." He absently rubbed a nasty scar running the length of one cheek. "Where you bound?"

"My sister's house." Nancy withdrew a letter from her coat pocket and checked the return address. "Thirteen Hundred East Cary Street."

"You're in luck." The trapper pointed to an uphill dirt road. "That there's Fifteenth Street. Follow it a block and turn left on Cary Street. Place is so close you could almost spit on it!"

"You're very kind, sir. I thank you."

The boatman touched the brim of his battered hat before tending to his furry cargo. Nancy followed his directions, pausing along the way to catch her breath and parse the surrounding chaos. Despite the cold, the waterfront hummed with wagons, carts and drays pulled by horses with blankets and bearskins over their withers. They were wrangled by bearded, rough-looking frontiersmen like the one on her boat. Beneath the constant shouts, creaking wheels and jangle of harness bells lurked a mysterious dull roar.

"One thing I'll say for Richmond," Nancy muttered to herself. "It's loud!"

She followed the trapper's directions and found Molly's home without difficulty. The plain, two-story wooden building, one of several in a block-long row, was neat and tidily kept, but when Nancy recalled tales of

Moldavia's grandeur, she realized Molly's fall from grace was as cataclysmic as her own. At least, she thought, she's not relying on anyone's charity.

"Darling girl!" Molly cried when she answered Nancy's knock. "What a wonderful surprise!"

Molly was the oldest of the sisters, and the twelve years between them dictated that they had never been playmates or confidantes. Nancy had always admired Molly's natural grace and elegance, still present even in her simple morning dress, but she hadn't expected the streaks of gray at her sister's temples.

"I'm happy to see you too." As she stepped inside and melted into her sister's warm embrace, Nancy realized how lonely she had been and how long since she had felt the touch of another human being. "Your last letter said you and David will help me find accommodations."

"Indeed, we will. You'll stay here for now. Luckily, one of our boarders moved out yesterday, and we haven't rented his room yet. I'd offer it to you permanently, but I know you have few funds, and we simply can't afford to give up a paying room."

"I understand. Just sleeping in a real bed will make me happy."

"A real bed?" Molly frowned as she took Nancy's hat and coat and ushered her into a small parlor all but swallowed by grand furniture. "What do you mean?"

Nancy started to respond but found her throat dry and raspy. "Might I have a drink of water?"

"It's bitter outside. Wouldn't you prefer coffee?"

"If it's not too much trouble."

"Not at all. Sit down and warm yourself by the fire. I'll be right back."

For the next hour, Molly listened in horror as her younger sister explained her shattered relationship with Judith, John's bewildering behavior and accusations, and the lamentable state of Tuckahoe.

Molly grimaced. "Judith was intolerable even when we were little. When she and Richard honeymooned with us at Presqu'ile, she was ugly to everyone, including me. I don't truly know how you endured her for so long. I once joked with David that the real reason I married him was to get away from my mean little sister."

"You didn't!"

"Oh, but I did. I even said a prayer for Richard when he proposed marriage. Poor man had no idea what he was getting himself into!"

"No, he most certainly did not."

"How did you get here from Tuckahoe?"

"The caretaker showed me how to flag down a bateau. A trapper and his mother were kind enough to give me passage and directions here. They wouldn't even accept payment."

"Thank heavens you're alright. Terrible things happen on that river and down by Shockoe Creek. We'll have to tell you what parts of town to avoid. Richmond might be the state capital but it's a still rough town." When she saw Nancy's despair, Molly hastily reassured her. "You'll be fine, my dear. City life is different, that's all. You'll learn how to comport yourself in no time."

"I hope so."

"I know so." Molly smiled. "Now come along and I'll show you your room. Are you hungry?"

"Starving." Nancy hadn't eaten since devouring the remainder of the purloined ham for last night's supper. "Do you mind if I lie down for a little while?"

"Not at all. I know how tiring travel can be."

Nancy removed her shoes and collapsed onto the bed, so exhausted that she fell asleep before noticing a single detail of the room.

32

There was a gentle knock at the door. Nancy awoke as her brother-in-law David poked his head into the room and whistled merrily. "Hello there, sleepyhead. Molly told me to ask if you're still hungry or want to sleep until tomorrow morning?"

"I'm so sorry." Nancy said groggily. "I guess I was more tired than I realized."

"No matter. Join us in the dining room whenever you like. Our boarders have already been fed, so we'll have the table to ourselves."

"Thank you, David."

"If you fall back asleep, I'm eating your Fayette pudding!"

"I promise I'll be right down."

Left alone to freshen up, Nancy was grateful that David had kept his sense of humor despite a string of financial setbacks. He had enjoyed great success as master of Presqu'ile plantation and served as U. S. Marshall of Virginia under Presidents President Washington and Adams. When Jefferson became President in 1801, however, David was ousted for his opposing Federalist views. Drowning in debt amid the tobacco-fueled recession, he was forced to sell his properties and pursue a drastically reduced existence. When Nancy entered the dining room and saw more furniture crowded into a small space, she knew what had happened. David noted her reaction

"Welcome to Little Moldavia," he said, pulling out her chair. "Molly couldn't bear to part with our furniture when we sold the house, so here it is. Some of it anyway."

"I know the scale is all wrong," Molly allowed, "but our boarders seem to appreciate the fine furnishings and it enables us to charge a bit more than the competition."

"As does your famous cooking," David added.

"I'm sorry I never visited Moldavia," Nancy said. "Tom Junior said it was one of the most beautiful homes he'd ever seen."

"The mahogany stairway is the finest in Richmond," Molly said, voice tinged with nostalgia. "And you would've adored the mirrored ballroom and octagonal dining room."

"No doubt."

"I'll walk you up there sometime. We can't go in, but I can show you the outside."

Not wanting to dwell on personal loss, Nancy changed the subject. She eyed a platter of pork chops with stewed winter squash, scalloped oysters, potatoes mashed with onions, sea kale resting atop buttered toast, and Johnny cakes. "What a lovely table. Everything looks and smells wonderful."

"Cooking and entertaining are my passions."

"That's no exaggeration," David said. "Her nickname at Moldavia was Queen Molly, and I've told her a hundred times she should put her recipes in a book for sale to the public."

"That's a wonderful idea!"

"But who has time to do it?" Molly asked. "We only have one servant girl, and I work harder than she does. People don't think running a boarding house is that difficult, but let me tell you—"

"Please, my dear. Pass the pork chops before they get cold." David regarded his famously garrulous wife with affection as he added, "Molly's motto is 'Why use one word when a dozen will do?'"

Dinner was lively with conversation and brought the first wine Nancy had enjoyed in years, courtesy of Judith's strict ban. Between Molly's opinions on everything imaginable and David's amusing anecdotes, Nancy was thoroughly entertained. She was not called upon to say much, but when a rare quiet moment settled over the table, she remarked on the food.

"One of the most delicious dinners I've ever had, Molly. Your boarders are very lucky."

Molly chuckled. "Surely you don't think this is their usual fare. If I fed them such bounty, we'd be bankrupt inside of a month. This was a special dinner in your honor."

"Then I'm honored indeed." Nancy smiled. "And very grateful for your offer to help me find a place to stay."

"Which means tomorrow will be a busy day," David said. "Richmond is bursting at the seams, but an old acquaintance of mine, Major John Pryor, may be able to help. He manages Haymarket Gardens, and his wife Anne runs a boarding house on Eighth Street. I mentioned you to her when Molly received your last letter. We'll call on them first thing in the morning."

"You're very kind."

"Not at all." He turned to Molly. "Now where is that Fayette pudding you promised?"

Despite her long nap, Nancy fell asleep easily. She awoke to a sky threatening snow, but it did not taint her good spirits. Further rejuvenated by Molly's hearty breakfast, she lingered over coffee until David finished his morning chores and announced that he was ready to call on the Pryors.

"Bundle up!" he said. "It's always colder down by the river."

The city was still waking up as they walked down Cary Street, and Nancy was again intrigued by a dull roar. "What's that strange noise?"

"You must mean The Falls." David offered his arm as they negotiated an uneven patch of frozen mud. "I'm so used to the sound I don't hear them anymore. They'll get much louder with the spring melt."

"Whatever I heard was muffled by other noises. Cities are certainly louder than plantations."

"True enough. Far more so in summer, I might add. In addition to more activity, especially on the docks, the heat means we can't close the windows to shut out the racket." When Nancy looked apprehensive, he said, "You'll get used to it. Everyone does. Ah! Here we are!"

David paused before a two-story frame house with a brick façade and small porch. Three chimneys poked through a flat roof, adding whorls of smoke to the gray skies. Enclosed by a white picket fence, it appeared homey enough, but Nancy's attention was caught by an enormous sign across the street, the garish entrance to Haymarket Gardens.

"You mentioned that place last night. What exactly is it?"

"Richmond's biggest pleasure park. All sorts of public attractions and amusements. Bowling, shuffleboard, quoits. Cockfights. Masquerade balls."

"Aren't those places a bit unseemly?"

"Not altogether, although the crowds can become rowdy late at night and it sometimes attracts—" He fumbled for a genteel explanation. "Shall we say, not the most highborn of ladies. Molly and I like the ice cream and coffee cakes on the lower part of the Dancing House and the terraces leading down to the James. The river views are wonderful." He smiled at the memory. "In any case, I don't believe you'll be corrupted by living across the street."

Nancy gave him a droll smile. "The maxim that comes to mind is, 'Beggars can't be choosers.'"

David squeezed her hand where it clung inside his elbow. "We've both learned a great deal about survival these past few years, haven't we? Our fine world is changing, Nancy. Disappearing in front of our very eyes, and we either adapt or wither away. I face forward as much as possible because I believe it's dangerous to look back. Molly doesn't agree. She's forever offering to show people Moldavia, but the idea is painful to me. Chatting about the past is tolerable, but looking at it is something I cannot do."

"I assure you I understand."

211

"No doubt you do, especially after what you said about the sad state of Tuckahoe." David gripped her arm as they climbed three icy steps to the porch. He lifted an iron doorknocker in the shape of a shell and dropped it with a loud thud. The door swung open after a moment, revealing a petite woman about Nancy's age with a feather duster in hand. A heart-shaped face was dotted with freckles and red curls peeked from beneath a mobcap.

"David Randolph, as I live and breathe!"

"Hello, Anne."

"Come in! Come in!" She chirped. "And who might this be?"

"This is Nancy Randolph, Molly's sister. I told you about her some weeks ago. She's in need of a room."

"I remember." She smiled at Nancy. "As luck would have it, you have two to choose from."

"I'm surprised." David turned to Nancy. "Anne's house is very popular with dockers and millworkers."

"They're a rough and tumble lot, but they're good men. I'm sorry to say two of them were attacked and robbed yesterday after coming out of Galt's Tavern on Nineteenth Street. One took a knife in the side, and the other nearly got an eye gouged out. I'm told those hooligans harden their fingernails with candle fire and use them as weapons! I tell you this town is getting worse by the day!" Anne changed the subject when she saw Nancy's horrified expression. "The rooms are upstairs, Miss Randolph. Come along."

The rooms were identical except for the views. The one overlooking Haymarket Gardens, Anne said, was noisier but welcomed a nice river breeze in the summer months. The other faced west and, she admitted, could be a furnace by July.

"I appreciate your honesty," Nancy said. "I was about to choose the other precisely because it didn't face the park, but this one's fine."

"Good. To tell you the truth, I've been longing for female companionship. Keeping company with workingmen isn't the easiest things in the world, but, mind you, I'm not complaining. I'm grateful to have a husband and a roof over my head and…oh, listen to me! Blathering like a fool when I should be behaving like a landlady." She spotted a patch of dust on a table top and dispatched it with her feather duster. "The room is two dollars a week including three meals a day, linens and towels."

Nancy weighed her limited resources and was pleased to learn that the rent fit her purse. "That's fine."

"Then it's all settled. I'll tidy the place and change the bed linens, and you can move in this afternoon." She gave Nancy a warm smile. "You're most welcome here, Miss Randolph. I hope we'll become friends."

"I hope so too, Mrs. Pryor."

"Then you can start by calling me Anne."

Nancy's spirits remained high and rose even higher after the evening meal. Because she was the only female guest, Anne invited her to dine with her and her husband, sparing her the coarse company of the male boarders. Major Pryor, who had served heroically in the Continental Army, was genial enough but left most conversation to his gregarious wife. When he excused himself after dinner, Anne invited Nancy to the parlor to enjoy a blazing hearth and glasses of madeira. She noticed Nancy staring at a wall lined with bookshelves.

"The major's library. Please feel free to read anything you like."

"That's most generous." Nancy tasted the madeira. "This is the second night in a row I've had wine. I pray it promises more good things to come."

"Yes, indeed." Anne clinked Nancy's glass and sipped. "I'm enjoying getting to know you and hope you'll be with us awhile."

"Thank you. I hope so too."

"I don't want to sound like a nosy landlady, but will you tell me a bit about yourself?" A frisson shot down Nancy's back when she thought of Glyntyvar. "I assure you

I'm not a gossip, and, believe me, Richmond is one gossipy little town."

Nancy studied the wine glass. "What did David tell you about me?"

"Only that you're his sister-in-law and that you needed a room."

Encouraged by the wine and a belief that Anne could be trusted, Nancy felt a sudden need to unburden herself. "In that case, there's something you should know, and it's best that you hear it from me." Anne was enrapt as Nancy revealed her troubled past, even daring to include the core of her woes. "My fiancé died along with our stillborn child. The scandal has dogged me ever since, and if you don't want a fallen woman living here—"

Anne's interruption stilled Nancy's fears. "Nonsense. It's an honor to have a Randolph under my roof. As for any scandal, I say it's much ado about nothing, if I may quote the Bard. A Negro midwife once told me half the brides in Virginia are pregnant on their wedding day. You're just one of the unlucky ones who got caught."

"A price I'm still paying."

Anne smiled warmly. "Not as far as I'm concerned."

"Thank you for that."

Over another glass of wine and more logs on the fire, Nancy was astonished to learn how much she and Anne had in common. Anne's father was also a planter, albeit not on the grand Randolph scale, who remarried after her mother's death, leaving her in the care of a spinster aunt who hated children. Anne didn't put it in words, but Nancy intuited that she married Major Pryor to escape her misery.

"So here we are then," Anne concluded with a laugh. "Two ladies who shed their gloves and fancy gowns and learned how to fend for themselves." She flinched when the front door banged open and shut. "Sounds like one of my wayward boarders is home."

A short, bandy-legged man, cheeks crimson with whiskey and cold, reeled into the entrance hall. "Evening, Miss Anne!"

"Good evening, Lucas. Did you have yourself a time?"

"I did, thank you." He doffed his cap. "Have you a visitor?"

"This is Miss Nancy Randolph. She has taken a front room."

"Lucas Stark, ma'am." An ill-chosen bow caused him to lose his balance and careen into the banister. He hastily excused himself and disappeared upstairs, leaving Anne bemused.

"He's such a shy soul I'm surprised to see him like that. Our boarders work so hard in the flour mill they usually retire right after dinner, but they occasionally get a bit rambunctious."

Nancy thought of John's drunken rants. "It won't bother me."

"Good." Anne drained her wine glass and adjusted the fire screen to prevent wayward embers from sparking onto the carpet. "I'd best say good-night. The major will be wondering why I'm up so late."

"I should retire too." Nancy paused in the doorway. "Thank you for sharing confidences and making me feel at home."

"I'm glad. And now good-night."

"Good night."

A bit tipsy from the wine, Nancy held her candlestick tight and gripped the banister as she climbed the stairs. Alone in her room, she giggled at her clumsiness in undressing. Giddiness was a new sensation, and she embraced it as she went to the window and peered into the night. The snow that hung over the city all day had materialized at last, undulating in white sheets driven by gusts from the James River. Nancy enjoyed the dizzying spectacle a few moments before fatigue drove her to bed. It was a good day, she thought, snuggling under Anne's generous supply of blankets. As she drifted toward sleep, she allowed herself a rare moment of optimism before asking herself the age-old question.

Could such contentment last?

33

Cities offer employment opportunities nonexistent on plantations, but despite her eagerness to work, Nancy was crippled by social dictates. Her prestigious surname, which she could not hide, barred her from employment in shops, stores and factories, and especially taverns and inns. She could retain respectability as a modiste or milliner but had no funds to finance such a venture. Her education qualified her for a position as governess or genteel companion, or a teaching position at a girl's school, but a request for references would expose her past and prove her undoing. Anne came to her rescue.

"If you help me around the house, I can lower your rent a bit."

Nancy was elated. "Oh, Anne! You're a Godsend!"

"Actually, I'm only thinking of myself." Anne winked. "You're my excuse to get rid of that worthless girl working for me now."

The arrangement was so successful that Nancy stopped fretting about her future. She never minded her routine duties because, unlike Judith, Anne was neither critical nor watched her like a hawk. One spring afternoon, Nancy was removing splattered candlewax on a parlor table when she spotted a copy of the *Virginia Gazette*. She was struck by the large front-page headline announcing that Aaron Burr, former United States Vice-President under Thomas Jefferson, was to be tried for conspiracy there in Richmond. Burr had attempted to carve an empire from America's recently acquired Louisiana Territory, and his trial was set for May 22, 1806. Presiding would be Chief Justice John Marshall, who, Nancy well remembered, had helped to acquit Richard thirteen years ago. Her cousin Edmund Randolph would appear on Burr's behalf, imparting a twinge of familial pride until she read further and learned that the jury foreman would be Congressman John Randolph of Roanoke.

"No!"

Nancy hadn't seen John in eight years, not since that horrible day when he accused her of murdering Richard and earned a slap knocking him to the ground. Even now, the idea of him being in the same city made her queasy. Nancy wanted to believe that he had forgotten about her and was now immersed in the politics of Washington City, but John Randolph was nothing if not unpredictable.

She looked up when the smell of tobacco preceded the major into the parlor. "Ah! I thought I left that paper in here. Reading about the trial, are you? It's the biggest thing to hit Richmond since that traitor Arnold set fire to the place. I noticed a couple of Randolph names in that article. Relatives of yours?"

"Cousins," Nancy replied.

"I don't know much about Edmund, but that John Randolph of Roanoke is always getting himself in trouble. I recollect when that young fellow was elected to Congress and took Washington City by storm, but when you start that high, the only way to go is down."

Nancy passed him the paper. "I haven't followed his career."

"Randolph's made a passel of enemies with his belligerent speeches, including President Jefferson. He so alienated the Democratic-Republicans that he formed a party of his own, some crazy thing called the Tertium Quid. Not long after it failed, he showed his displeasure by bringing his hunting dogs onto the senate floor." Pryor clucked. "I consider that downright disrespectful."

"Nothing he does surprises me."

"You know him then?"

"His late brother married my sister."

"Is that right?"

218

Nancy nodded and resumed working on the stubborn candlewax. She was delighted to know John's career was in shambles but wanted to hear no more. Happily, Pryor changed the subject.

"The town is going to be jumping when that trial starts. Taverns and inns are already filling up, and the Gardens will be packed. That's why I've installed something called the Flying Gig. It can move people two hundred yards in a single minute."

"Goodness!"

"Yes, indeed, Miss Nancy. Folks are calling this Burr business the trial of the century."

"Is it really so important?"

Pryor was amused by her naivete. "Most assuredly. The mayor is predicting record crowds over at the Capitol. Treason charges aside, most Virginians admire Burr because he shot and killed Alexander Hamilton, and they'll turn out in droves to cheer him on. I'd be there myself if I didn't have to run things across the street." Pryor folded the newspaper and slapped it against his open palm. "Which reminds me I'd best get back to work."

Alone again, Nancy put John out of her mind and hurriedly finished her housework. She'd promised Molly to help repair their mother's needlepoint samplers and would be late if she didn't leave soon. She paused just long enough to give herself a cursory glance in the hall mirror, and wished she hadn't. Her worn, twice-mended gingham dress made her long for something fresh and new. Rather than dwell on impossibilities, she grabbed her bonnet and went outside. A steady breeze from the waterfront bore the scent of pitch and sweat and golden Virginia leaf and snatched at her hat when she started up the hill to Cary Street. She was surprised to see Molly heading in her direction.

"Shall we take a walk, little sister?" Molly asked.

"I thought we were to work on Mama's samplers."

"They can wait. It's too pretty a day to stay indoors, and I promised to show you Moldavia. Afterwards, we can walk over to the Capitol. Didn't you say you wanted to see it?"

"No!" Nancy blurted.

"What? Why not?"

Nancy explained about seeing John's name in the paper. "The notion of seeing him makes my skin crawl. He's my worst nightmare."

"I understand, dear, but he'll hardly be at the Capitol this far ahead of the trial. Now come along. After Moldavia, I'll show you the fine stores on Main Street. My favorite is Ellis & Allen. Of course, all I can afford are cotton hose, but you'll swoon over the cashmeres and swansdowns."

Molly didn't exaggerate. Richmond boasted a full city block of stylish milliners, modistes, haberdashers and shoemakers that left Nancy gasping. Once again, she yearned for something new and smart, a hopeless notion further fueled when she saw the beautifully dressed creature exiting a shop.

"Molly, look!"

Nancy pointed at a young woman wearing a snowy white walking dress with loose sleeves and rows of ribbands fastening the front. A scarlet chip hat with a cascade of egret plumes matched the parasol clutched in her gloved hand.

"She could have stepped from a French fashion magazine." Molly squinted. "Do you suppose that dress is muslin or sarsenet?"

"I can't tell, but look how beautifully it moves, light as air. Let's get a closer look." They had gone only a few steps before Nancy froze. "It can't be!"

"Can this be Nancy Randolph?"

"God help me!" Nancy whispered to Molly. "My other nightmare."

Gabriella Harvie Randolph Brockenbrough advanced on the sisters like a galleon under full sail. Her effusiveness was absurdly transparent. "And your sister, Molly. Dear me! How fortunate to happen across not one but two Randolph ladies!"

"Good afternoon, Gabriella," Molly managed, trying to be civil. Nancy said nothing.

"What brings you two to Richmond?"

"We live here," Molly replied.

"How enchanting. I can't imagine why I haven't seen you. Then again, the social whirl here is so overwhelming I suppose one can't attend everything." She brushed aside a feather tickling her forehead. "Do you live nearby?"

"Toward the river."

"What a surprise." Gabriella simpered. "I didn't know there were any respectable neighborhoods down there. My husband, Dr. Brockenbrough, built me a lovely place up here on Twelfth Street. He's President of the Bank of Virginia, you know." When her smugness elicited no response, Gabriella stepped close enough for Nancy to smell her perfume. "Alas, your prediction that Richmond society would spurn me never came to pass."

"Your memory fails you," Nancy said, undaunted. "I made no mention of society, only said there was no room amongst decent people for larcenous parvenus. I've no doubt that still holds true since new houses and titles mean nothing."

Gabriella glared at Nancy's threadbare dress. "Spoken like someone who has neither."

Nancy stiffened. "Have you nothing better to do than insult people you impoverished by stealing their fortunes?"

"People who kill their own family deserve far worse!" Gabriella shot back. Seeing the shock on Molly's face, she said, "My husband is good friends with John Randolph whose brother she murdered. John is staying with us at present, and I can't recall a more charming cavalier." She turned back to Nancy. "I'll give him your regards."

"Precisely what someone of your low station would suggest." Nancy tasted delight when Gabriella's pale face flooded with color.

"How dare you!" Outraged, Gabriella squeezed the handle of her parasol so hard it broke apart. She hurled it to the ground. "See what you've done!"

"It's your own fault," Nancy said coolly. "Even whores know to hold a parasol by the ring through its nose, not by the handle."

"Nancy!" Molly said, appalled by her sister's language.

"You might also consider changing that vile perfume. Perhaps something that doesn't carry the stink of mendacity. Come along, Molly!"

The memory of Gabriella, red-faced and fuming on Main Street, was an image Nancy would cherish to the end of her days.

34

The Burr trial dragged on. With no rain since June, searing winds turned Virginia's tobacco fields into rattling brown wastelands, and the hellish heat crippled man and beast. The enthusiastic crowds coming to the Burr trial began thinning in July, and were gone by September 1 when a verdict of not guilty was announced to a Virginia Hall of Delegates empty of spectators. Once Burr's supporters heard the news, however, they flocked to Haymarket Gardens to celebrate. It was also an excuse to take their minds off the miserable heat.

Major Pryor was overjoyed. He stationed himself at the main gate to greet his regular customers and welcome new ones, pointing out this attraction and that. Pryor knew the Gardens were frowned upon by the town's elite, but their disapproval was drowned out by the constant click of the turnstile. He wished Anne could share his triumph, but respected Nancy's dislike of crowds and knew Anne was keeping her company. The two had fixed a spot on the roof to catch any breeze off the river and watch fireworks the major had saved for the occasion. They were chatting about nothing in particular when Anne reached into her dress pocket and retrieved an envelope.

"I almost forgot. Someone left this on the front porch this afternoon."

"It's probably from the little Baine girl across the street." Nancy used a fingernail to break the adhesive seal. "I've been helping her with her schoolwork, and she delights in sending sweet notes. She's such an adorable little—oh, no!"

"What is it, dear?"

"John Randolph." She sighed, exasperated. "But how did he know where…oh! Gabriella of course. No doubt she

223

told him about seeing Molly and me on Main Street, and no doubt it wasn't difficult for a congressman and a bank president to determine where I live." Anne said nothing as Nancy read on, her face cloaked in disgust. "He's starting up again, making the old accusations that I killed Richard, but now he's added prostitution to his litany of lies."

"What?!"

"He claims that my proximity to the Gardens is so I can offer gentlemen my...how did he put it?" She reread the letter. "My 'unspeakable services.'"

"One wonders how he knows where such women gather."

Nancy folded the letter and squinted into the fast-fading sunset. "Yes, one does."

Anne was appalled. "The man must be insane, Nancy. Why else would he continue these outrageous lies?"

"Because he's a bitter, vindictive serpent who'll stop at nothing to drag me through the mud." Nancy looked up when the first fireworks blazed across the darkening sky. "It's ironic that John and Gabriella have become allies since he was the first to warn our family about her scheming. Then again, the man lies whenever it suits him and loves spinning his outlandish tales in taverns. He calls them the white man's slave grapevine, and with Richmond having so many taverns and, as you say, its fondness for gossip...well, it's only a matter of time."

"I certainly hope not," Anne said sadly. "You'll ignore that note of course."

"Yes, but no doubt it's not the last."

"Honest to God, I've never heard of such shameful behavior, and from an elected official no less. I've come to know you well, Nancy Randolph, and I've seen only good things. You work like a dog. You help children. You're generous to a fault. Is there no legal avenue you could pursue to—?"

"I don't dare meet him in a court of law. No doubt he'd forge letters and pay witnesses to lie in support of his libelous accusations."

"You'll do nothing?"

"I've no other choice."

Anne was unconvinced. "I'm going to ask the major for advice. If he can't help, perhaps he knows someone who can. He has some influential friends from his military days."

"That's very kind, but I think the less said the better."

Both looked back to the skies when the fireworks intensified, cascading across the heavens with dazzling colors. The women were close enough to hear applause from the appreciative crowd and a roar of delight when the explosions reached a thundering crescendo. Clouds of acrid smoke glowed beneath the light of a half-moon before being shredded by the wind. The ballroom orchestra struck up a lively tune designed to draw patrons onto the dance floor. It was, Nancy sadly recalled, one of the tunes she and Colonel Gibbes danced to that long-ago night in Williamsburg. It also revived the hated memory of Judith's spiteful scheme to prevent Nancy from a second encounter with the genial officer. Nancy was sick to death of hate-mongering relatives controlling her destiny and wondered, yet again, if this senseless punishment would ever end.

She had her answer within the week.

Nancy and Anne were enjoying one of their late evening chats when they heard a slammed door and commotion in the entrance hall. Lucas Stark appeared alongside Clarence Jenkins with whom he shared a room. Their clumsy posturing and red faces announced they'd been in the taverns. While Jenkins clasped the newel post for support, Stark, who was slightly more sober, lurched into the parlor and glared at Nancy.

"Is it true?" he shouted.

Guessing what was coming, Anne got to her feet. "You've had too much to drink, Mr. Lucas. Off to bed with you." She directed her gaze next to Jenkins. "You too, sir."

"Is it true?" Lucas repeated. "I want to know if it's true."

"As I said, Mr. Lucas—"

"Never mind, Anne." Nancy also rose to face the man squarely. "Is what true, Mr. Lucas?"

Lucas shrank from Nancy's imperious bearing but quickly recovered. "Is it true that you're the Jezebel of Virginia?"

"Quite true, sir," Nancy declared. "Is there anything further you'd like to know?"

Thoroughly flummoxed by her unexpected response, Lucas fumbled for words. When he failed to regain control, Jenkins leapt into the ugly conversation.

"We heard that you had your brother-in-law's baby and then killed it and him too," he slurred. "Why ain't you in jail, girlie?"

"And how come you be renting to whores and murderers?" Lucas demanded of Anne.

Awakened by loud voices, Major Pryor grabbed his robe and went downstairs to investigate. He looked from one man to the other. "What's all the shouting?"

Lucas pointed at Nancy. "We was down at Rockett's Landing where we heard about this she-devil. It's a sorry state of affairs when a decent, hard-working man finds himself living under the same roof with the likes of her!"

Pryor, who knew nothing of Nancy's history, was lost. "What on earth are you talking about?"

Anne was adamant. "These men must go to their rooms at once!"

Feeling no need to question his wife, the major barked, "You heard the lady. Off with you. Now!"

"We'll go," Lucas snarled, shooting Nancy a nasty leer before grabbing Jenkins and shoving him toward the stairs. "But come tomorrow, by God, we'll be leaving this den of iniquity for good!"

No one spoke until they heard the slam of an upstairs door. Pryor looked helplessly from one woman to the other. "What in God's name happened?"

Anne pecked her husband's check and straightened his nightcap. "It's late, my darling. I'll explain tomorrow."

"But what did Lucas mean about a den of iniquity and leaving for good?"

"He was drunk, that's all. Now off to bed." Pryor grumbled but did as she asked.

"It's I who should leave," Nancy said ruefully.

"I won't hear of it," Anne declared. "Why would you even say such a thing?"

"Because this proves, as I predicted, that John Randolph would use taverns to spread his filth. Those men are certainly not the only ones to hear the stories. I'll be talked about all over Richmond."

"Oh, Nancy!"

"If Lucas and Jenkins leave, others may follow, and it won't be easy to replace them with my scandalous name hanging overhead. A boarding house's reputation attracts a certain clientele, and you and the major can't afford this black mark."

Anne was at odds with herself. "But I don't want you to leave. I should hate to think I was responsible for you having to move yet again."

"I appreciate your words, but it can't be helped. There's no way to fight John Randolph, especially with Gabriella as an ally."

Anne was shamefaced. "I know I promised to talk to the major, but it slipped my mind." She put her hands on Nancy's shoulders. "We're both upset, so it's not the time to make important decisions. Please sleep on it, and we'll discuss it in the morning."

"I thank you, dear friend, but that will only delay the inevitable." Nancy moved to the open window where a weak breeze struggled to invade the small hot room. She stared into the darkness and said, "Richard and I grew very close the last months before he died. We talked about many things, one of which is now especially fitting. He said that he would never understand how a single moment given to love could reap a lifetime of sorrow." She sighed wearily. "It's time I did something I should've done years ago."

"What's that?"

"I'm going to leave Virginia."

"You can't mean that! Where will you go and what will you do?"

"That must remain my secret," Nancy replied firmly. "If no one knows, perhaps even John won't find out. That is my only hope of finding peace."

Part 7

"It is what a man thinks of himself that really determines his fate."

-Henry David Thoreau

35

"In quitting Virginia," Nancy wrote to St. George Tucker, "every chord of my heart burst asunder."

But, quit she did, and headed north, joining the throngs of Americans making their young nation the most mobile in the world. While the early colonists subscribed to the notion of remaining "within the sound of the parish bell," a restless new breed was on the move via wagon, stagecoach, riverboat, horseback and even on foot. Nancy spent almost a year in Newport, Rhode Island, before resettling in Fairfield, Connecticut, where fate set her in motion yet again. Abigail Pollack, a New York widow visiting Fairfield friends, took an immediate liking to the well-bred Virginian, and when Nancy returned her feelings, Abigail invited her to be her companion in her boarding house on Greenwich Street in Manhattan.

The idea of a city of 90,000 souls with polyglot neighborhoods aswarm with immigrants was daunting, but Nancy allowed herself to be swayed. By the summer of 1808, she was living in a working-class neighborhood of wooden rowhouses only eighteen-feet wide. Backyards held vegetable gardens (fenced to deter wayward hogs), smokehouses, cisterns, woodpiles and the requisite privy. Families lived upstairs with the ground floor serving as work space. In Richmond, Nancy had learned a valuable lesson about living with people not of her station and was thus comfortable among the Village's carriage makers, carters, carpenters and joiners. With her small salary as Abigail's companion, life was good, and best of all, did not include John Randolph.

Nancy's greatest pleasure was her continued correspondence with St. George Tucker. He alone knew her whereabouts and kept them a secret along with other intimate confidences. A few weeks after Nancy sent her new address,

Tucker mentioned a long-time New York friend, Gouverneur Morris, whose acquaintance might be advantageous. Tucker had met him in 1785 when Morris visited Virginia to negotiate a tobacco contract for his half-brother, Robert, and was entertained at Tuckahoe where he met Colonel Randolph's herd of offspring. Nancy had no memory of that meeting, but when Morris returned three years later, when she was thirteen, she vividly recalled the mortifying moment when four-year-old Harriet pointed at the distinguished visitor's pegleg and asked if he were a pirate!

As summer melted into fall, Nancy settled into a contented regimen. She took long walks and found endless diversions in the hustle-bustle of Manhattan Island. The waterfront with its raucous wharves, fifteen on the Hudson and twice that many on the East River, fashioned a circumferential vista of ship masts and spars which, when coupled with the city's spires, cupolas and rows of tall buildings, offered a vista Nancy found dazzling. She treated herself to window shopping the expensive specialty shops on Maiden Lane, and was awed by the five-story City Hotel on Broadway which drew the carriage trade with elegant dining and the finest wine cellar in New York. One bright October day, under cloudless turquoise skies, she was returning from the Fly Market with a basket of apples for Abigail when she spotted a commotion on Greenwich Street. Chased by a dusty tribe of screaming street urchins and making a great clatter of wheels and horseshoes on cobblestones, a stylish coach-and-four drew up in front of the Pollack boarding house. Nancy watched, mystified, when a liveried footman leapt down from the driver's seat and opened the coach door. A tall, smartly dressed older gentleman stepped onto the sidewalk, adjusted his beaver hat and waved politely to the ogling crowd. Nancy's bewilderment ended when she saw his wooden leg.

"Gouverneur Morris!" she gasped. "It must be!"

Nancy started for the house but hesitated until Morris had gone inside. She wished she was wearing something more presentable than a dowdy cotton frock, but all she could do was tuck wayward strands of hair under her bonnet and adjust it to a smarter angle. That done, she marched into the house as Abigail was greeting her caller.

"Ah, here she is now!" Abigail said. "Nancy, you have a visitor."

The man doffed his hat and bowed to reveal a receding hairline of thick white curls. When he straightened, Nancy decided his sloping forehead and hawkish nose were redeemed by full lips and dark, heavily lashed eyes. Those eyes delivered a steady, unsettling gaze.

"Gouverneur Morris, at your service, madam."

"Sir." Nancy curtsied. "I have heard much about you from my dear friend, St. George Tucker."

"As I have heard of you," he replied. "Please allow me to apologize for dropping in unannounced. I was tending to a bit of business at the Tontine, and, since I was near your neighborhood, I presumed to call."

"The Tontine?"

"A coffee house on Water Street and Wall. It's a gathering place for stock traders." He smiled. "Nothing of interest to ladies."

"I see." Taking a cue from Abigail who discreetly waved toward the parlor before excusing herself, Nancy said, "Will you have tea, Mr. Morris?"

"Thank you, no. I've only a few minutes as I'm due home by nightfall. I live at Morrisania at the top of the island. At least I did when I left yesterday morning." He chuckled heartily. "I suppose one should never leave one's home in the hands of rogues and rowdies."

"I beg your pardon."

"That my home is in such disarray is precisely why I've come calling, Miss Randolph. My household staff is untrained and incompetent because they lack the firm hand of someone who understands the importance of manners and gentility. I have gone through a succession of housekeepers incapable of managing this motley lot and have finally reached the end of my rope." His wooden leg thumped against the floor when he shifted to a more comfortable position. "Some time ago, I wrote Mr. Tucker of my dilemma which prompted him to mention your regrettable circumstances. He believes, and I wholeheartedly agree, that what Morrisania needs are the services of a gentlewoman to command respect and get the household running smoothly."

Nancy's pulse quickened. "I see."

"I realize of course that it's presumptuous on my part to approach a lady such as yourself without warning and credentials, but I believe Mr. Tucker will vouch for my character."

"There is no need for apology for either manners or character, Mr. Morris. I've known Mr. Tucker all my life and assure you he is someone whose judgment I would never question. That you are his good friend is more than sufficient proof of your standing."

"I'm honored and pleased to hear that, dear lady. May I presume that you will at least entertain my offer of a position at Morrisania?"

"You may indeed."

"Splendid. I must travel upstate on business for some months but will contact you upon my return. In the meantime, please feel free to write me here." He handed her a card. "No doubt you have a number of queries regarding my offer."

"There's certainly much to consider, Mr. Morris. At present I confess to being a bit overwhelmed."

"Understandable. Understandable." Morris bowed again and backed toward the door. "It has been a great pleasure, Miss Randolph. Until next time then."

Nancy curtsied again. "Until then, sir."

She opened the door and watched Morris pop his hat back into place and thump for the carriage with his distinctive lopsided stride. Without an assist from the footman, he climbed into the coach, turned toward Nancy and tipped his hat as he pulled away, pursued by the same crowd of raucous street children. Nancy was enjoying the peculiar sight when Abigail appeared beside her.

"Imagine that!" she exclaimed. "One of our nation's fathers in my own house!"

Nancy turned to her. "What do you mean?"

Abigail was astonished. "You don't know that Mr. Morris wrote the Preamble to the Constitution? That he signed the Articles of Confederation and was a minister to France and a New York senator. He even delivered the eulogy at Alexander Hamilton's funeral!"

"Good heavens! All that!" She considered her ignorance. "Thank goodness you know all about politicians."

"Only the New Yorkers, dearie. Especially those from the old families. I know for example that Mr. Morris is very wealthy and one of the city's most eligible bachelors, even at his age. He must be close to sixty by now. I've always wondered why no woman was able to snare him. Of course, there was all sorts of talk about that Frenchwoman."

Nancy was intrigued in spite of herself. "Frenchwoman?"

"When he lived in Paris. Adelaide Something-or-Other. She was a novelist of some renown. Mr. Morris is apparently drawn to ladies of letters."

"There were others?"

"Oh, my, yes! He was involved with a poetess named Sarah Morton. A married woman, mind you, but it was her sister Fanny who caused the real scandal. When Fanny came to live with Sarah, she was seduced by Sarah's husband, a Mr. Perez, and had his child. When the truth got out, poor Fanny took an overdose of laudanum. It was worthy of a sentimental novel."

Nancy's throat went dry upon hearing a tragedy so similar to her own. She swallowed and said, "How in the world do you know all this?"

Abigail chuckled. "Because I'm an old busybody who makes it her business to know such things and aren't you glad I do?"

Nancy laughed too. "I suppose I am."

"So tell me, dearie, why did he come calling?"

"A mutual friend told him of my situation, and he's offered me a housekeeping position."

"How splendid! I'd certainly hate to lose you, but it sounds like a golden opportunity."

"Perhaps a little too golden," Nancy said slowly.

"You sound dubious."

"Not by choice."

"What do you mean, child?"

Nancy valued Abigail's friendship and support, but, unlike with Anne, had never confided intimate details about her past. She had learned early on about the older woman's fondness for gossip, a reality confirmed by Abigail's eagerness to repeat Gouvernor Morris's rumored peccadilloes.

"Only that my life has been such that I no longer accept things at face value. I have been cast aside and set adrift too many times to follow a new path without great caution."

"But surely you have no cause to question a man of Mr. Morris's stature."

Nancy gave her a wry smile. "I'm a thirty-four-year-old spinster, Abigail. I must question everything and everyone."

36

When six months elapsed with no word from
Gouverneur Morris, Nancy wondered if her past had caught
up with her again. As always, she turned to her champion for
answers, asking Tucker if he supposed Morris had heard John
Randolph's vile propaganda. Tucker's response included the
surprising revelation that John had severed their relationship.
Things began souring when John openly broke with President
Jefferson whom Tucker ardently supported and endorsed
James Monroe over Tucker's choice, James Madison, in the
1808 Presidential election. It collapsed altogether when
Tucker severely chastised his stepson for harassing Nancy.
Tucker believed John's fierce reaction was rooted more in an
irrational hatred of Nancy than their political differences, and
encouraged her to be forthright with Morris about the
scandal. This she did in the most difficult letter she had ever
written, her future dependent upon a few telling words.

"You expressed concern over your credentials," she
wrote, "when the concern should be for mine. A series of
unjust accusations have plagued me for many years and
caused me uncountable distress and hardship. I am so weary
of persecution that I vowed never to impart my distress to
anyone, but your kind and generous offer dictates otherwise.
I cannot consider accepting it without cautioning you against
taking into your home a woman whose honor has been
compromised and inviting a situation wherein you could be
subjected to the same slander as myself."

The weeks that ensued, with no reply, worsened
Nancy's fears. She grew nervous and irritable, and when
Abigail queried her, Nancy blamed it on melancholia and
assured her landlady it would pass. She did her best to appear
cheerful during the Christmas season, but when the new year,
1809, brought no word from Morris, she despaired anew. By

February, she was abandoning all hope when a letter arrived on the fourth day. Nancy held her breath as she raced through Morris's alarming tale of an illness in Schenectady severe enough to warrant rewriting his will, along with a harrowing account of an Albany January so ferocious that the ink froze in his inkwell. Finally, she reached the words she yearned for.

"Talk not of gratitude, madam. I once heard, but have no distinct recollection, of events which brought distress into your family. Dwell not on them now or trouble yourself with the judgment of others."

Nancy wept so loudly with relief that Abigail rushed to investigate. "My dear! What has happened?"

"A lifeline!" Nancy cried. "I've been thrown a lifeline!"

Nancy and Morris continued their correspondence through the remainder of the winter and into spring. She was thrilled by letters filled with rare wit, compassion and intelligence, and was further pleased when Morris proved himself a gentleman of the highest order regarding treatment of his housekeepers.

"The fine ladies who visit me have never harbored an idea injurious to the virtue, as they call it, of my housekeepers. They are right, for certainly I have never approached any of them with anything resembling desire."

Nancy needed to hear no more. She wrote Morris that she was at his disposal whenever he chose to return to the city, and received a prompt reply that he would come for her on the morning of April 29. After breakfasting on Dutch waffles and fruit preserves at Fraunces Tavern, which elevated his already fine mood, Morris arrived shortly before ten o'clock to find Nancy packed and waiting in the parlor. After a tearful good-bye to Abigail, she was helped into the carriage by Morris's footman and, joined by the man himself, was off to Morrisania.

"We are escaping but barely," Morris remarked as the carriage was swallowed by the throng of traffic heading north on Broadway.

"Sir?"

"Day after tomorrow is Moving Day," he reminded her.

"You're right. I'd quite forgotten."

Nancy had seen the alarming phenomenon soon after arriving in New York. On the first day of May, all leases expired simultaneously, flooding the city with those seeking new homes, offices and shops. For twenty-four hours, the streets were inundated with thousands of desperate souls in carts, coaches, wagons and drays creating such chaos that everyone else stayed indoors.

"It's not something I wish to witness a second time. Mrs. Pollack said she was reminded of the biblical exodus or people fleeing the plague." Nancy smiled wistfully. "She is a kind soul and has been good to me. I will miss her."

"I do hope you don't regret your decision to leave."

"Not at all. I've been looking forward to this day with great anticipation. The idea of new experiences is exhilarating."

"Are you a seasoned traveler?"

"To the contrary. I had never been outside Virginia until two years ago. I spent a little time in Rhode Island and Connecticut, but was not much impressed by either." She paused before adding, "That's not altogether true. The ocean views in Newport were lovely, and I discovered that I love the smell of salt air."

"As do I. You'll be pleased to know we can smell the sea from Morrisania, if the wind is right."

"I'm most anxious to see it for myself."

"I pray you don't reconsider once you meet your staff."

"Your letters have suitably prepared me, although I admit to some trepidation after such vivid descriptions." She conjured his words. "Two Irish hooligans, a shy Frenchman, an Englishwoman, three Negroes and…who have I forgotten?"

"A quarrelsome German, two more girls and a surly laundress with the unlikely name of Clara Cheer. She can be infuriating, but I tolerate her because she's a genius with my shirts." He shifted his weight to get more comfortable. "Miss Randolph, if you knew my travails in acquiring even this wretched staff, you would understand my frustration. As Mr. Tucker told you, I am a very busy man and have scant time for domestic issues." He pointed to the expanse of land ahead of them. "In fact, I'm currently consumed with work on the Commissioner's Plan for a Manhattan grid system above Fourteenth Street. The streets will run east to west and be numbered instead of named. The same will be true of the wider avenues, which will run north and south."

"It sounds most ambitious."

"Of necessity, since the street numbers will total over two hundred and we must not repeat the chaos of downtown which, as you know, is a bewildering jumble of streets. It will also simplify the purchase of land by creating standard-sized lots." When Nancy didn't comment, Morris said, "Most anything related to transportation is of great interest to me. In fact, I've been accused of suffering from canal mania."

"What on earth is that?"

"An obsession with canals. I spent some time in Europe after the war, and saw the miracles accomplished by canals in Amsterdam and Antwerp and especially the Forth and Clyde Canal in Scotland. I was so enamored that I, with Mayor Clinton's support, have been fighting for a canal connecting the Hudson River with the Great Lakes. It will give the city a tremendous advantage over other ports and slash transportation costs."

"It sounds like a splendid idea, Mr. Morris. Why does it require a fight?"

"Cost, plain and simple. Plus, a plague of unimaginative senators incapable of envisioning the future. I can sympathize to an extent considering the canal will be over three hundred miles long with a drop of almost six hundred feet from Lake Erie to the Hudson, but we must think of our great city's future."

"Such a project will surely require a great number of locks," Nancy ventured.

"Close to fifty I imagine." Morris weighed the unexpected remark. "How would you know about such things?"

"My father had a large library at Tuckahoe which, alas, I eschewed for sympathetic novels. It wasn't until I moved to a boarding house in Richmond that I availed myself of other sorts of books. Most dealt with military matters since they belonged to a former army officer, but many were about history and travel which captivated me in a way no sentimental novel could."

"You read about canals?"

"A short history, beginning with the one built by King Darius connecting the Nile River with the Red Sea."

Morris was delighted. "Darius is one of my heroes. He also constructed a series of roads to facilitate communication in his vast empire."

"With a series of men and fresh horses to carry communiques with great speed."

Morris leaned back and regarded her with admiration. "You astonish me, madam!"

"Sometimes I astonish myself," Nancy declared, recalling her lively talks with Anne and Major Pryor. "I didn't know I had so much curiosity until given the opportunity to explore it and engage in enlightening conversation."

"It sounds as though you were in prison."

"In a manner of speaking, I was."

Nancy immediately regretted her confession, worried it might lead to unwelcome questions, but Morris was distracted when the carriage swerved too late to avoid a large pothole. The resulting jolt and fierce bang made Morris fear a broken axle, but the carriage rumbled on, smoother now along the paved turnpike.

"I have complained endlessly about lack of repairs along this stretch," he grumbled. "It's the only highway leading south into the city, and there's no reason for it to be forever pocked with holes."

"It's still superior to some of our Virginia highways which are little more than horse-tracks," Nancy observed. "And I must say that the countryside is lovely."

Some distance back, the rows of tightly-packed buildings had given way to farmhouses and stretches of open land greening with the approach of summer. Now, as Nancy and Morris approached the halfway point of their journey along Manhattan's thirteen-mile length, forests of maple, beech and towering sassafras and sycamore pressed in close. At some points, limbs intertwined to create a canopy. Red-winged blackbirds darted through the branches, scarlet shoulders dappled with sunlight and startling against the green.

"I can't remember a more charming drive," Nancy said. "I almost hate to see it end."

He smiled. "Shall I slow the carriage?"

"That's not necessary, but what a kind offer. Thank you, sir."

"Madam," he said with a nod.

If Gouverneur Morris was half this considerate as an employer, Nancy allowed herself to imagine her future finally held promise. Only time would tell.

37

"My people came from Wales over a hundred and fifty years ago," Morris explained as the coach ascended a hillock alongside the Harlem River. "I bought the house from my half-brother Robert at the end of the war. It had been looted by the British, so it needed a great deal of repair." Nancy noted that his deep voice acquired a dreamy quality as he continued. "Morrisania is more than a home to me, Miss Randolph. It's flight from the world, an escape, if you will, that rejuvenates me when I return from my constant travels. I can sit on the terrace overlooking the river and breathe the most salubrious air in the world." He fell silent as the coachman crested the hill and the mansion rose into view. He turned to see Nancy's reaction as he said, "Welcome to Morrisania."

"Oh, my!"

The three-story stone-and-stucco mansion reined over sixteen hundred acres including landscaped grounds dotted with shade trees. Three chimneys and a half dozen dormer windows pierced a roof surmounted by a handsome belvedere. On the second floor, a 130-foot-long covered terrace graced by lacy ironwork ran the length of the house. Beneath it, in the center, was the front door. When the coachmen brought the carriage to a halt, Nancy trembled with a rush of emotion that did not go unnoticed.

"Dare I suppose you are thinking of Tuckahoe?"

"I could not help myself," she admitted. "The houses look nothing alike but they share an unmistakable air of welcome. My mother used to say that Tuckahoe belonged to its guests."

"A charming lady, I recall, and a magnificent hostess." Morris alit from the carriage with remarkable dexterity and stepped aside so the footman could assist

Nancy. He turned toward the house when the front door swung open. "Shall we?"

Nancy reacted with a start when she saw the middle-aged woman holding the door. A red-faced blousy sort in rumpled clothing and ratty mobcap, she managed a clumsy curtsy and stepped aside.

"Miss Randolph, this is Clara Cheer." Nancy nodded. "Clara, this is our new housekeeper."

"Ma-am," Clara muttered. She closed the door and walked away until Morris called after her.

"Where is the rest of the staff, Clara?"

"Hanging from the trees for all I know. I figured somebody oughta open the door for ya."

"I appreciate that." Clara mumbled something about tending to her wash and disappeared. Morris chuckled and looked at Nancy. "A delight, isn't she?"

"She makes me warier than ever about the rest of your staff."

"You'll be fine. All they require is a firm hand from someone who can command their respect."

"What was the previous housekeeper like?"

"A sweet old soul who allowed everyone to run roughshod over her. I couldn't bear another tearful outburst, so I let her go." Morris gestured toward a high-ceilinged great hall with a magnificently carved plaster ceiling. "Please feel free to explore your new domain. I'll be back momentarily."

"As you wish, sir."

As Morris thumped away, a fading beam of sunlight drew Nancy's eye to fine French parquet floors scarred by his pegleg. She wandered into the parlor to marvel at exquisite furnishings and a superb collection of tapestries, paintings and sculptures, all the appurtenances of means. She was less impressed by the veneer of dust on everything.

"The place is a disgrace!" she whispered to herself.

She found more of the same upstairs, beautiful furniture cloaked with grime, and carpets that hadn't been aired and beaten in months. Sun-faded curtains served up more neglect, but her mood lightened when she ventured onto a terrace with a vista so picturesque it begged for an artist's paintbrush. Bright sunlight cast dark shadows across the uppermost tip of Manhattan Island and New Jersey beyond. The hushed beauty was such that Nancy ignored the flutter in her breast warning that this, like everything else, could be abruptly taken away. She breathed in the restorative air Morris described earlier and, drawing from her last untapped well of strength, decried the old fears.

"Begone!" Nancy muttered to herself, or so she thought. She had been so lost in the moment that she hadn't heard the telltale thump of a wooden leg.

"Did you say something, Miss Randolph?"

"I was just thinking out loud, sir." She indicated the view. "This needs only a frame to become a painting."

"What charming imagination. I've spent countless hours here but never had that notion." He was clearly pleased. "Did you like the house as well?"

"It's lovely, but I must be frank."

"Please do."

"Those rooms have not seen a feather duster or cleaning cloth in months. Some of the upstairs windows are so grimy they barely admit light, and the whole house urgently needs airing out. The situation is dire."

"I trust not too dire for someone such as yourself."

"Not at all, but if I am to succeed, it's essential that the staff does not question my judgment and that I have total control." Nancy took umbrage when Morris burst into laughter. "You find me amusing, sir?"

"My apologies, madam. My reaction was because I've never seen tenacity wrapped in such a proper package."

"Oh."

"Furthermore, I'm delighted to discover you a force to be reckoned with." He chuckled again. "Your declaration is quite similar to one I made to the King of France. Louis was, alas, not as amused."

Nancy joined in his laughter. "I should like to hear about your time with the king. I'm fascinated by all things French and…oh!" She stopped abruptly and looked down. "Forgive my presumption, sir."

"Presumption?"

"My role is that of housekeeper, not some lady engaging in badinage. I had no right to overreach."

"Then perhaps we should strive for a middle ground."

Nancy demurred. "With all due respect, sir, we both know that isn't permissible. There are strict rules dictating the relationship between housekeeper and employer."

"You think so, eh?" Morris swept his arms wide. "You see all this land, Miss Randolph? This is my private kingdom where I alone determine what is and is not permissible. In my realm, I will discuss whatever I like with whomever I like whenever I like. *Honi soit qui mal y pense!*"

"Shame be to him who thinks evil of it," Nancy translated. "A bold philosophy, sir."

"Do you find it agreeable?"

"I do," she replied, suddenly moved to change the subject. "As is that lovely breeze. I can smell the sea just as you said."

"Take a moment to enjoy it if you like. Afterwards, I will show you to your office and introduce you to the staff."

"No need to wait." Nancy untied her bonnet as she preceded him back inside the house. "The lion's den awaits."

Chuckling at her little joke, Morris ushered her to a downstairs room in the rear of the house where Cora Cheer had assembled the staff. He looked at each in turn. "This is Miss Nancy Randolph," he said in the authoritative tone used to cow veteran politicians and arrogant planters. "She is Morrisania's new housekeeper and is to be treated with respect. Anyone who fails to do so will answer to me." He nodded to Nancy and left.

Quick inventory told Nancy that Morris's phrase "motley lot" was no exaggeration. She was appalled by slovenly dress, dirty clothes, and hygiene so pungent she ordered the window opened. She asked each person to state their name and position and memorized their responses. When they finished, she told them to wait outside so she might interview each privately. Using a check list made before she left New York, she designated duties, from cleaning, dusting and serving meals to mending clothes, drawing water, hauling wood and emptying the slops. That done, she reassembled everyone and delivered her prepared address.

"Our responsibility is to provide Mr. Morris with a clean house run by a polite, orderly staff. Mary Hannigan will make uniforms for each of you, so kindly meet with her straight away so she may take measurements. It will take time to get things organized and running smoothly, but if we work together, it can be done to everyone's satisfaction. Are there any questions?"

"I've got one, miss." This from Pádraic Monahan, one of two Irishmen Morris had termed hooligans. Monahan was probably this side of thirty, but hard drinking had aged him well beyond. The ripe smell of whiskey had not passed unnoticed when Nancy was alone with him.

"Yes, Mr. Monahan?"

"How about giving us a kiss?" He guffawed noisily, but fell silent when his rudeness was ignored by the others. He was further shamed by Nancy's response.

"I'll consider no requests whatsoever, Mr. Monahan, until you draw a sober breath." When he scowled, she added, "If that's not to your liking, the door is there. Morrisania has no place for drunks and rowdies." She scanned the gathering, noting both grins and frowns in response to her ultimatum. She turned again to Monahan, now staring at his feet like a scolded schoolboy. "Mr. Morris told me that your misconduct forced the departure of my predecessor. Rest assured that if you repeat such disobedience, it is you who will depart, not I. Are there other questions?" The silence in the room was near tangible. "No? Very well then. Tomorrow will be a very busy day, so everyone be about your business."

Nancy was relieved when the staff dispersed without grumbling. Morris was right, she thought. A few might be beyond salvation, but most of these poor souls just needed a fair but firm hand, the sort her mother wielded with Tuckahoe's servants. She inspected the drawers in her new desk, refilled a bone-dry inkwell and went searching for Morris. She heard him conversing outside the front door, and, upon investigation, found a coach bearing two fashionable young ladies in muslin carriage dresses with sarsnet mantles. One wore a turban adorned with swan feathers, while the other sported a chip hat like the one favored by Gabriella. Nancy hastened to retreat, but not before Morris noticed her.

"Ah! Miss Randolph!" He turned to his visitors, Hetty and Elizabeth McCourt who lived on a nearby estate. "This is my new housekeeper."

"I certainly hope she's more capable than your last one, Gouverneur," Hetty laughed. "The poor old thing."

"At least this one's younger," Elizabeth added, earning herself an elbow in the ribs from Hetty.

Morris looked displeased by their haughtiness but said nothing. When the awkward moment hovered, Nancy curtsied and went back inside, waiting in the great hall until the jangle of harness announced the carriage's departure. She opened the front door when she heard Morris approach. He was surprised to find her waiting.

"Miss Randolph. Have I forgotten something?"

"My quarters, sir."

"Of course. Of course. Forgive me. I have much on my mind. I'd even forgotten I'm dining with the McCourt sisters this evening."

"Certainly, sir."

Morris gave her directions to her room on the top floor and excused himself to dress for dinner. Nancy climbed the stairs, each step weighing heavier than the last as she thought about the smartly-dressed beauties in the carriage. Inside her room, she gave the unmade bed and cloudy dormer window a cursory glance before chiding herself.

You'd best forget what Mr. Morris said about a middle ground. You're his servant now, same as Clara Cheer and Pádraic Monahan. If you forget that, even for a moment, you could lose everything.

38

Morris departed Morrisania the next day for a series of upstate business trips, leaving Nancy to a true baptism by fire. For a full week, the house echoed with shouts, threats, weeping and words of gratitude as the staff adapted to her demands. The Negro cook, Florence, was volatile as cooks often are, but Nancy discerned sweetness beneath the steely facade and negotiated a lasting truce. Alain Ferrier, the shy, quiet Frenchman, proved eager to learn the duties of a gentleman's gentleman, and although the cleaning girls were slow to learn, patience and encouragement made them blossom. The rest, even Pádraic Monahan and the temperamental Clara Cheer, eventually fell into the routine Nancy demanded to make Morrisania a source of pride for its owner.

As the staff mastered their duties and required less attention, Nancy found time to renew her correspondence. She had written Tucker shortly after arriving at Morrisania, thanking him for her new position. Self-assurance buoyed, she broke her silence and wrote to her siblings, even Judith. Their letters trickled back, bearing good wishes from Molly and news from Patsy that Tom and the ever-quarrelsome John had come dangerously close to dueling over political differences. Judith wrote that special schooling for Saint had failed to help him speak and that John now lived at Roanoke plantation where, with over four hundred Negro workers, he was the biggest slaveowner in Charlotte County. Despite his wealth, John continued to disdain a grand manor house and remained in the log cabin. Well acquainted with his misanthropy, Nancy was unsurprised to learn that he lived alone. Morris wrote that he would be finishing his business in Buffalo earlier than expected. On his return date, Nancy saw that everyone was groomed, uniformed and lined up to greet him in the great hall. His surprise when she opened the door made her heroic efforts worthwhile.

"By George!" he boomed gleefully. "Have I come to the wrong house?"

"Welcome home, sir." To Morris's delight, Nancy's curtsy signaled the others to bow as well. "I trust your trip was enjoyable."

"It was a great success, as, it seems, were your efforts here."

"Thank you, sir." Nancy gave the staff a nod of approval and dismissed them "That will be all."

"Now I truly feel like the lord of the manor," Morris effused as he saw more bows and an orderly dispersal. "You've worked miracles, Miss Randolph, and I should like to hear about them over supper. You will join me, yes?"

"I instructed Florence to prepare something special for your homecoming," Nancy said evasively. She gestured toward the stairs. "If you'd like to go to your room, your valet Alain will help you change."

"Alain?! The mousy little Frenchman?"

"He's quite the gentleman's gentleman now. I believe he will surprise you."

"It would seem, dear lady, that you have considered everything."

"That is my intent, sir."

"Except you didn't respond to my dinner invitation."

Ever concerned about their delicately balanced relationship, Nancy fumbled for a response. "I'm honored, sir. Only—"

"You're still in my employ, are you not?"

"Of course."

"Then kindly do I ask and for heaven's sake wear something else. These past few weeks, I've seen nothing but hotel and café uniforms, and I'm thoroughly wearied of them."

Nancy was uneased by Morris's request, but did not resist further. Dinner was his idea, after all, and she was

250

merely following orders. Thank goodness she had the foresight to have Mary Hannigan make her a new dress when she finished sewing uniforms for the staff. As she headed outside to the kitchen to confer with Florence, Nancy found herself humming all the way.

The chandelier dispersed much-multiplied candlelight onto a dining table gleaming with china, crystal and freshly polished silver. Nancy was pleased to see the girls had done a fine job and needed only to straighten a single oyster fork before achieving perfection. Intrigued by the china's botanical pattern, Nancy picked up a plate and ran a fingertip along a ribbed stem with convex leaves. Most unusual, she thought. When she heard Morris approaching from the great hall, she replaced the plate and gave herself a quick check in the pier mirror. To satisfy a housekeeper's need for a dress for special occasions, Mary Hannigan had created a lilac satin half-full dress with white silk frost work. A double row of silk trim dipped low across the bosom, and a delicate white lace cap provided an elegant touch atop Nancy's upswept hairdo. It was fancier than necessary, but Nancy had indulged herself with her first new dress since her days at Tuckahoe.

She turned when Morris's reflection materialized over her shoulder. "Good evening, sir."

"Madam." His eyes flickered over her dress but he made no comment as he circled the table before ending up at her side. "This room looks completely different. Another splendid job."

"Thank you, sir."

"How did you come to choose that particular china?"

"Florence told me it was your favorite. Such a striking pattern."

"I brought it back from London. There's a story behind it you may find interesting." While Morris took his seat at the other end of the long table, Nancy sat and picked up a tiny dinner bell to summon the first course. Morris watched, impressed, as two girls in crisp white aprons deposited bowls of steaming Mulligatawny soup before quietly disappearing. "I know I'm repeating myself, but you truly appear to be a miracle worker."

"I'm pleased to report the staff has been cooperative, although admittedly not without a few wrinkles. I considered replacing a few, but so far everyone remains in service."

"Even Mr. Monahan?"

"Mr. Monahan, to my great surprise, has an affinity for woodworking. Thanks to him, the servant's stairway no longer has a railing riddled with splinters." Nancy picked up her soup spoon. "Please tell me about the china."

"The pattern is called Blind Earl for George William Coventry, the fifth Earl of Coventry. After a hunting accident left him sightless, he sought something that he could recognize by touch, which explains the distinctively raised design."

"I hadn't imagined such a touching history."

"Nor I. I was attracted to it as much for the beauty of the design as empathy for the earl. Such a thing often exists between people who share, shall we say, physical shortcomings." When he paused to taste the soup, Nancy anticipated his next words. "I've been intending to explain about my leg, you see, and despite it not being ideal dinner conversation, I would like to tell you now."

"If you wish."

"I wish it were the result of some great heroic feat, but, alas, it was only a carriage accident when I was twenty-eight. A rearing horse startled by a loud noise." Morris spared Nancy the gruesome details of snagging his left leg in the spokes of a turning wheel, dislocating the ankle and crushing several bones. "Unfortunately, I was traveling at the time and told by a country doctor that without amputation, I would die of gangrene. When I returned home, my personal physician said the diagnosis was hasty and that the leg could have been saved."

"How unfortunate. Yet, you've not let it hinder you."

"Nor will it," Morris asserted. "I can dance, ride, and climb church steeples. I've even ridden river rapids." He gave his wooden leg a playful slap. "My old friend here gives me the occasional slip in the mud, but we've managed well enough over the years."

"I admire your optimism, sir."

"It's not optimism, Miss Randolph. Such deeds cannot be undone, and I see no gain in bemoaning them." He cocked his head. "Did I see a smile?"

"Your philosophy is familiar, Mr. Morris. I've said more than once that regrets are worthless."

"What a delight to know we share such acuity!"

"Sir."

Soup course completed, they savored oysters from Long Island Sound and fresh flounder fried and served with brown butter. Nancy led Morris into a discussion of his recent business trip and tried hard to understand the surveying and engineering details of the massive Erie Canal project.

"The journey was not without incident, however, as I took a good spill on the muddy shore of the Mohawk River." He paused to admire a rainbow thrown through crystal when a servant refilled his wine glass, then chuckled. "I ruined a brand-new suit and nearly cracked my noggin, but my clumsiness was to blame, not my wooden leg. In fact, the thing once saved my life."

"Oh?"

"I was appointed Minister to France by President Washington back in ninety-two, hardly a propitious time for visiting with the country on the brink of revolution. When it came, I was caught up in the Reign of Terror. Royalty, nobility and the aristocracy were being hunted by bloodthirsty Paris mobs, whom I unfortunately encountered when my coachman took a wrong turn near the Bois de Boulogne. Because I was in a fancy closed carriage, the rabble assumed that I was the enemy, so they surrounded my coach and began rocking it back and forth. I'll not pretend that I wasn't terrified. I knew my only hope for survival was to prove I wasn't French, so I threw open the door, stuck out my wooden leg and yelled that I was an American patriot who lost his leg in our war against the British. It helped that I speak French with a heavy accent, and I escaped in one piece."

"Good heavens!"

"But what have we here?" Morris marveled at the arrival of guinea fowl and leg of lamb along with a host of fresh vegetables from Morrisania's lush gardens. "Florence has outdone herself."

"The poor woman was never given the opportunity to show her skills because your previous housekeeper requested only basic foods."

"That was my fault," Morris confessed. "These last few years, I was away more often than home and was content with simple fare. Chicken or venison or fish, a few vegetables."

"I hope you approve the change."

"Dear lady, I am delighted with everything you've done. The house is spotless, the servants efficient and deferential and the food is sublime. Bringing you here was one of the wisest decisions of my life."

"I'm humbled, Mr. Morris," Nancy said softly. "Now, if you like, I've arranged for dessert on the terrace. It looks to be a clear, starry night, and I'm hopeful of a breeze from the river."

"A delightful idea. Once again, you've thought of everything." Nancy jumped when Morris's deep voice boomed across the table. "Good heavens! Where are my manners?!"

"Sir?"

"All evening long, I've been conversing with a beautifully turned-out lady and have said not one word about her dress."

Nancy colored beneath the flattery. "Mary Hannigan made it. Another of your underused staff. The woman is a wizard with the needle."

"I am astonished, Miss Randolph. The more we talk, the more I learn about unearthed treasures that have been here all along."

"That's my job, sir."

"And well done it is." Morris sipped his madeira and tucked into the lamb. He chewed thoughtfully and said, "Fate is such a nebulous thing. A simple suggestion in an old friend's letter and here we are. It's all rather amazing, is it not?"

"Amazing indeed, sir."

39

By autumn Morrisania was running like clockwork. Nancy had excellent relationships with the staff, especially Mary Hannigan, and even engaged in some light-hearted banter with Clara Cheer. The servants were not the only ones drawn to Nancy's natural warmth and caring nature. As she and Morris spent more time together, Nancy acknowledged a drift toward something beyond friendship. Her first notion that Morris might view her as more than a servant came with his declaration that he governed his realm as he chose and cared not a fig what others thought, but she dismissed the notion when he left to dine with the glamorous McCourt sisters. The question rose again with their first dinner together, but faded when he attended plays, balls and various fetes in New York, with a different woman on his arm each time. Nancy remembered Abigail Pollack's portrait of Morris as a notorious lady's man, but no such behavior was in evidence at Morrisania where he treated her with the utmost respect. Nancy was further perplexed when Morris began spending less time in the city, and made their dinners together a nightly occurrence. As they continued to share confidences, Nancy not only felt an attraction but succumbed to emotions she believed dead and buried. But could this celebrated man of the world possibly share her feelings?

To distract herself from endless speculation, Nancy sought escape through reading. Once Morris made his vast library available, she immersed herself in works he recommended along with those of her own choosing. She also devoted more time to correspondence, but revealed no sensitive thoughts about him to anyone, not even Tucker or Patsy.

Morris's quiet curiosity about Nancy had him writing letters as well. He had been honest in stating that he cared nothing about her past, but knew that someone of his standing was obliged to get facts. Because he considered any sort of confrontation unbefitting, he contacted his longtime confidante John Marshall, now Chief Justice of the United States. "You have perhaps heard," Morris wrote, "that Miss Nancy Randolph of Tuckahoe is employed in my household. She had earlier apprised me of unfortunate events causing her to fall upon troubled times and expressed fears that our association might direct calumny toward me." His request for information on "Miss Randolph's reputation and her standing in Virginia society" yielded precisely the response Morris yearned for. Marshall replied that the Randolphs were among the finest families in the state, and that he once successfully defended her brother-in-law Richard in a defamation case. Marshall attributed the case to "rumor which, with its usual industry, spread countless stories invented by the malignant and magnified by those who love to fan the flames with manufactured details." Marshall added, to Morris's further relief, that, "If any other indiscretion was ascribed to that young lady, the suspicion has never reached my ears."

Armed with that knowledge, Morris moved swiftly. On Christmas eve, 1809, the day after Marshall's letter arrived, Morris requested Nancy's presence in the parlor for afternoon refreshments. She had, to his delight, seen that the house was handsomely decorated for the holiday season, and the room was aromatic with evergreen boughs and logs hissing and crackling in the fireplace. Sensing that the meeting was important, Nancy wore the fancy apron reserved for company and saw that her brown curls fell becomingly from a crisp linen cap. Her intuition proved correct when Morris appeared in his best afternoon suit.

"Please," he said, indicating the silk settee. Nancy sat, hands folded in her lap, and waited with trepidation. "As gentlemen my age do not have time to squander, I will get directly to the point. Since your arrival at Morrisania, my dear Miss Randolph, I have, to my surprise and great joy, found myself attracted to you and, yes, falling in love. I may be deluding myself with hopes that the feeling might be reciprocated since I am, after all, twenty-two years your senior. If, however, you can find it in your heart to make an old man happy in his sunset years, please hear me out."

A tremor pricked the nape of Nancy's neck and burned hot when Morris dropped to his good knee with impressive grace. Her hand was somehow in his, and his words seem to come from somewhere far away.

"Will you do me the great honor of becoming my wife?"

There was no hesitation. "Yes, Mr. Morris, I will." Nancy rested a hand atop his and added shyly, "For I have fallen in love with you as well."

The two were suddenly on their feet, embracing for the first time as Nancy struggled with the truth of the moment. What she heard next heightened the challenge.

"I wish us to marry on Christmas day."

She gasped in alarm. "But that's tomorrow! Your entire family is coming to dinner, and I must tend to a million—!"

Morris laughed heartily. "It would hardly do for Mrs. Gouverneur Morris to continue her duties as housekeeper. I'm certain our excellent staff can manage."

"But—" Nancy protested, ever dutiful.

He silenced her with a kiss on the forehead. "My family is rarely all together, so this is the best time to impart our happy news. We'll marry in the morning and announce it at dinner." Morris considered the scene. "Of course, the adults will suspect something when they see you without your apron."

"A wedding gown!" Nancy gasped. "I have none!"

Morris was embarrassed by his thoughtlessness. "Please forgive me. Might you not wear that lovely gown made by Mary Hannigan?"

Nancy considered his request and made a surprising decision. "I shall be married in my oldest dress, sir. It's thrice-mended, but I wish to acknowledge its years of service and my newfound good fortune."

Morris beamed. "What a charming sentiment. Your quick mind and good heart never cease to astonish me." He reached inside his jacket and produced a slender box. "May I offer these as compensation for a wedding gown?" Nancy opened the box to reveal a necklace of perfect pearls. "They were my mother's favorites. No one has worn them since her passing."

"They're beautiful," Nancy murmured as Morris draped them around her neck and closed the clasp. They laughed together at the image of a uniformed housekeeper wearing such riches. "This afternoon seems more dream than real. It's even a bit frightening."

"Will you permit me one more surprise?"

"Of course." Nancy took a deep breath. "Although I'm not certain my heart can bear more excitement."

Morris embraced her again before leading her to a table where a bottle of wine and two glasses gleamed. He uncorked a bottle bearing the Hapsburg royal crest, a two-headed eagle.

"I've saved this for years, waiting for a special occasion. I can only hope that you don't object to a wedding gift intended for another bride." He gave her a glass of pale Tokay. "This was given to Marie Antoinette on the occasion of her marriage to King Louis the sixteenth of France, by her mother the Empress Maria Theresa of Austria."

"Good heavens!"

"You must also forgive me for serving a dessert wine with no dessert, but our relationship is no stranger to idiosyncrasy."

"For which I am most grateful." Nancy sipped the rich Tokay. "Absolutely delicious. How in the world did you come by it?"

"Honestly, I'm proud to say." He winked. "Although when one is minister to a country in the midst of revolution, all manner of odd opportunities present themselves. This bottle appeared on my Paris table quite unexpectedly when…my darling girl!" Morris set aside his glass and took Nancy into his arms. "Why these tears on such a joyous occasion?"

"They're tears of gratitude," she replied.

"Gratitude for what, my love?"

"For you, my darling Gouverneur." Nancy was all smiles as she used his Christian name for the first time. "For you."

Part 8

"Thus, so our lives glide on, slander sounds like distant thunder."

-Nancy Randolph Morris

40

At ten o'clock on Christmas morning, 1809, with Clara and Alain acting as witnesses, Nancy Randolph of Tuckahoe wed Gouverneur Morris of Morrisania. Officiating was Reverend Y. Walker Brooks who, despite a last-minute summons and a harrowing journey over icy roads, radiated conviviality throughout the ceremony. Afterwards, Gouverneur asked Nancy to change into her best gown and remain upstairs until he assembled the family in the parlor. Only then did he dispatch Clara to fetch his bride and announce to the gathering that he had important news. When Nancy appeared in the doorway, a lovely vision with her late mother-in-law's pearls gleaming at her throat, he extended his hand.

"Please join me in welcoming the newest member of our family." His voice brimmed with pride as Nancy swept across the parlor and took his hand. "Allow me to present Mrs. Gouverneur Morris."

After some rumbles of disbelief, one relative after another stepped forward to congratulate the couple. Gouverneur knew such felicitations masked resentment from those expecting to inherit his vast estate. Heading this contingent was his nephew David Ogden who had long counted on boosting his troubled finances with his uncle's largesse and never imagined the old man would wed or leave his fortune elsewhere. He was barely cordial, but Gouverneur was too happy to care. After devouring Florence's splendid Christmas goose, the guests trickled home, leaving Nancy and Gouverneur alone. Before they retired to his bedchamber, he made a series of personal confidences to his new wife. Nancy had prepared herself for seeing his knee without the wooden leg, but she knew nothing of another deformity. When Gouverneur was ten-years-old, he accidentally overturned a kettle of boiling water and scalded his left arm. A hideous scar ran from shoulder to wrist, and although he offered to keep his nightshirt on, Nancy assured him she was not distraught.

"Physical perfection matters not in our union," she assured him. "Now blow out the candles, husband, and come to bed."

For the next few months, Nancy regained happiness she believed forever lost. She shared her joy with select family members, most eagerly with Tucker. "Your long-lost child," she wrote, "became the wife of one who, like yourself, personifies every generous and truly noble quality." Tucker was so pleased that he published an announcement of the marriage in the *Richmond Enquirer*. Any Virginians pondering the fate of Nancy Randolph now had their answer.

When Gouvernor had business at the Tontine, he encouraged his new wife to accompany him so she might visit her old friend Abigail and patronize the modistes and milliners lining Lower Broadway, Williams Street and Maiden Lane. Because Nancy had been told to spare no expense, merchants along those streets were elated when Morris's elegant coach-and-four drew up before their shops. She indulged her long dormant passion for fine fashion, and soon acquired a wardrobe envied by the wealthiest women in the city. Nor did she lack opportunity to display her finery. Gouverneur's prominence ensured that he and Nancy were sought-after guests in the best homes, dined at the elegant City Hotel and attended the theater on opening nights. Gossip about the mysterious Virginian who had captured the heart of New York's most eligible bachelor bloomed anew, but this time the talk was flattering. Yes, Gouverneur had married his much-younger housekeeper, but criticism was hushed by the revelation that her bloodlines were bluer than most of New York's oldest families. The Morrises entertained lavishly and often, with invitations to Morrisania becoming the most coveted in the city. Two of their guests were James and Ellen

Sharples, illustrious English artists who immortalized the couple with pastel portraits. Back home in London, Ellen spoke effusively about the grandeur of Morrisania and Nancy's sublime skills as hostess. Her opinions were typical.

Nancy's dream life continued as Gouverneur took her on a series of excursions. In 1810, the New York legislature finally approved the Erie Canal project and named him head of the commission to select the best route. Nancy accompanied him upstate to inspect the region and was treated to the unforgettable spectacle of Niagara Falls. They also visited a community of celibate Massachusetts Shakers where they heard a sermon exhorting them "to abandon worldly pursuits, enjoyments and the conjugal pleasures." Nancy was amused when Gouvernor declared this a "most unnatural doctrine." The next year she was given a tour of Washington City while Gouverneur and his friend, New York City mayor, DeWitt Clinton, sought federal funding for the canal. The government turned them down, but they found solace in a dinner at the President's House where Nancy drew the admiring eye of another stylish lady, Dolley Madison. Far less welcome was a chance encounter with John Randolph while she toured the unfinished Capitol. She was shocked when he not only behaved cordially but engaged in polite conversation with Gouverneur about England's increased meddling in American affairs. Conviviality between the men was such that Gouverneur, despite knowing of John's vicious animosity and to Nancy's horror, invited him to Morrisania. The gesture was not, as Gouverneur told her, in pursuit of reconciliation, but a demand that John show her the respect she deserved. Knowing his unstable nature, Nancy was relieved when John said ongoing trade disputes with England would keep him in the capital. His concern was validated the following June, 1812, when Congress declared war on Great Britain. Bitter memories of British occupation during the fight for independence prompted New York City to fortify itself so thoroughly that the British never even attempted to lay siege. This insulated Nancy and Gouverneur from the war and, on February 9, 1813, they welcomed a son, Gouverneur Morris II, whom they nicknamed Gouverno. Gouverneur was ecstatic to be a father at age sixty-one, and, along with Nancy, doted on the boy. David Ogden, further angered by another impediment to his uncle's wealth, nicknamed the baby after Napoleon's Russian adversary, General Kutuzof. The reference was clear when Ogden pronounced the name "cut us off." No one dared repeat the joke to Gouverneur, but another relative, Gertrude Meredith, criticized Nancy in a letter. Gouverneur replied that no less than the Chief Justice of the Supreme Court had endorsed his wife and that he hoped Gertrude didn't mind if he "endeavored to suit myself instead of you."

With the war dragging on, Nancy's correspondence with Judith was infrequent. As expected, Judith carped about her ill health, her mutable relationship with John and her struggle for survival. Nancy took her sister's complaints with a grain of salt until she learned from Tucker that Bizarre had burned to the ground and that Judith now occupied a small house in Farmville. Nancy sent money but, forever scarred by her sister's cruelty, never considered inviting her to live at Morrisania. Judith's lamentations continued into 1814 when Saint, who remained hopelessly deaf, proposed to a cousin and was refused. When Saint was sorely unhinged by the rejection, John took him to Roanoke where physicians dubbed his scribbled inanities the "ravings of a madman." John also tried to help with Tudor, financing his education at Harvard, but Judith's younger boy was also headed for disaster.

In April, 1814, unbeknownst to Judith or John, Tudor wrote his Aunt Nancy for money. Nancy generously complied, only to receive a second request a few weeks later. Tudor, for unexplained reasons, had left school and was trying to get home to Virginia but made it only to Providence, Rhode Island. Again, Nancy sent money, only to receive a third letter asking if he could come to Morrisania. When he arrived in August, Nancy saw no resemblance to the little boy she had adored and tended so many years ago. Tudor was now eighteen, aloof and distant like his mother, but it concerned Nancy far more that he was gravely ill. She promptly put him to bed and summoned a physician when the boy began hemorrhaging blood from his lungs. Fearing he might meet the same end as his Uncle Theo, Nancy sent money to Judith and urged her to come at once. Judith arrived within a week and was relieved to find her son much improved. Nancy was as shocked by Judith's haggard appearance as Judith was by her sister's robust glow of happiness. Differences somehow fell by the wayside, and the two coexisted so amiably that Judith suggested inviting John for a reunion. Wanting to please the pitiable Judith and remembering Gouverneur had already invited John to Morrisania, Nancy conceded. It would be the first time the three were together since she slapped John sixteen years ago, a memory she secretly cherished.

The first week in October, Clara Cheer, now housekeeper, announced the arrival of a carriage. Secure in her role as Gouverneur's wife and mistress of a grand estate, Nancy shunted aside her reservations about John and, with calculated hauteur, swept outside to greet her old nemesis.

"Dearest cousins!" John called upon seeing Nancy and Judith. He waited for assistance from the coach and hobbled forward with the aid of a cane. "How marvelous to see you both."

"Welcome to Morrisania," Nancy said as John kissed Judith on both cheeks. When he approached her with the same intent, however, Nancy retreated. She might allow him under her roof, but she could not abide his touch. His face reddened, but he said nothing.

Seeing John's embarrassment, Judith tried to smooth the awkward moment. "What happened to your leg?"

"An act of carelessness on my part. Two days ago, I was at the Port Conway Inn when I was roused to catch the stage at three in the morning. In my somnambulance, I lost my footing on a steep staircase and took a tumble. The pain is in both my leg and shoulder, but no matter. How's my nephew?"

"Much better. He's anxious to see his famous uncle."

"Shall we go inside?" Nancy said.

"Not yet," John said, taking in the splendor of the Morris estate. He clucked with admiration. "Well, well, cousin dear. It appears you have done quite nicely for yourself."

Nancy stiffened. "Gouverneur and I are most content here."

"As well you should be. It must have been quite a shock to find yourself mistress of a house full of servants instead of being one yourself."

"For heaven's sake, John!" Judith cried. "We must be grateful that Nancy has found security after…after all our misfortunes."

John's narrow shoulders rose and fell. "I suppose we must move on. Am I forgiven for my frankness?"

"No, you are not," Nancy replied frostily. "And if you wish to remain here, you'll curb that sharp tongue."

He bowed with exaggerated humility. "As you wish."

Nancy remained leery although John was on his best behavior as he and Gouverneur had a spirited discussion of the war. As with everything else, John had strong opinions on the British burning of Washington City and their current threat to Richmond, and he didn't hesitate to air them in loud rants. Then again, he could radiate civility and charm as he did at dinner with amusing commentary on his fellow congressmen and blunt candor about himself.

"I am roundly despised and defamed by both parties, no doubt because I've never been reticent about my personal views. Our cousin Edmund, my less than memorable tutor, drove me to distraction with his mercurial principles, so I publicly called him a chameleon on the aspen, every trembling, ever changing. Martin Van Buren was such a monster of stealth and duplicity, I accused him of rowing with muffled oars." Warming to audience laughter, John added, "Then there's poor Benjamin Hardin, that enthusiastic but roughhewn Kentuckian who sounds like a carving knife whetted on a brickbat."

Even Nancy enjoyed his japes, Gouverneur more so. "Have you an opinion of my fellow New Yorker, Edward Livingston?"

"Ah, yes. The inimitable Mr. Livingston." John drained his wine glass and signaled for more. It did not go unnoticed that his speech was growing slurred. "He is a man of splendid abilities but utterly corrupt. He stinks and shines like rotten mackerel by moonlight."

When Gouverneur stopped laughing, he said, "Tell me, John. Are your powerful enemies the reason you failed to be re-elected?"

"Along with a hundred weaker souls upon whose sensitive toes I have trod," John replied airily. "I confess that I miss the challenge of politics but have found contentment at Roanoke. The place summons me like a siren whose call I am powerless to resist. You surely feel the same about this magnificent garden spot."

"Yes, I do, and Morrisania returns my affection. As Nancy has often heard me say, the best fertilizer for an estate is the master's footprint."

John's high-pitched cackled so startled the young woman pouring Gouverneur's wine that she nearly dropped the decanter. She finished and hastily retreated to a corner.

"On that amusing note," John concluded, "I shall retire for the night. Please convey my thanks to the cook for a most agreeable meal."

"I don't know what we'd do without Florence," Nancy said.

"Starve perhaps," John muttered. He rose unsteadily and exited the dining room, leaving a table of bemused faces in his wake.

"That," Gouverneur pronounced, "is one of God's strangest creatures."

Tudor, who'd said nothing all evening, resented the criticism. "Uncle John is my hero!" he declared. "I wish I were just like him."

"Be that as it may," his mother said wearily, "it's time you and I retired too."

Judith trailed Tudor upstairs, leaving Nancy and Gouvernor to linger over Florence's caramel custard. Gouverneur kept his voice low as he made a dark confidence about John's peculiar behavior. "You think him drunk, yes?"

Nancy shrugged. "Something I've seen countless times."

"It isn't merely drink, Nancy. I've seen that comportment before. He's taking opium."

"Opium?!"

"You may have heard raised voices while we were discussing the war."

"Judith and I both did."

"You've told me John's behavior can be erratic, but this was in the extreme. Controlled and convivial one moment, madly irascible the next. Much more telling were his constricted pupils, definite signs of opium use. You may think he got it from a doctor in Port Conway, but I assure you it's not new."

Nancy considered. "Perhaps he began using it when a horse crushed his foot several years ago. Then again, John's had poor health as long as I've known him."

"That combined with his history of volatility and cruelty suggest a very troubled soul. You know, there are many in Washington City who believe your cousin is mad. He's caned men in congress, challenged others to duels, and after witnessing tonight's behavior and knowing Saint's sad story, it makes me wonder if lunacy is John's legacy."

"Mr. Tucker and I have discussed it more than once," Nancy confessed.

"John Randolph clearly possesses a formidable intellect, but is cursed with a weak, deformed body and an explosive nature he cannot control. Filling himself with opium and whiskey is a dangerous business for one already poisoned with bitterness. We must always be mindful."

"That fact was seared into my soul years ago," Nancy said, "but this time I'm not concerned."

"And what is that, my dear?"

"The same reason I didn't object when you proposed inviting him here." Nancy smiled and took his hand. "You, of course."

41

John left the next morning with plans to linger in New York City before continuing home to Roanoke. Bad luck with horses continued when his carriage veered into a construction site on Courtland Street, struck a pile of rocks and overturned. His old wounds were exacerbated by a knee injury that left him hobbling worse than ever. He took up residence at Bradish's Boarding House on Greenwich Street, only a few blocks from Abigail Pollack's establishment, where Judith and Tudor often kept him company and ran errands. One morning while John was perusing the newspaper in bed, his landlady announced a caller he didn't know.

"A gentleman named David Bayard Ogden," Mrs. Bradish said. "Says it's a family matter."

"My leg devils me fiercely today," he said. "I'll receive him here."

Ogden's clothes and manners proclaimed a gentleman of means, and he wasted no time in explaining his visit.

"We have a mutual enemy, Mr. Randolph."

His declaration earned one of John's trademark cackles. "My list of enemies runs to the moon and back, Mr. Ogden. Pray be more specific."

"My uncle is Gouverneur Morris. It is his wife Nancy to whom I refer."

John's soul stirred as the old loathing was rekindled, but because the man was a stranger he proceeded with caution. "Why do you imagine I harbor ill-will toward the woman?"

"Our friend, Harmanus Bleecker told me as much."

"Ah, yes. He knows my history with Mrs. Morris quite well. Dear Harmanus. We exchanged portraits, you know."

"So, he said."

Interest stoked, John indicated a chair. "Please sit and share your opinion of the lady in question."

"I believe her to be a fortune hunter taking advantage of an old man whose judgment is unsound."

"Such suspicions are hardly surprising, given the lady's record of wantonness and manipulation."

"True, but she has dared go even further by claiming her child, who is set to inherit Morrisania, was sired by my uncle. I have it on good report that the father was a servant at Morrisania who was subsequently discharged."

"Ho!" John was gleeful with the news. "And how might we best use such a delectable secret?"

"I suggest a frank letter to Gouverneur exposing his wife's true nature. He will surely see the wisdom in ridding himself of this thieving termagant and directing his funds to their rightful heirs." Ogden coughed and cleared his throat. "I believe that you, sir, with your legendary command of language, are just the gentleman to write such a revelatory letter."

"That, and more," John muttered.

"Sir?"

John ignored Ogden's query, mind drifting to something Tudor said a few days ago when they were reminiscing about Bizarre. The boy was three when he saw his Aunt Nancy knock his Uncle John to the floor. A few years later, Tudor said he overheard his mother accuse Nancy of murdering his father. Realizing he had found a kindred spirit with an equally gaudy imagination, John plumbed his nephew's memory further. The remainder of the boy's recollections were petty and forgettable until Tudor mentioned a slave named Billy Ellis.

"What about him?"

"Aunt Nancy taught him how to read, and Mama said it was so they could exchange secret notes."

John didn't bother asking if Tudor had read these notes or why he thought they contained secrets. He was far more concerned with gleaning the worst imaginable accusation to levy against Nancy. The merest hint of sexual congress between a white woman and a Negro man was anathema in Virginia and would immeasurably enrich and revive the old rumors.

"Mr. Randolph?" Ogden said again.

"Forgive me, sir. When I embark upon certain projects, my enthusiasm sometimes renders me lost in thought."

"Does this mean you'll write the letter?"

"I can think of no more rewarding way to pass the day."

John motioned for his visitor to fetch paper, quill pen and inkwell from the nearby desk and bore a malevolent grin as he arranged them on his bed tray.

"Shall I share this good news with the family?" Ogden asked.

"In time, Mr. Ogden." John winced as he shifted his aching limbs into a tolerable position and reached for the quill. "Good morning to you, sir."

Alone again, John began composing the most malevolent missile of his life. It mattered not that it contained no shred of truth. He wanted only for the world to hear his accusations, and if it toppled Nancy from her lofty perch, he would be doubly rewarded. An ache for revenge surged through his long fingers as he dipped the pen into the inkwell, touched it to the paper and scratched out his litany of lies.

"Dear Madam," he murmured.

He began with a resurrection of the events at Glyntyvar twenty-two years ago, accusing Nancy of killing her bastard child and destroying the reputations of his brothers, Theo and Richard. To this, he reiterated the charge that she murdered Richard, an accusation he declared was corroborated by Richard's son, Tudor, and added Gabriella's claim that Nancy worked as a Richmond prostitute. His final volley was the claim of miscegenation. John took special delight in referring to Billy Ellis as Nancy's "personal blackamoor."

Referring to their reunion after so many years of estrangement, John wrote, "Chance has thrown you under my eye, and what do I see? A vampire that, after sucking the best blood of my race, has flitted off to the North, and sunk her harpy fangs into an infirm old man. If Morris be not deaf and blind, he must sooner or later unmask you unless he, like my poor brother Richard, dies of cramps in his stomach. Repent before it is too late!"

John's eight-page letter was addressed to Morris to ensure he saw it. Its purpose was, after all, to bring Gouverneur to his senses by alerting him to his wife's transgressions. He mailed the letter on All Hallow's Eve, 1814, and afterwards shared the most inflammatory snippets with allies whom he knew would spread his lies. When his accusations were made public, a variety of camps arose. A few loyal constituents, who would've believed a claim that the moon was made of green cheese, were as obsequious as ever, but unlike 1792, when the scandal was new, John now had a reputation for choosing flamboyance over fact. Most people believed his vicious attack on the well-respected Morrises was rooted in jealousy, the pathetic cry of a lonely, sexless, widely despised bully. Far more dismissed John Randolph of Roanoke as insane.

Gouverneur urged Nancy to ignore the letter, but he could only watch in uneasy silence as she paced the parlor, letter clenched in her fist. Before his eyes, she became someone else. Even her voice was different, markedly lower and edged with anger, as she declared her intent.

"He has gone too far with his lies about poor Billy Ellis. A kinder, gentler soul I've never known, devoted to his wife and children. He made toys for Saint and Tudor, and they absolutely adored him. That's why I simply cannot divine Tudor conjuring such an unspeakable lie. Cannot! Cannot!"

Her pacing increased along with her fury. Back and forth, her skirts swished so fast they extinguished the candle beside Gouverneur's chair.

"I've wasted years as a helpless, hopeless victim of this madman's lies and incessant hounding. I was stripped of all weaponry, humiliated and abandoned, but I now have a beloved husband to defend me and a child to protect. I am no longer a woman lost and alone, but one well-armed for battle." She stopped pacing and faced Gouverneur, eyes ablaze with resolve. "Be it known, here and now, that I am formally declaring war on John Randolph of Roanoke."

Gouverneur smiled his approval. "In that case, I will be proud and privileged to help you mount the charge."

"I thank you for that, dearest, but this is a very personal campaign." She kissed him quickly and went in search of quill pen and paper. Encouraged by her husband's vow, Nancy composed a rebuttal containing over seven thousand words and quoted letters from Judith, Tudor and John himself expressing their love and devotion to her. Wishing to leave no issue unaddressed, she acknowledged the birth of Theo's stillborn child, thereby putting to rest speculation about the fateful night at Glyntyvar. Her conclusion was the literary equivalent of scorched earth.

"I observe, sir, in the course of your letter, an allusion to one of Shakespeare's tragedies. I trust you are by this time convinced that you have clumsily performed the part of 'honest Iago.' Happily, for my life and my husband's peace, you did not find him a headlong, rash Othello. For a full and proper description of what you have written and spoken on this occasion, I refer you to the same admirable author. He will tell you it is a tale told by an idiot, full of sound and fury, signifying nothing."

When she finished, Nancy had a commanding indictment, as much document as letter, but her master stroke was yet to come. Shortly after the new year, 1815, she mailed the letter not only to John but to his political adversaries, including First Lady Dolley Madison. To ensure that the letters reached the widest possible audience, she encouraged her recipients to freely circulate them. Such an act from a woman was unprecedented, as tradition dictated that ladies confine their political endeavors to organizing dinners, writing poems and essays and appearing in plays and tableaus. Nancy's daring act delivered her adversary's long overdue comeuppance and shamed John into silence.

She never heard from him again.

Gouverneur, immensely proud of Nancy, remarked that the peace achieved from her wildcat machinations was eclipsed only by the Treat of Ghent signed by President Madison on February 18 accepting the surrender of Great Britain. The War of 1812 was over, and while Nancy rejoiced in the return of peace, her family news was less welcome. In March, Tudor's lung ailments returned, and he was dispatched to the more wholesome climate of the Mediterranean. He sailed from Norfolk in April but, too ill to travel beyond England, died at age nineteen. Nancy's feelings were mixed. She had loved Tudor when he was a child, only to have him demean her with lies about Billy Elliot. Six months later, Judith followed her son in death, taken by fever in Richmond. As with Tudor, Nancy had conflicting emotions, but told Gouverneur that she hoped Judith had found peace at last.

"I don't believe my sister had a single day of pure happiness in her entire life."

By May, 1816, with John silenced, Judith and Tudor deceased and Saint institutionalized in Philadelphia, Nancy closed the Bizarre chapter of her life and entered a period of pure joy. The snows in New York had retreated, the earth warmed and it seemed as if the whole world was in bloom. She often took her morning coffee on the terrace to enjoy the sweeping beauty of Morrisania and followed it with a solo walk about the vast estate. Her favorite destination was a hillside apple orchard overlooking the Harlem River, especially now when it was a showy spectacle of pink and white blossoms. One morning she was reaching for her sun bonnet when a deep voice asked if she might welcome male companionship. She had become so accustomed to the thump of Gouverneur's wooden leg that she hadn't heard his approach and turned to find him and three-year-old Gouverno wearing their best hiking togs along with hopeful smiles.

"My favorite two gentlemen!" she cried, heart full to bursting. "By all means, come along."

42

With the Erie Canal project slated to begin next year, Gouverneur retired from public life and devoted himself to life at Morrisania. He and Nancy enjoyed a mild summer refreshed by river breezes and occasionally pungent salt air from Long Island Sound. They rarely accepted dinner invitations or ventured into the city, preferring to play with their lively, ever-curious son, correspond with old friends or simply enjoy each other's company. His retreat of choice was a corner of the terrace affording him a view of what he dubbed Nancy's "unframed painting." Today, as September waned, the borders of that painting blushed with scarlet and gold, and the background was a rich, cloudless blue. Nancy found him ensconced in his favorite chair, sharing masculine humor with Alain who, having lit his master's pipe, bowed and disappeared. Gouverneur waved his pipe at Nancy and beckoned her closer.

"Come join me on this perfect day."

"It *is* perfect," she concurred, settling into a chair beside him. "Something about it reminds me of Virginia. I cannot say what."

Gouverneur noted the envelope in Nancy's hand. "A letter for me?"

"After a fashion." She drew two pieces of paper from the envelope and passed one to him. "It came in Patsy's response to my request to visit. It appears she is not the only one who wishes to welcome us to Monticello."

"Oh?" Gouverneur wore a wry smile as he unfolded the page. "Well, what do you know? A personal invitation from President Jefferson himself." He pursed his lips as he finished the note. "He writes that he would be 'happy indeed' to receive us at Monticello and assures me of his 'continued esteem.'"

"Why, pray tell, would the principal author of the Declaration of Independence not admire the Penman of the Constitution?" Nancy teased.

"Because of our long-standing and very celebrated political differences, that's why." Gouverneur chortled. "But if Thomas is willing to tender an olive branch, I'm certainly willing to accept it and seek something we can discuss without fireworks."

"Then we can go?"

"Of course, my dear, but are you quite certain you want to go back to Virginia? It's been what? Eight years?"

"Almost nine," Nancy replied with a nostalgic sigh. "The time seems right as I will be returning in triumph with my loving husband and son. I know things will be different with Judith gone and the family scattered more than ever, but Virginia still tugs at my heart. Not as much as you, of course." She squeezed his knee affectionately, but yanked her hand away when Gouverneur winced with pain. "Oh, dear! Is it the gout?"

"Alas, yes. It's been especially troubling these past few days."

"Shall I have Florence prepare something special for dinner?"

"You mean bland of course." Gouverneur snorted. "The French exist on wine and rich desserts, and I didn't see them suffering."

Nancy dodged this old discussion. "What would you have me do?"

"The only thing that truly helps is elevating my leg." As if on cue, the ever- vigilant Alain reappeared to slip a gout stool under Gouverneur's leg, careful to minimize the discomfort of movement. "Merci, Alain. Much better."

Nancy glanced at Alain. "Some tea might help as well."

"Right away, madam."

Gouverneur sighed. "I know I've remarked on it many times, but I continue to be astonished by the miracle you wrought at Morrisania, turning a pitiful shipwreck into a sleek vessel manned by a well-drilled, handsomely uniformed crew."

Nancy smiled. "You're certainly waxing poetic today."

"True enough, so kindly indulge me." Gouverneur puffed on his pipe and exhaled a stream of bluish smoke. "This year has made me reflective, no doubt because I'm now the age of my father when he died."

Nancy was discomfited by the remark. "Why should that matter?"

"It reminds me of my mortality."

"I wish you wouldn't speak of such things, especially when our happiness is so complete."

"Then allow me to share something I wrote to John Parish last week." He took her hand. "I told him that being a little severe with ourselves and a little indulgent with others is the key to happiness. To love one's friends, to be beloved by them, is the best means to brighten our lives. It's simple, yes, but it has served me well."

Nancy squeezed his hand. "I'm grateful for friendships every day, especially dear Tucker. Had he not made your acquaintance those many years ago and thought to write you of my predicament…well, the consequences are too dreadful to contemplate."

"I've also considered that, and how odd that our paths crossed twice while you were a child. Fate certainly took her time bringing us together."

"She did indeed, and, speaking of children, it's time I roused Gouverno from his nap. Shall I bring him here?"

"Later, if you will. Our conversation has left me with a desire for correspondence. Please have Alain bring my lap desk. I'll have tea later."

"As you wish, darling."

Gouverneur enjoyed a few more draws on his pipe before Alain reappeared with the lap desk. Deciding to write his old friend, Tucker, he thrust a quill into the inkwell and began a paean to marriage. "Nancy has much genius, has been well-educated, and possesses an affectionate temper, industry and a love of order. That I did not marry earlier is not to be attributed to any dislike for that connection. On the contrary, it has long been my fixed creed that as love is the only fountain of fidelity, so it is in wedded love that the waters are most pure. The postulate was that I find a woman who could love an old man!" Gouverneur praised his son as well, but expressed concern for the boy's status with certain family members. "Nancy and I see Gouverno almost every minute of every day and are delighted by the benevolence that warms his little heart. The sweet tyke has beguiled even the most avaricious of his uncles and aunts who would have been pleased had he never seen the light of day."

Gouverneur finished the letter and set aside the quill when his last sentence stirred an old fear. In addition to his worsening gout, he had not told Nancy about a deepening distrust of his nephew, David Ogden. Well before Gouverno's birth, Ogden strove to get himself declared executor of his uncle's will, going so far as naming his eldest son, Gouverneur Morris Ogden. When that failed, Ogden, who was perpetually overextended despite a successful law practice, remained a pesky fly that Gouverneur swatted with small loans and gifts of cash. Last fall, when Ogden had been especially needy, Gouverneur co-signed a mortgage on some upstate properties and accepted his nephew's promise of quick repayment. Consumed with Erie Canal matters, Gouverneur had forgotten about the mortgage, and now chided himself for not monitoring the transaction. As he considered Ogden's other greedy actions, he decided it was time to get his nephew's hand out of his pocket once and for all. Toward that end, he wrote his lawyer, Moss Kent and requested a new will switching Ogden's bequest to another nephew and reaffirming a prenuptial agreement giving Nancy a $2600 annual pension plus the use of Morrisania for life. The remainder of his estate went to Gouverno with Nancy and Kent as co-executors. Establishing Nancy as final arbiter in all estate matters gave her significant discretionary powers, including sole authority to divide the estate if Gouverno predeceased her. Gouverneur felt better when he sealed the letter, certain that these new conditions would render Ogden, and other fortune hunters, impotent.

"Your tea, sir." Gouverneur looked up when Alain slid a tray onto a nearby table. "Will there be anything else?"

"Post this letter straight away," Gouverneur replied. "And kindly remove this desk. It's suddenly grown heavy."

Right away, sir." As he retrieved the desk, Alain watched with alarm when Gouverneur's face turned an unearthly white. As he slumped into a dead faint, the quill slipped from his hand and fluttered to the ground. "Sir!" Alain cried. "Sir!!"

Voices were distant and muddled. Gouverneur opened his eyes and, as the fog of pain lifted, recognized his bedroom, but closed shutters and flickering candles hid the time of day. He struggled to sit up but, failing to find sufficient strength, fell back against the pillows. The bedroom door was ajar, enabling him to hear voices in the hall. Nancy sounded urgent.

"There's nothing more to be done, Dr. Hosack?"

"I regret to say, medicine doesn't know a great deal about gout. It usually manifests itself in the big toe and often strikes older men who...may I speak frankly?"

"Please do."

"It strikes older men who were dissolute in their youth. This is why we suggest avoiding wine and other spirits which will exacerbate the situation. I also recommend rest and a plain diet. Gout is not called the disease of kings without reason."

"I'm afraid Mr. Morris believes otherwise."

"His beliefs aside, you must keep him away from rich food and drink."

"I'll try my best." Nancy's next words were inaudible until she asked what cause Gouverneur to faint.

"An extreme bolt of pain can trigger loss of consciousness, and I'm afraid there will be more such incidents. You must prepare yourself to see your husband suffer." When he saw Nancy's horror, the old physician touched her shoulder. "Keep your spirits up and stay well, Mrs. Morris. You'll need your strength for the coming trials."

Nancy thanked the doctor and send him on his way. When she entered the bedroom and approached the bed, it was clear to Gouvernor that she was struggling for composure. Her valor touched his heart, and he raised a hand before she could speak.

"I heard what Hosack said."

"Oh, my darling!" she cried. "What are we to do?"

"Come lie here beside me." Gouverneur closed his eyes and flinched with pain as he made room for Nancy on the bed. "For now, let's just be together."

43

Gouverneur's attack of gout was a horrid bellwether ushering in weeks of agony. Nancy remained close, doing her best to make him comfortable. She brought Gouverno when his father asked to see him and fought tears when the little boy threw his arms around his father's neck and hugged him tight. She knew this was a painful ordeal, but Gouverneur never complained.

"My child's love is a burden I happily endure."

On October 26, Gouverneur rallied enough to tolerate a visit from Moss Kent and finalize the changes to his will. As word spread through the family that Gouverneur was critically ill, Ogden came sniffing around on November 4. Gouverneur refused to see him, and told the doctor that his nephew was an ongoing menace.

"I have done everything in my power to protect my wife and son against his villainy," he lamented. "The rest is in God's hands."

When the gout triggered blockage in Gouverneur's urinary tract, Dr. Hosack summoned every instrument in his arsenal to ease the man's suffering. Nancy watched helplessly as Gouverneur was bled again and again, fed laxatives and subjected to cupping and enemas. He was given ever-increasing doses of laudanum, and when that failed, Hosack resorted to gum guaiacum. Nancy was sadly reminded of Richard's final hours when she and Judith were desperate to relieve his suffering. Nothing worked.

By the next day, Gouverneur's pain was so intense that Dr. Hosack advised Nancy to wait outside the sickroom. She refused at first, but when Gouverneur's constant groans tore at her heart, she retreated to the hall and instructed Clara to keep Gouverno out of range of his father's cries. Moments of quiet ensued when Gouverneur fainted or lapsed in and out of consciousness. Sometime after midnight, when mercy dispatched a moment of peace, Hosack summoned Nancy who held her husband's hand while he quoted poetry, only a little of it intelligible. Nancy could only watch, vision blurred by tears, as Gouverneur's body convulsed again and again. His screams chilled her blood.

"Dr. Hosack!" she cried. "Please help us!"

The old physician shook his head. "There's nothing more I can do, Mrs. Morris. His system is hopelessly blocked now. It's only a matter of time."

"Days? Hours? Minutes?" she pleaded. "Tell me!"

"That, I do not know."

After another violent convulsion, Gouverneur, face scarlet and glistening with sweat, grabbed the doctor's shoulder and pulled him close. He whispered something Nancy could not understand, and when Hosack asked to be alone with his patient, she did not question him.

"I'll be just outside the door, doctor."

Paralyzed by fatigue and fright, Nancy collapsed onto a divan, oblivious when Clara covered her with a blanket. Unraveled by exhaustion, she fell asleep, unaware that the doctor, under Gouverneur's orders, dispatched Clara on an errand that would have horrified both women had they known its purpose. Inside the sickroom, the physician took Clara's spare corset, dismissed her and sliced it with a scalpel. He extracted a slender shaft of whalebone and, with great reluctance, passed it to his patient.

"Please don't do this to yourself," Hosack pleaded.

Gouverneur ignored him and threw off the sheets. He yanked up his nightshirt to expose his agonized flesh. "You said I will die if I can't urinate. If you won't remove the blockage, I'll do it myself!"

"The pain will be excruciating!"

"I've lost a leg and burned off half an arm, man! I'm no stranger to pain!"

The frustrated physician fumbled in his medical bag for a leather mouth strap. "At least bite down on this."

Nancy's sleep and the leather strap insulated her from Gouverneur's choked cries as he inserted the whalebone and waged a final, frantic battle to clear his urinary tract. She dreamed of Morrisania. It was autumn, like now, and the fields were dotted with hay bales. They broke free of their staves and spiraled high into the air before shattering into a shower of straw that buried her. She fought to break free but someone shook her shoulder and dispelled the nightmare. Dr. Hosack stood over her, whispering words she couldn't understand. Nancy threw off the blanket and ran into the sickroom. The doctor had drawn a quilt to Gouverneur's chest to spare her the horror of the bloody sheets beneath. Agony ended, Gouverneur's face had softened and he appeared at peace as Nancy pressed his lifeless hand to her lips.

"My love," she whispered. "My life."

Hosack closed the bedroom door behind him as the long-case clock in the hall began to chime. It was five o'clock, Wednesday morning. The date was November 6, 1816.

At Nancy's insistence, Gouverneur's funeral was the next afternoon. The service was brief with only a few family members, servants, farmhands and neighbors in attendance, and he was buried in the cherry orchard. Three-year-old Gouverno couldn't comprehend what had happened. He knew only that he couldn't find his father and brought some to tears when he asked again and again, "Where's Papa?" For the next few weeks, Nancy and her son cocooned themselves at Morrisania. Her grief was such that she wished to remain isolated forever, but a letter from Moss Kent arrived on the first day of December requesting a meeting. Nancy assumed it was in regard to the will, but when she received the attorney in Gouverneur's study, his grim demeanor announced it was nothing so simple.

"I'm afraid your husband's concerns about David Ogden were well-founded."

Nancy's throat went dry as dormant fears stirred. "What concerns?"

"Last summer he suspected his nephew was involved in some questionable transactions, so he changed his will. Unfortunately, he didn't know the extent of Ogden's misdeeds." Kent removed a sheaf of legal documents from his satchel and spread them on the desk. "Last year, Ogden persuaded Mr. Morris to co-sign a mortgage and promised to make all payments himself. Not only did he default on those payments but secretly took out a second mortgage which he was granted on the strength of your husband's good name. He has now defaulted on both. By my reckoning, Ogden has defrauded Mr. Morris of one hundred seventeen thousand dollars and made him liable for his own debts."

"But how can this be? Gouverneur took great pains to protect his son's birthright and make certain that I was taken care of as well. He told me so many times."

"Your husband was a very generous man, Mrs. Morris, but like everyone else he was only human. He trusted Ogden because he was family, and when he suspected wrongdoing, he attempted to undo it. Unfortunately, Ogden was so skillful in hiding the defaulted mortgages that Mr. Morris knew nothing about them. I didn't uncover them myself until his death required that I examine every aspect of his financial records."

Nancy grappled with an old enemy. "When family is involved, you must trust no one and always expect the unexpected." She glanced over the attorney's shoulder at the pastel portraits of herself and Gouverneur. "Have I no legal recourse?"

"Technically, yes, although I would advise against it. Mr. Ogden is a powerful force in New York's legal circles. His nickname, 'Sledgehammer of the Courts' is not, I regret to say, undeserved. He is, in effect, untouchable."

"Even by someone so clearly wronged?"

"Especially so," Kent replied ruefully.

"So, I'm to be dismissed as a poor, defenseless widow?"

"Not altogether." He passed Nancy a business card. "Munro & Sons are excellent financial advisors. I suggest you contact them immediately as it's only a matter of time before you hear from the creditors."

"Creditors!" Nancy cried. "Dear God! My poor Gouverneur is barely gone, and I must deal with creditors?!"

"I'm very sorry to be the bearer of such bad news, Mrs. Morris. Please remember that I'm available whenever necessary." When Nancy fell silent, Kent rose and buttoned his jacket. "Very well then. If there's nothing else—"

"There…is…nothing…else," Nancy managed weakly. "If you'll kindly see yourself out."

"As you wish, madam. Good afternoon."

Alone again, Nancy sank deep into Gouverneur's favorite leather chair and weighed this latest calamity. She knew there was no blaming him. He had trusted Ogden as he had trusted her, never questioning their characters or imagining betrayal until it was too late.

"Trust," she whispered. "Why must it ever be such a fragile, elusive thing?"

She stared at Gouverneur's portrait for a long time, as though he might offer advice. After a moment, she felt him urging her to seek the man who brought them together. Nancy withdrew stationery from the desk and began a letter to St. George Tucker. Of all people, he would best know what to do, and she drew comfort from that knowledge. She followed that with a letter to Munro & Son requesting a meeting as soon as possible. After dispatching the coachman to New York with the letters, Nancy sought her only other source for solace. She found Gouverno on the terrace with Clara, riding a rocking horse sent by "Uncle" Tucker for his third birthday. The little boy's gleeful laughter was a reminder of the blissful naivete of childhood and how she must help him keep it as long as possible. Gouverno was in the eye of her latest hurricane, and the possibility that his legacy could be wrested away, like her own, burned Nancy's eyes with tears. She backed away lest he see her. No, she thought. My son must never know defeat.

As Nancy hoped, a letter filled with advice arrived swiftly from Tucker. She was also pleased by her first meeting with Peter Munro, a gentleman her age whose impeccable credentials and genteel manner quickly won her trust. Within a week of their first meeting in New York, he called on Nancy at Morrisania where he pronounced her predicament, "Ominous but not insurmountable." She listened closely as he revealed his divide-and-conquer battle plan. "Some of these claims can wait, but you must deal immediately with the most pressing. We'll begin with Mr. Morris's Albany properties."

"Albany properties?"

Accustomed to dealing with widows ignorant of their late husband's finances, Munro hastened to reassure her. "You need not concern yourself with details, madam. That's my job. You may think me harsh, but we must be as ruthless in raising cash as your creditors in their efforts to secure it."

"I understand, Mr. Munro. Please continue."

Munro riffled through a stack of papers for an inventory list and delivered the disheartening news. "You will start by selling off the majority of your furniture, artwork and silver." Munro peered at her over the tops of his bifocals. "You must also give up the pension bequeathed in your husband's will."

"I see." She swallowed. "Is there more?"

"I'm afraid so." Munro looked back at the list. "You must mortgage Morrisania."

Nancy struggled to control her quavering voice. "All of it?"

Munro scratched away with his pencil. "All but fifty acres. You can hold onto the house." He started to add something, but didn't.

"You were going to say 'for now,' were you not?"

"You're too quick for me."

"I need to know the worst, Mr. Munro."

"Soon you must dismiss all but the most essential household staff. Their salaries are a considerable expense."

"Mr. Morris and I considered them worth it," Nancy said, suddenly drained. "What about the farmhands?"

"As long as the farm is profitable, by all means keep them on."

"Is that all?"

Munro nodded and tucked away his papers. "These measures will keep the wolf from the door."

"For now," Nancy added with meaning.

Munro stood. "I admire your mettle, Mrs. Morris. Most ladies would be weeping and wringing their hands at such news."

Nancy rose too. "I consider that sort of behavior a waste of time."

"I'll contact you in a few weeks. I want to brief you before the first of several meetings I'll arrange with banks."

"As you say." Nancy saw him to the door before summoning Clara to the office. "Please assemble the staff in the great hall. I'm have to deliver some unfortunate news."

By the end of the week, Morrisania's household staff was reduced to Clara, Florence and a single indentured servant girl, Hannah Simon, for cleaning. Most of the servants had been there since before Nancy's arrival, and she bade them all a tearful good-bye. That unpleasantness behind her, she called on Rafaello Iannucci, the overseer who had kept the estate running smoothly for almost three decades. Iannucci was a crusty Sicilian who didn't relish taking orders from a woman, but Nancy won his respect with a plan to keep food on everyone's table. Four hundred acres would be planted in corn and potatoes for a cash crop and taken to market along with apples, pears and grapes. Iannucci hired migrants to work the fields, freeing him to tend the cattle, sheep and swine.

Under Munro's tutelage, Nancy also proved her mettle with banks, quickly determining who was and was not acting in her best interest. She surprised Munro by insisting he sue three men for unpaid debts to her husband and was awarded twenty-four thousand dollars. When attorney James Hamilton, the son of Gouverneur's good friend, Alexander Hamilton, took her to court over her refusal to pay what she considered overblown fees, she forced an out-of-court settlement for half of what he demanded. Peter Munro confided that she was the most capable female client of his career.

Nancy's struggles were far from over, however, and she barely managed to extinguish one financial fire before another flared in its place. By 1818, budgeting still further, Nancy tearfully released Clara and Florence and struggled to make do with only Hannah. Once again, she was reduced to household chores. "I rise early and toil constantly. Each day is alike, but one does what one must," she wrote Tucker. "Thank God my darling boy is everything the fondest mother could wish for."

Nancy's ferocious tenacity and commitment to protecting Gouverno carried her through the leanest years, and by 1820 she had paid her debts in full and put Morrisania on such firm financial footing that it could again be fully staffed. She located and happily rehired Clara and Florence, both of whom brought welcome nostalgia to the house. Sitting on the porch with Gouverno beside her, knowing Morrisania was safely his, Nancy found, if not total happiness, a reassuring contentment that served her well.

44

For the next fifteen years, Nancy's life remained peaceful and largely uneventful. The notable exception was Gouverno who, at twenty-two, had become a proper gentleman as intelligent as he was handsome. Tall and blonde with deep blue eyes and an engaging smile, he could easily have followed in his father's libidinous footsteps, but Nancy's tutelage directed him elsewhere. She committed herself to providing an excellent education, and was thrilled when Gouverno proved an eager student. She encouraged his interest in transportation and city planning, doubtless inherited from Gouvernor, which led to the offer of a position in the New York City mayor's office. Knowing he would have made his father proud gave her immeasurable pleasure.

When she wasn't spending time with Gouverno, Nancy devoted her time to compiling a genealogy of the Morris family and corresponding with family and friends. She was especially keen to maintain relationships with the younger Randolphs and earned a reputation for generosity with frequent gifts of cash. One by one, her generation was passing away. She had little contact with William or Harriet, and by 1835, Jane, John and Elizabeth were gone, along with Molly and her husband David who had helped during her difficult Richmond days. Thomas Junior had, to no one's surprise, died of drink, leaving Patsy in much reduced circumstances at Edgehill after Monticello was lost to creditors. Tuckahoe had also left the family, mismanaged by Gabriella's son, the usurper Thomas. When Virginia's husband William Cary died twelve years ago, their heavily mortgaged plantation, Carysbrook, was also sold, forcing Virginia and her six children to live on the charity of others. All had survived, and Virginia now resided in Alexandria, an agreeable village across the Potomac River from Washington

City. She had authored several successful advice books and held a teaching post enabling her to rent a comfortable cottage for herself and Patsy, her only unmarried child. Virginia had been a devoted correspondent and valued confidante over the years and repeatedly begged Nancy to visit, as did Patsy who longed to meet her mysterious New York aunt. "As I am most anxious to meet you, surely you will someday agree," Patsy wrote. "For I have always heard that a tale of distress would find ready access to your heart." Nancy was moved by the girl's earnest entreaty, but insisted that her world was her son and Morrisania.

One sunny May morning, warm enough to breakfast outside, Gouverno joined his mother on the porch. He bussed her cheek and helped himself to tea and some of Florence's delectable scones.

"I finally finished your genealogy papers on the Morrises."

"Any surprises?"

"Quite a few. I didn't know that great-grandfather Lewis moved here from Barbados."

"In 1670. The same year another of your great-grandfathers, William Randolph, came to Virginia. I always thought that an interesting coincidence."

"I wish I knew more about your side of the family, Mother. I've always wondered who had more politicians and lawyers, the Randolphs or the Morrises."

"I suspect both have had more than their fair share."

"Which brings me to something I've been meaning to ask."

Nancy sipped her tea and studied him over the rim of her cup. "Oh?"

"Isn't it time I met my Virginia relatives?"

Nancy's hand trembled a bit as she placed her cup back in its saucer. "I'm afraid almost all my brothers and sisters are dead."

"Not Aunt Virginia."

Nancy's eyebrows rose. "Is there a conspiracy here?"

"What do you mean?"

"Earlier this week I had letters from both Virginia and her daughter, begging me to visit and bring you along."

"No conspiracy, Mother. Only a coincidence, but it's a good one. I have a few weeks before I begin work for the mayor and would relish some travel before I settle in."

"Your father loved travel too," Nancy smiled. "He gallivanted all over Europe before we met, and he took me on trips upstate. I even saw Niagara Falls. We had marvelous times."

Gouverno grinned. "So, it's settled then. We'll visit Aunt Virginia."

"It's no such thing!" Nancy wanted to sound firm, but knew she was weakening. "Although I suppose it's only fair that you meet my side of the family." She sighed. "For better or worse."

"That's wonderful. Thank you." Gouverno relished a rare victory over his famously determined mother, but suddenly reconsidered. "Forgive me for being insensitive. I didn't consider that the trip might be difficult for you."

"Well, I'm assuredly not as young as I once was but...oh. You mean Glyntyvar, don't you?"

He nodded. "I was glad when you told me about it, Mother, but since Aunt Virginia was with you that night, will seeing her cause pain?"

"I appreciate that, my darling, but those old memories long ago ceased troubling me. The truth is that a desire to visit Virginia has slumbered in my heart for some time. It seems that you were all it needed to be awakened."

"I'm so pleased."

"As am I." Nancy leveled her gaze. "And I should not be surprised if you've already thought about transportation."

Gouverno looked sheepish. "Sometimes I think you know me better than I know myself."

Nancy was sixty-one, her sister forty-nine, but the age difference was swept away when they fell into each other's arms, weeping tears of joy at finally being together.

"There were times," Virginia declared, "when I despaired of ever seeing you again."

"I had the same fears," Nancy confessed, "but thank the Lord we're together again."

"Yes, indeed."

"Where's Patsy?"

"Down the street visiting friends. We didn't know what time you were arriving, but she'll be home in time for supper." Virginia peered over Nancy's shoulder at the young man assisting the coachman with luggage. "That's Gouverno, of course. What a dashing figure he cuts in those smart traveling clothes. And so tall!"

"He's certainly his father's son." Nancy leaned close. "Remind me to tell you something amusing."

"Tell me now!" Virginia insisted. "You could always make me laugh."

"Later," Nancy whispered. "It's not for my son's ears."

They hugged again before Gouverno was introduced and the three went inside. The cottage was modest, but large windows made it appear light and airy. They settled in the parlor where Nancy sank into a comfortable divan.

"This is such a welcome relief after those hard seats in the stagecoach."

Gouverno sat beside her. "It is indeed. Those rough roads didn't help. I promise you, Mother, if I had known the trip was going to be this difficult, I would never have suggested it."

"Stop apologizing, dear. We're here now, and that's what matters." Nancy's eye was caught by something when Virginia brought in a tea service. "My goodness! Is that grandmother's sugar bowl?"

"I hoped you would notice."

"But how on earth did you get it?"

"I stole it from that hateful witch Gabriella. Heaven knows she stole enough from us." When Gouverno burst out laughing, she said, "Has your mother told you about her?"

"A little. She was not, I believe, very popular in family circles.".

"An understatement if I ever heard one."

"But how did you manage such a thing?" Nancy asked.

"I took it when Tom moved us children to Monticello."

"You were only four years old!"

"Yes, I was. You know how mean Gabriella was to me and how she kept telling us children not to touch anything that wasn't ours. Well, I did much more than touch that little sugar bowl, and it's been mine ever since."

"I'm astonished," Nancy laughed. "My own little sister, a sneak thief."

Gouverno nodded approval. "I'd consider that sugar bowl a badge of honor, Aunt Virginia."

"Thank you, my dear." She passed him a cup of tea. "Would you like some sugar from my ill-gotten sugar bowl?"

"By all means."

Gouverno sipped his tea in polite silence, mind drifting elsewhere when his mother and aunt began reminiscing. He wanted to pay attention but his mind was dulled after the wearying trip. Fearing he might fall asleep and embarrass himself, he stood and stretched.

"If you ladies will excuse me, I need to stretch my legs."

"Of course," Virginia said. "Downtown is only a few blocks to the right out the front door, but promise you won't be gone long. We're dining in an hour or so."

"I promise." Gouverno bowed to both women and left them to their memories.

"That young man has charm to burn," Virginia declared. "I love him already and Patsy will adore him."

"She wrote the sweetest letter last year. I'm most anxious to meet her."

Virginia laughed. "And I'm most anxious to hear that amusing story unfit for Gouverno's ears!"

"In truth, it's more vengeful than amusing." Nancy explained how David Ogden had, in his ceaseless efforts to get his hands on Morrisania, revived John Randolph's defamatory lies and attacked Nancy's moral character. "His favorite accusation was that Gouverno was the illegitimate son of one of our gardeners. Of course, I knew my best defense was time."

"Time?"

"I had only to wait until my sweet boy began to resemble his father, which, unhappily for Mr. Ogden, happened early on."

"That must have been a bitter pill for him."

"Oh, yes. For John Randolph too."

"That awful man! How can you even speak his name?"

"It no longer bothers me, especially now that my old nemesis is gone."

"I didn't know that. When?"

"Two years ago. St. George Tucker wrote that he was half-mad, addicted to alcohol and opium and a total pariah. He was alone except for his manservant who reported that John's last word was, 'Remorse!' I haven't given him a sustained thought since." Nancy paused. "You appear apprehensive, my dear."

"You could always read me like a book." Virginia frowned and fussed with a lacy cuff. "It's just that…well, there's something we must talk about."

Nancy knew what was coming. "Glyntyvar."

"It still troubles me."

"Poor darling. You were only six years old."

"Yet I remember it vividly."

"I've wished so many times that you hadn't been there. It was a terrible ordeal, especially for a child."

"It's no one's fault, Nancy. Not really." Virginia fidgeted with the napkin in her lap. "And yet—"

"And yet?"

"It remains a mystery."

"If your memory is vivid, my dear, there should be no mystery. You know what happened."

"I know only that there was a stillborn baby, and that Richard took it away. It was what I heard afterwards that confused me. Adults can be so careless about what they say in front of children."

Nancy had a rush of dread. "What do you mean?"

"I heard over and over that everyone lied at the hearing. Richard. Judith. The Harrisons. Even the lawyers." Virginia leaned close, whispering as though someone might overhear. "Did they lie, Nancy? Did they?"

At last, Nancy thought. It's finally time for the truth.

"Yes, they did, Virginia. Every one of them lied to protect to Richard's reputation and mine as well. They lied that I had an attack of colic and that there was no baby, and they employed the most powerful lawyers in the state to reinforce their lies. Those were very different times, Virginia. Honor had to be maintained at all costs, even to the point of hiring legal counsel you could ill-afford. Patrick Henry eventually sued Richard for non-payment. Richard was humiliated, and I was terribly ashamed because none of that would've happened had I not borne a child out of wedlock."

"What a hateful twist of fate. Had Theo not died and the two of you had married...what is it, Nancy? You have such a faraway look. Forgive me for mentioning Theo. I'd no idea his name would affect you so."

"It isn't that." Nancy went to a window facing the street. She watched an empty farmer's wagon as it rattled home from market, followed by a fancy carriage filled with laughing young people. "There's more to the story, and I hope it rests easily with you."

"I think I've already guessed, but please go on."

Nancy remained at the window a bit longer before facing her sister. "I loved Theo dearly, but he was not the father. He might have been had his health not failed, but the poor soul was so frail toward the end that it wasn't possible." She drew a long breath. "I was so grief-stricken at his passing that I welcomed Richard's efforts to comfort me. Neither of us intended for what ensued to happen, but happen it did, and you witnessed the unfortunate aftermath."

Virginia nodded. "As I suspected."

"And you don't think badly of Richard and me?"

"Never. My darling William and I knew passion before we were married, so I am in no position to judge. A similar tragedy could have befallen us as well. Life has so many odd twists and turns."

Nancy returned to the couch. "If I've learned anything from those terrible years, it's what a wicked weapon the tongue can be. If the slaves at Glyntyvar had kept silent, no one would have been the wiser, and my world would not have been destroyed."

"And yet fate has brought you back to Virginia in triumph." Virginia squeezed Nancy's hand. "Is it possible that you might stay here with us?"

"I would consider it if I were alone, but I want Gouverno to take advantage of his father's old friends and connections. When Mr. Ogden began his ugly accusations, I learned who my allies were and, more importantly, who they were not. Those most loyal, I'm pleased to say, are also the most influential and will help my son's career. In fact, he soon begins a job in the mayor's office."

"The Mayor of New York?!"

"The same."

Whatever else Nancy might have said was lost beneath peals of laughter as Gouverno and Patsy burst into the room. There was little family resemblance save chestnut hair and large, inquisitive blue eyes, and the difference in height was startling. With Gouverno standing well over six feet, Patsy barely reached his shoulder. She was a pretty

299

picture in a pale blue afternoon dress and matching parasol. Her smile lit the room when she saw Nancy.

"Aunt Nancy!"

"Darling girl!" Nancy smiled and opened her arms when Patsy rushed to embrace her. "How lovely you are."

"Thank you."

Nancy glanced at Gouverno. "I see you've met your cousin."

"I certainly have," he smiled.

"I recognized him right away," Patsy gushed. "Of course, it helped that I saw him coming out of our house. He must be the handsomest man in Alexandria, and look at those clothes! He makes our local boys look like country bumpkins!"

"Such talk, Patsy," her mother chided. "You'll embarrass Gouverno."

Gouverno politely demurred. "Not at all, Aunt Virginia. I'm flattered."

"Now I'm the one who's embarrassed," Patsy cried, making everyone laugh when she patted her pink cheeks. "How long before supper, Mama? Might I show Gouverno the river?"

"Yes, dear, but don't forget the time and wander off."

"I won't." Patsy gave her mother a quick kiss before taking Gouverno's arm. The two vanished as fast as they had appeared.

Virginia and Nancy shared a look. "They'll wander off, of course."

"Of course, they will and who can blame them? At that age, wouldn't you rather be strolling with some dashing cavalier than dining with two old widow women?"

"Heavens!" Virginia laughed. "You make us sound awful."

"Then I'll just say that they're far more interested in each other's company than ours." Nancy helped herself to a teacake. "How old is Patsy now?"

"Almost sixteen. I know parents aren't supposed to have favorites, but I couldn't help myself."

"I can see why. She's so vivacious and warm. Affectionate too."

"All weapons she mercilessly uses on her poor mother."

"As children will do." Nancy picked up the sugar bowl and traced its pattern with a fingertip. "I suppose this is the last of it."

"What do you mean?"

"I mean it's all that's left of Tuckahoe. A little piece of porcelain." She put the sugar bowl back in place. "I hope whoever lives there now has children who will appreciate how special it is."

"I wish I'd spent my whole childhood there like you."

"I wish you had too, Virginia. There were times when those happy days were all that stood between me and madness."

"What do you mean?"

"When things were at their absolute worst, when I felt helpless and trapped, I escaped through memories of Tuckahoe. I thought about the smell of Mama's perfume, her rose garden, of running through the boxwood maze. I thought about the dogwood trees in spring when they looked like clouds come down to earth."

"I remember. So beautiful."

"If I concentrated hard enough," Nancy continued, "I could make myself dream about Tuckahoe and those dreams, even after I woke up, somehow gave me the courage to go on. I suppose that sounds ridiculous."

"Not at all. When I was little, you were always telling me fanciful stories and filling my head with dreams."

"So I did." Nancy smiled. "Dreams have served me well, sister dear. They're how I survived when the real world became too much."

Epilogue

In 1835, Gouverno Morris married Martha "Patsy" Jefferson Cary. Two years later, Nancy died peacefully in her sleep at Morrisania, age sixty-three. She was deeply mourned by Gouverno who built St. Ann's Episcopal Church in her honor as her given name was Ann. She and Gouverneur were reinterred in the church graveyard and repose there to this day. Gouverno became a railroad magnate and served as President of the New York & Harlem River Railroad. He also developed Port Morris into a thriving commercial port and donated land for a working man's community called Morrisania Village. He and Patsy had three children, the first of whom was a son named Gouverneur Morris III.

Bibliography

Boudin, Powhatan, *Home Reminiscences of Randolph of Roanoke.* Danville and Richmond VA: Clemmit & Jones, 1876.

Brookhiser, Richard, *Gentleman Revolutionary: Gouvernor Morris, The Rake Who Wrote the Constitution,* Free Press, 2004.

Chastellux, François Jean, Marquis de, *Travels in North America, in the Years 1781,1782 and 1783*, Chapel Hill: University of North Carolina Press, 1963.

Crawford, Alan Pell, *Unwise Passions,* New York: Simon & Schuster, 2005.

Dabney, Virginius: *Richmond, The Story of a City*, New York, Doubleday, 1976.,

Daniels, Jonathon, *The Randolphs of Virginia, America's Foremost Family*, New York: Doubleday & Co., 1972.

Eckenrode, H. J., *The Randolphs, The Story of a Virginia Family*, New York: The Bobbs-Merrill Company, 1946.

Gaines, William H., Jr., *Thomas Mann Randolph Jefferson's Son-in-Law,* Louisiana State University Press, 1966.

Johnson, Gerald W., *Randolph of Roanoke, A Political Fantastic*, Minton, Balch & Co., 1929.

Joseph, Robert, *The Tobacco Kingdom*, Durham, Duke University Press, 1938.

Kierner, Cynthia, *Scandal at Bizarre,* New York, Palgrave Macmillan, 2004.

Larkin, Jack, *The Reshaping of Everyday Life, 1790-1840,* New York: Harper Perennial, 1981.

Meade, Robert Douthat, *Patrick Henry, Practical Revolutionary*, Philadelphia: Lippincott, 1969.

Morris, Gouverneur. *The Diary and Letters of Gouverneur Morris*, edited by Anne Carey Morris, New York: Scribner's Sons, 1888

Randolph, Mary, *The Virginia Housewife, Or, The Methodical Cook,* Washington, 1824.

Randolph, Sarah N. *The Domestic Life of Thomas Jefferson*, Charlottesville: University of Virginia Press, 1871

Sawyer, Lemuel, *A Biography of John Randolph, with a Selection from his Speeches,* New York: William Robinson, 1844.

Stadiem, William, *A Class by Themselves: The Untold Stories of the Great Southern Families.* New York: Crown Publishers, 1980.

Swiggers, Howard, *The Extraordinary Mr. Morris*, New York: Doubleday & Co., 1952.

AFTERWORD

When I began researching *Defamed,* I soon realized that Nancy Randolph's story was far more than a stunning fall from grace. It is, by turns, a jeremiad, a saga of survival, a tale of redemption, and, ultimately, a cautionary tale as it chronicles the perils of an elitist patriarchal society, the oppression of Southern white women, and the collapse of a dynasty devoured from within. *Defamed* is also an indictment of the hypocrisy, duplicity and frayed moral fabric of post-revolutionary Virginia. Richard Randolph's examination defense, based on lies deployed by no less than Patrick Henry, will resonate with modern readers disillusioned by a manipulative press and corrupt politicians using alternate realities to market self-serving agendas. *Plus ça change, plus c'est le même chose.*

Nancy's story was immeasurably enriched by a cast of admirable, endearing, despicable and ruthless characters. John Randolph of Roanoke was by far the most challenging to recreate. Vicious and acerbic, he could also be generous and highly principled, as evidenced by a will granting freedom to his slaves. His physical peculiarities were likely caused by Klinefelter Syndrome, discovered by endocrinologist Harry Klinefelter in 1942. It strikes males with two or more X chromosomes and can render them beardless, impotent, and soprano-voiced, along with other genetic aberrations. Randolph's erratic behavior in his later years has been attributed to opium addiction, alcoholism and mental illness. Coupled with the early deaths of his brothers Richard and Theodorick and his nephew Tudor, along with the madness of his deaf nephew Saint, one might conclude that this branch of the Randolphs was withered by inbreeding.

In describing the food of the period, I was delighted to learn that Nancy's sister Mary (Molly) published America's first regional cookbook in 1824. *The Virginia Housewife: Or Methodical Cook,* continues to sell today and provides an invaluable window into eighteenth-century dining. Mary's dishes found their way to my characters' tables, and her tips on home management and proper manners were also of great use. Mary earned another niche in history as the first person interred in what became Arlington National Cemetery.

Nancy's youngest sister, Virginia, authored advice books, poetry and novels under the pseudonym "A Lady of Virginia." In addition to Patsy, who wed Gouverno Morris, two more of Virginia's children made excellent matches. Her son Archibald and daughter Mary married children of Scottish peer, Thomas Fairfax, 9th Lord Fairfax of Cameron, which meant brothers and sisters shared in-laws. As if marrying first cousins wasn't confusing enough!

Despite a superb education and advantageous marriage to Thomas Jefferson's daughter Patsy, who bore him twelve children, Thomas Mann Randolph Jr. was a study in self-destruction. He managed to become a Virginia senator, U. S. Congressman and Governor of Virginia before alcoholism and an uncontrollable temper brought his ruination. After years of abuse, Patsy and the children returned to Monticello where she took pity on her sick, penniless husband at the end of his life. Thomas died in 1828, two years after Thomas Jefferson. Faced with mountainous debts, Patsy sold Monticello in 1831.

Gabriella Harvie and her father John were the wild cards. John was a well-respected lawyer and wealthy planter, so why would he marry his daughter to a longtime friend, thirty-one years her senior and in questionable mental health? (Marriages between young women and older men were common, but this extreme difference surely raised eyebrows.) The obvious answer is greed. Harvie wanted to add Tuckahoe to his collection of Virginia plantations, which he achieved by disinheriting Thomas Randolph Sr's ten children by a first marriage. It's unknown whether Gabriella was a pawn or if she masterminded the scheme. What is certain is that she mistreated her stepchildren, especially Nancy, and pressured her husband to marry Nancy off and make her unquestioned mistress of Tuckahoe. The marriage ended with Randolph's death three years later, and Gabriella made a second lucrative marriage to John Brockenbrough, president of the Bank of Virginia. It was in her grand Richmond home, which served as the White House of the Confederacy during the Civil War, that Gabriella and John Randolph fabricated tales of Nancy's prostitution. The house is handsomely restored and open for tours, although vastly changed from Gabriella's time.

St. George Tucker was the character I most admired, not only for his impressive career and enlightened views on slavery, but for his compassionate treatment of Nancy. He alone remained a lifelong friend and directed her turbulent life toward a happy ending. Tucker and his first wife Frances had five children, and second wife Leila had two of her own. In the interest of simplicity, I did not include them. Tucker's elegant home, visited in the book, remains one of the most prominent in Williamsburg. Unfortunately, it is accessible only to benefactors and closed to the general public.

The Morris family left an admirable, unblemished legacy. Gouverneur's beloved Erie Canal, deemed an engineering marvel, was completed in 1825. Gouverno found great success as a railroad mogul, and, in an ironic twist of fate, reunited the Morris and Randolph families by marrying his first cousin, Patsy Jefferson Cary. Their grandson, Gouverneur Morris IV, was a popular pulp novelist and short story writer. Several of his works were adapted for films including *The Man Who Played God* (1932) and *The Penalty* (1920) starring Lon Chaney. Their great-grandson, Philip Bonsal, was a U. S. Ambassador to Cuba. The great estate, Morrisania, was razed around 1905 and became a low-income Bronx neighborhood. St. Ann's Episcopal Church's African-American and Hispanic congregation worship alongside the celebrated patriot buried there with his once-infamous wife. Gouverneur Morris High School boasts several famous graduates including Colin Powell, Milton Berle, Jules Dassin, Armand Hammer and Arthur Murray. As of 2002, the building houses four specialty high schools and is called the Morris Campus.

While researching the book, I was happily surprised to discover a personal connection to the Randolphs. In 1670, my sixth great-grandfather, Daniel Llewellyn, Jr. sold property on Turkey Hill Island to Nancy's great-great grandfather, William Randolph. I also learned that my 6th great uncle, John Stith Jr., wed Mary Randolph, William's daughter, making Nancy a relative, albeit very distant, by marriage.

-Michael Llewellyn
Fredericksburg, Virginia

AUTHOR'S NOTES

Because the language of Jeffersonian America is stilted and pretentious to the modern ear, I sought a palatable bridge between the two but flavored the story with direct quotes from Patrick Henry, John Marshall and Thomas Jefferson, and the letters of Nancy Randolph, Judith Randolph, John Randolph, St. George Tucker, John Marshall and Gouverneur Morris. I encountered three spellings of Randolph Harrison's plantation - Glenlyvar, Glentivar and Glyntyvar – and settled on the last. Gouvernor Morris's Christian name, French for "governor," is pronounced both Gover-*neer* and *Goo*-veneer.

Of all the plantation homes in Nancy Randolph's world, only Monticello, Roanoke and Tuckahoe survive. All may be toured. Tuckahoe, after being sold in 1830, returned to the family in 1898, purchased by a consortium of Randolph and Jefferson descendants. Shortly afterward, Tuckahoe made a victorious early test of the National Historic Preservation Act when Virginia announced plans to route a state highway through the property. Tuckahoe was prominently featured in the 2014-17 television series, *Turn: Washington's Spies*.

Acknowledgments

I am deeply indebted to Bill and Susan Beck, owners of Beck's Antiques in Fredericksburg, for granting me access to their collection of vintage and rare books about the Randolphs of Virginia. I am also grateful to the owners of Tuckahoe Plantation and their staff for allowing me to tour my heroine's childhood home, see the window glass etched with her mother's death date and wander the tranquil gardens.

I must also thank Alan Pell Crawford, author of *Unwise Passions: The Story of a Remarkable Woman and the First Great Scandal of Eighteenth Century America*, and *Scandal at Bizarre: Rumor and Reputation in Jefferson's America* by Cynthia A. Kierner. Their nonfiction accounts of Nancy's life provided invaluable background information and were instrumental in shaping key scenes. Kudos also go to Jan Smith Patterson for another excellent editing job and to my cousin Christa Thomas for her beautiful cover illustration and design.

On a more personal note, heartfelt thanks to Jennifer Calvert, Brenda Hamilton, Patty Iannucci and Fran Slaterbeck along with other friends and family members generous with their support and encouragement over the years.

Made in the USA
Middletown, DE
09 January 2026

26218882R00172